"One of these days, Michelle, you're going to trust me, and we're going to make glorious, fulfilling love....

"But I won't rush you." Jonathan unlocked the door and kissed the top of her head. "Get a good night's sleep, angel. I'll see you in the morning."

As if Michelle could sleep when her entire body was clamoring for him! She was deeply troubled by Jonathan's powerful hold over her. Was it more than just sexual attraction? Could she possibly be falling in love with him?

Michelle rejected the idea! He was simply a very experienced man who knew how to get what he wanted. And yet...she admired everything about him. He was intelligent and thoughtful. He was warm and kind—when they weren't arguing. He was every woman's dream...and perhaps her ultimate undoing....

Dear Reader,

In the spirit of blossoming love, Special Edition delivers a glorious April lineup that will leave you breathless!

This month's THAT'S MY BABY! title launches Diana Whitney's adorable new series duet, STORK EXPRESS. Surprise deliveries bring bachelors instant fatherhood...and sudden romance! The first installment, *Baby on His Doorstep,* is a heartwarming story about a take-charge CEO who suddenly finds himself at a loss when fatherhood—and love—come knocking on his door. Watch for the second exciting story in this series next month.

Two of our veteran authors deliver enthralling stories this month. First, *Wild Mustang Woman* by Lindsay McKenna—book one of her rollicking COWBOYS OF THE SOUTHWEST series—is an emotional romance about a hard-luck heroine desperately trying to save her family ranch and reclaim her lost love. And *Lucky in Love* by Tracy Sinclair is a whimsical tale about a sparring duo who find their perfect match—in each other!

Who can resist a wedding...even if it's in-name-only? *The Marriage Bargain* by Jennifer Mikels is a marriage-of-convenience saga about a journalist who unexpectedly falls for his "temporary" bride. And *With This Wedding Ring* by Trisha Alexander will captivate your heart with a tale about a noble hero who marries the girl of his dreams to protect her unborn child.

Finally, *Stay...* by talented debut author Allison Leigh is a poignant, stirring reunion romance about an endearingly innocent heroine who passionately vows to break down the walls around her brooding mystery man's heart.

I hope you enjoy this book, and each and every story to come!

Sincerely,

Tara Gavin
Senior Editor and Editorial Coordinator

Please address questions and book requests to:
Silhouette Reader Service
U.S.: 3010 Walden Ave., P.O. Box 1325, Buffalo, NY 14269
Canadian: P.O. Box 609, Fort Erie, Ont. L2A 5X3

TRACY SINCLAIR

LUCKY IN LOVE

Silhouette®

SPECIAL EDITION®

Published by Silhouette Books
America's Publisher of Contemporary Romance

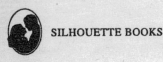

SILHOUETTE BOOKS

ISBN 0-373-24167-4

LUCKY IN LOVE

This edition published by arrangement with Harlequin Books S.A.

® and TM are trademarks of Harlequin Books S.A., used under license.
Trademarks indicated with ® are registered in the United States Patent
and Trademark Office, the Canadian Trade Marks Office and in other
countries.

Printed in U.S.A.

TRACY SINCLAIR

began her career as a photojournalist for national magazines and newspapers. Extensive travel all over the world has provided this California resident with countless fascinating experiences, settings and acquaintances to draw on in plotting her romances. After writing fifty novels for Silhouette, she still has stories she can't wait to tell.

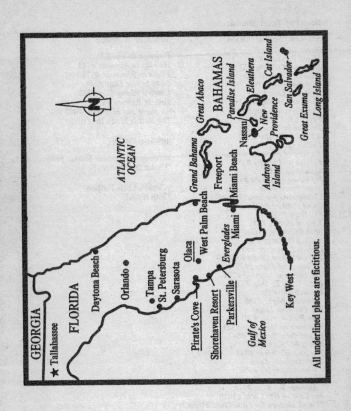

GEORGIA

★ Tallahassee

FLORIDA

Daytona Beach

Orlando

Tampa
St. Petersburg
Sarasota

Olaca

Pirate's Cove

Shorehaven Resort

Parkersville

West Palm Beach

Everglades

Miami

Gulf of
Mexico

Key West

ATLANTIC
OCEAN

Grand Bahama

Freeport

Miami Beach

BAHAMAS

Great Abaco

Paradise Island

Eleuthera

Cat Island

San Salvador

Nassau

New
Providence

Andros
Island

Great Exuma

Long Island

All underlined places are fictitious.

Chapter One

Michelle Lacey had just turned on the eleven o'clock news when the telephone rang.

"I hope this isn't too late to call," Evelyn Lacey said. "I know you don't usually go to bed early."

"No, I was just watching television. Is everything all right, Mother?"

"It couldn't be better! I'm so glad you talked me into coming here. I've having a marvelous time."

That was good to hear. Evelyn had reacted negatively when Michelle suggested a trip to Florida. The way she reacted to everything since her husband died a year previously. Michelle had been concerned about her formerly vivacious and fun-loving mother, especially after a bout with the flu that winter left her wan and debilitated.

"It's a good thing you got out of New York when you did." Michelle glanced out the window of her Manhattan apartment. "We're having another snowstorm."

"I'm almost embarrassed to tell you it was eighty degrees here today," Evelyn said.

"I'm delighted for you. Is your cough improving?"

"It's all gone fortunately, because I don't have time to be sick." The older woman laughed. "There's too much to do here. Lucky and I drove into town for lunch at a darling little café yesterday. The food is really excellent here at Shorehaven, but it's nice to try other places for a change. Then last night we played bridge with the Mackenzies and won again, as usual. Lucky's nickname really fits him."

Michelle knew that Lucky was Warren Richfield, a man her mother had met at the resort. She'd spoken of him often in the last couple of days. They seemed to be spending a lot of time together.

"I just got back to my room and I couldn't wait to tell you about the fabulous party the hotel gave tonight," Evelyn continued. "The theme was A Night In Las Vegas. They had dice tables and roulette wheels, every kind of gambling device. It was such fun. Lucky taught me how to play blackjack and shoot craps. He's awfully good at both of them."

"He seems to be quite a gambler," Michelle remarked neutrally.

"Only as a hobby. Lucky is an inventor. But I guess I already told you that," Evelyn said with a little laugh.

"No, you only mentioned that he's handsome and charming. What kind of work does he do?"

"I just told you, he's an inventor."

"Very few people make a living from that. Does he have some other kind of job?"

"He doesn't need one. Whatever he invented must have been quite lucrative. He's very wealthy."

"How do you know that?" Michelle persisted. "Because he told you so?"

Evelyn's voice cooled perceptibly. "I don't think I like

your attitude, Michelle. Lucky is a friend of mine. I don't talk about *your* friends in a derogatory manner.''

"I wasn't criticizing him, Mother. I merely wondered how much you knew about him. Sometimes people exaggerate to make a good impression. It doesn't mean you can't enjoy their company, but you have to take what they tell you with a grain of salt."

"Lucky isn't like that. He's quite modest about his accomplishments. Everybody here at Shorehaven likes him—especially the single women." Evelyn gave a breathless little laugh. "A lot of them are green with envy because he seems attracted to me."

"He shows good taste," Michelle replied noncommittally. "Has he ever been married?"

"He's a widower. His wife died more than five years ago." Evelyn's voice sobered. "Lucky understands how hard it's been for me since your father died. He had trouble adjusting to his loss, too."

"You told him what a happy marriage you and Dad had?" Michelle asked casually.

"Of course, and what a good husband he was. Lucky was impressed that Richard left me so financially secure."

Michelle stifled a groan. "It isn't like you to discuss personal matters with a stranger. Was that really wise?"

"Lucky isn't a stranger, and he's not some kind of confidence man, either, as you seem to be implying. The subject came up naturally when he was telling me about a new invention he's been working on. Lucky expects it to be a real gold mine."

"What is it?"

"I don't know exactly. Some kind of safety device for airplanes. The aircraft companies are always looking for things like that, so I asked if I could invest in his company. He wasn't keen on it at first. He said I'd be better off in blue chip stocks. I had to convince him that I could afford to take a small risk."

"Good Lord, Mother, don't you know when you're being conned? It's the classic gambit and you fell for it! He mentions a great opportunity, pretends to be reluctant to let you in on it and then allows himself to be persuaded. The man makes his living fleecing inexperienced women like you!"

"That's insulting! You're saying the only reason Lucky is attracted to me is for my money."

"That wasn't what I meant at all. I'm sure he enjoys being with you," Michelle said carefully. "But if he's as wealthy as you say, doesn't it seem a little odd that he'd need your money to help finance his invention?"

"He doesn't *need* it, he was doing me a favor. I'm really disappointed in you, Michelle. Lucky is the first man who's made me feel alive again since your father died. I would think you'd be happy about it, instead of trying to make me feel guilty about enjoying his company."

"That certainly wasn't my intention. I'm delighted to see you taking an interest in life again. I'm just concerned that Lucky will take advantage of you. You're not experienced at handling investments. Dad did all of that."

"You're right, but I have to learn to make my own decisions now that he's gone."

"With proper guidance," Michelle insisted. "What you need is a good, reputable financial advisor."

"I might be inexperienced, but I'm neither stupid nor incompetent," Evelyn said crisply. "I wish you'd stop treating me like a doddering old woman. I'm only fifty-three, which is by no means over the hill yet. That's young enough to get married again, for heaven's sake!"

Now Michelle was definitely alarmed! After her father died, her mother had led an increasingly reclusive life. She wouldn't even accept a dinner invitation from a widower she'd known for years. The thought of marriage was surely the farthest thing from her mind. Did Lucky plant the idea, thinking she was wealthier than she actually was?

It was a situation that needed delicate handling. Michelle tried to warn her mother subtly, without seeming to criticize. It was no use. The discussion became heated. Finally Michelle was forced to back off before she did any more damage.

"Well, I'm glad you're enjoying yourself, anyway" she said, changing the subject rather awkwardly. "I wouldn't mind a little warm weather myself. This snow just won't quit. Maybe I'll fly down and join you for a few days if I can get some time off."

"I'm a little old to need a chaperone," Evelyn said dryly. "Or a nursemaid. Don't you think I know you want to check Lucky out?"

"I'd be interested in meeting him, but the eighty-degree weather is more of an attraction," Michelle lied. "If you don't want me to come, just say so. Maybe you don't want Lucky to know you have a twenty-six-year-old daughter."

"That's nonsense! I've told him all about you. I'd be delighted to see you—as long as you promise to remember your manners."

"Don't worry, I probably won't be able to get away. I'll talk to you soon, though."

Michelle's blue eyes were stormy and her soft mouth was set in a grim line as she hung up the phone. Wild horses couldn't keep her away.

Michelle was a buyer at an exclusive women's shop on Fifth Avenue in midtown Manhattan. It was an interesting job with a fair amount of responsibility. She couldn't take off at a moment's notice as she would have liked. But after explaining that it was a family emergency, she did arrange to leave the following day after work.

That gave Lucky two more days and a night alone with her mother, but it couldn't be helped. If he succeeded in getting his hands on Evelyn's money, she would need this job to support both of them, Michelle thought somberly.

* * *

She spent two tense days worrying about what Lucky was up to, but when the plane landed in Olaca on the west coast of Florida, Michelle's spirits couldn't help lifting. The tropical breeze that greeted her was such a delightful change from the frigid blasts in New York.

The scenery added to her pleasure. Tall palm trees formed a lacy pattern against the indigo sky, and white sand beaches glimmered in the moonlight as her taxi drove along the waterfront.

Michelle hadn't told her mother she was coming. She'd left it as a vague possibility, wanting to catch Lucky off guard. As it turned out, a surprise was waiting for Michelle, as well.

The desk clerk at Shorehaven told her that Evelyn was in the dining room. Since it was getting late and she didn't want to miss seeing her mother, Michelle checked in, but didn't waste time going to her room. She took her key and told the man to have her suitcase taken to her room.

Most of the guests had finished eating. There were only a few groups of people still in the dining room. Evelyn was sitting at a table with two men. The older one was obviously Lucky, so Michelle didn't bother with the younger one. She paused in the doorway to inspect Lucky and form her own judgment.

He was a handsome man with a full head of silvery hair and a tanned face that had laughter lines around the eyes. He was wearing a sport jacket and a shirt open at the throat. A casual outfit, but Michelle knew clothes. Lucky's were expensive, which was in keeping with his image as a wealthy businessman on vacation, she thought cynically.

Before she could come to any other conclusions, Evelyn spotted her in the doorway. "Michelle, darling!" She rushed over to kiss her. "Why didn't you tell me you were coming? Lucky and I would have been there to meet your plane."

"I wasn't sure until the last minute that I could get away," Michelle explained.

"You should have called from the airport before you left New York." While she was talking, Evelyn led her over to the table where the two men rose politely. "This is Lucky," she said proudly.

The older man smiled and took Michelle's hand in a grip that was firm, but not punishing. "I feel as if I already know you. Evie talks about you all the time."

"She told me about you, too," Michelle answered, trying to sound pleasant.

"And this is Lucky's nephew, Jonathan Richfield." Evelyn indicated the younger man.

Michelle felt a shock of awareness. He was exactly the kind of man she'd always been attracted to—with unhappy results. He was in his early thirties, with the tall, lithe physique of an athlete. He was also the darkly handsome type she preferred, but this one wasn't merely a plastic male centerfold. His strong face was full of character and his gaze was direct.

Jonathan was treating her to the same thorough scrutiny, with the same underlying disapproval. She was a real beauty, he told himself. That long silky black hair and wide blue eyes could make a man want to believe anything she told him. And that slender yet curved body was an even more powerful incentive. The thought of holding her nude in his arms made Jonathan's loins throb. A night of love with her could make him forget they were adversaries. None of these thoughts showed on his face. His expression was austere rather than admiring.

"It's so nice that both of you young people are here at the same time," Evelyn remarked. "Perhaps you can keep each other company tonight. I wish you'd told me you were coming, Michelle. Lucky and I made a date to play bridge."

"Don't worry about me," Michelle said. "I could use a

quiet night watching television. Tomorrow we can spend the whole day together, just the two of us," she added deliberately.

"We can do that at home." Her mother wasn't fooled by this display of filial devotion. "Wouldn't it be more enjoyable to have Lucky drive us all to Pirate's Cove? It's supposed to be very scenic and there are nice shops nearby. One of the women here told me about them. She got some lovely things there."

"I'll be happy to take you," Michelle said. "Men don't like to shop, Mother."

"You've met the wrong kind of men." Lucky smiled. "Evie and I have checked out most of the stores around here."

"He loves to shop," Evelyn said.

"That's news to me," Jonathan drawled. "Aunt Agatha could hardly drag him out of his workshop for meals. She was his wife," he added deliberately.

"I've always been sorry that I didn't spend more time with her," Lucky said soberly. "When you're young you think you have all the time in the world. I've had to learn to slow down and smell the roses." His expression lightened. "Shall we go take the Mackenzies to the cleaners, Evie?"

She glanced at her watch. "They're probably waiting for us, but I don't want to leave Michelle alone on her first night here."

Before Michelle could repeat her assurance that she didn't mind, Lucky said, "There's no reason for her to be alone. Jonathan can show her around."

"Thanks, but I haven't even been to my room yet," Michelle said swiftly. "I have to unpack."

"How long can that take?" Lucky asked dismissively. "You can do it later. Wouldn't you prefer to stroll around the garden with a handsome young man?"

"I'm sure a handsome young man like Jonathan has already made plans for the evening," Michelle answered, repeating Lucky's description ironically.

"I don't happen to have any plans, but I would have been happy to change them for such a charming lady," Jonathan drawled.

"Then that's settled." Lucky was oblivious—or chose to ignore—the veiled animosity between the two young people. The air fairly crackled with their tension. "Jonathan will give you an orientation tour of Shorehaven. It has everything you could possibly want from a resort."

"I'll look forward to seeing it tomorrow," Michelle said firmly. "I'm sure Jonathan is just being polite, and I really do need to unpack before my clothes get too wrinkled."

"All right," Evelyn said. "I'll go with you. You'll have to make my excuses to the Mackenzies, Lucky."

"You don't have to give up your evening for me," Michelle protested.

"It's only a bridge game," Evelyn said airily. "I'm sure you can get another partner, Lucky."

"I've found the partner I'm comfortable with."

They exchanged a meaningful smile before Evelyn turned back to her daughter. "You're sure you don't want to let Jonathan show you around?"

The last thing Michelle wanted was to spend the evening with Jonathan. He didn't seem exactly taken with her, either. Had Lucky called in his nephew—if Jonathan was indeed related to him—to help him pull off the scam? That could be the reason for his thinly masked hostility. He was annoyed with her for showing up and possibly upsetting their sure thing.

But Michelle knew she was outmaneuvered for the moment. How open to persuasion would her mother be if Michelle was a liability from the moment she hit town?

Gritting her teeth she said, "I guess I can do my unpacking later."

"Splendid!" Lucky said. "Come on, Evie, our pigeons are waiting to be plucked."

After they'd gone, Jonathan looked at Michelle moodily. "Well, I guess we might as well go. Where would you like to start, inside or outside?"

"Wherever you like," she replied indifferently.

"The grounds are quite extensive." He glanced at the gray high heels that matched her gray wool suit. "Will you be able to walk in those shoes?"

"Yes, they're quite comfortable."

He shrugged. "If you say so."

As they walked across the lobby a young woman was coming toward them. She had a sweet, but rather plain face, and a slightly dumpy figure. Her eyes lit up when she saw Jonathan.

Without even glancing at Michelle, she said in a breathless rush, "I was hoping I'd run into you. The bingo game is about to start. Are you going to join us? Ruth went ahead to get a table."

"I'm afraid I can't make it tonight, Winnie. Perhaps next time."

Jonathan's smile was not only charming but subtly personal, as though they'd shared some magic moments—an unlikely premise. A woman like this would never interest him, which confirmed Michelle's opinion that Jonathan's charm was as phony as he was. In a con man's world, everybody was a prospective mark.

She had to admit, however, that Jonathan was really awesome when he wanted to be. That handsome face and superb body would make any woman want to believe she was special to him. This one looked dazzled, even though he'd refused her invitation.

"Well, okay, then I guess I'd better go," she said reluctantly. "Ruth is waiting for me."

"Tell her I said hello."

When the woman had left, Michelle remarked ironically,

"You certainly got acquainted with the other guests in a short time. You and your uncle are very gregarious."

"Your mother is, too. She and Lucky hit it off as soon as they met and exchanged what might be called vital statistics," Jonathan drawled as he led her across the lobby.

"I don't doubt it," Michelle said evenly. "Mother is a very open person. She hasn't learned to be guarded with strangers."

They went out a side door onto a broad terrace with tables and chairs. Beyond the terrace were beautifully manicured lawns bordered by flower beds.

As they started down one of the graveled paths Jonathan turned his head to glance at her sardonically. "I'm sure your mother can take care of herself."

"I wish I shared your confidence. You might as well know, I'm here to see that nobody takes advantage of her."

"What a coincidence. I'm playing the same watchdog role over Lucky. He's usually very astute about people, but Evelyn is clever. She slipped in under his guard."

Michelle stopped dead in the middle of the path. Her blue eyes were dark pools in the moonlight, but the anger in them was unmistakable. "Are you implying that my mother has designs on your uncle?"

"I wouldn't put it quite as politely, but that's the general idea," he said insultingly. "Lucky is a very wealthy man. A lot of women have tried to get their hands on his money. It always amused him because he realized what they were up to—until he met Evelyn. She's a real pro, but she still won't get away with it."

"I can't believe you're accusing my mother of being a fortune hunter, when it's your uncle who is after *her* money!"

"Don't be ridiculous! Lucky is a multimillionaire."

"That's the story you'd like everyone to believe. Where would he get that kind of wealth? He told Mother he's an inventor. How many inventors can even support themselves without a regular job?''

"Not many, but Lucky is a genius. When he was still a young man he invented a new type of gasoline infusion valve that revolutionized the automotive industry. He could have retired on that one invention alone, but since then he's gone on to develop half a dozen other important devices.''

Michelle's face expressed her skepticism. "If he's a genius, why haven't I ever heard of him?''

"How much do you know about heavy manufacturing?'' Jonathan countered mockingly.

"Okay, so it isn't my main interest, but I should have heard his name,'' she said stubbornly.

"There are a lot of people who make important contributions without becoming famous for them. Your mother evidently recognized Lucky's worth,'' Jonathan observed dryly.

"It's the other way around,'' Michelle said indignantly. "He very adroitly found out how much my father left her, and now he's trying to fleece her out of it.''

"That's utter nonsense! Lucky could—'' Jonathan stopped abruptly and began to laugh. "We sound like two little kids, arguing about whose father is the richest.''

When he wasn't being hostile, Jonathan was a devilishly attractive man. She could just imagine how easily he could talk a woman into bed. At least the ones he conned got something in return, she thought cynically. His sexual prowess must be fantastic.

She was annoyed when an image of his taut, naked body flashed through her mind. Naturally he'd be great in bed. That was his natural environment!

Fixing her eyes only on his face, Michelle said, "It's obvious that we won't ever agree, but at least we understand each other.''

"That's another instance where you're wrong.'' His frown was back as he inspected her lovely face. "I don't understand you at all. You're young, clever and beautiful. You could be successful in any number of fields if you worked hard and stuck to it. Why don't you get an honest job instead of hanging around resorts, helping your mother prey on unwary older men?''

"I *have* a job!" Michelle answered indignantly. "A very good job that I had to leave to fly down here and protect my mother from you people."

"What kind of work do you do?" he asked skeptically.

"I'm a buyer at Barrington's on Fifth Avenue. And as far as working hard and sticking to it, I started in the stockroom while I was still in college and worked my way up to my present position. You might try it some time," she taunted. "The money isn't as good, but the feeling of satisfaction is very rewarding."

"I'll admit that Lucky gave me my first job, but I like to think I've lived up to his expectations."

"I don't doubt that for an instant!"

A muscle pulsed in his square jaw. "Has anyone ever told you that you're a very annoying woman?"

"No, you're the first. I get along well with most men," she said pointedly.

"That's understandable." He looked her over insolently. "If you were as nice to me as you are to your marks, I'd do my best to please you, too."

His knowledgeable inspection gave Michelle the uncomfortable feeling that he was seeing her without her clothes, assessing the size and firmness of her breasts, the rounded contours of her hips. A warm tide swept over her—because of her wool suit, she assured herself. It was much too warm for this climate. She wanted to take off her jacket, but she was afraid he would think he was getting to her.

"We both know how we feel about each other, so there's no point in discussing it any longer," she said crisply. "Can we go in now?"

"If you like, but I haven't shown you the lily pond. It's very romantic in the moonlight," he said mockingly.

"Save it for somebody who's interested." She started back up the path to the hotel.

"I won't take that personally, since I know you're uncomfortable," he said, falling into step beside her.

"You don't bother me in the slightest," she replied haughtily.

Jonathan's eyes gleamed with amusement. "I was referring to your outfit. It's scarcely suitable for the tropics. Just looking at you makes me warm."

Michelle glanced at him sharply, but his expression was bland. "I got here late and I didn't want to take time to change," she explained.

"You could at least remove your jacket."

"Then I'd have to carry it. Since the obligatory tour is over, I'll wait till I get to my room."

"We're not through yet. I haven't shown you the indoor facilities. There's an extensive library and a well-equipped exercise room, among other things."

Why would he want to prolong this charade, Michelle wondered? Jonathan wasn't enjoying himself any more than she was. He was simply taking a perverse delight in aggravating her, she decided.

"I think I'll skip the rest of the attractions," she said.

"If you like. Just be sure you don't tell Lucky and Evelyn that it was my idea to end the evening at nine o'clock."

Michelle hesitated in the middle of the lobby. Her mother would feel guilty if she found out—and Jonathan would make sure she did. But Evelyn would also be annoyed at her for not being more receptive toward Lucky's nephew. She'd never believe how tricky Jonathan was. He'd use any means to drive a wedge between Michelle and her mother.

She gritted her teeth. "Okay, show me the damn gym!"

"When you put it so charmingly, how can I refuse?" he asked derisively.

The workout room was filled with all the most up-to-date exercise equipment. In addition to rowing machines, stationary bikes and treadmills, there were weights, pulleys and even a padded leather sawhorse. The whole place was cluttered with equipment.

Since the gym wouldn't normally be used at this time of night, the air conditioning had been turned down. Michelle was suffocating in her wool suit and lavender turtleneck pullover, even though that was silk rather than wool.

"I was wondering how much longer you could stand being all bundled up," Jonathan commented, watching with interest as she took off her jacket. The soft silk pullover clung to her body closely, outlining her breasts.

Michelle ignored the flash of male awareness on his face by turning to survey the room. "Does anybody use all this stuff on a vacation?"

"I presume so. The bulletin board in the lobby says they have classes with a trainer every morning. I suppose people come here to work out after overeating at dinner the night before."

"Have you been to any of the classes?"

"No, I'm not much for organized exercise."

"You must do something to stay in such good shape."

Jonathan's lean body was perfectly proportioned and he moved with catlike grace. One of the big cats—a tiger, or perhaps a sleek black panther stalking its prey. In Jonathan's case that would be women, Michelle thought scornfully.

"I'm glad you think I'm in good shape," he drawled. "A compliment is the last thing I'd expect from you."

"It was merely an observation," she answered coolly.

"I should have guessed." Crossing his arms over his impressive chest, he leaned against the padded horse and looked her over clinically. "It's obvious that you don't need exercise classes, either."

"Don't spoil your image by trying to flatter me. You're not very convincing."

"Actually I was being truthful. You have a body that could make a man want to take you to bed and keep you there for a week. If it was *my* money you were after I might chance it, but I don't intend to let you and Evelyn take my uncle to the cleaners."

"He's the one with the pie-in-the-sky schemes," Michelle said angrily. "He asked Mother to back his latest invention."

"She must be very wealthy. Lucky's ideas cost serious money to develop."

"I've been trying to tell you she *isn't* rich! She has enough to live on comfortably—or at least she does if I can prevent your uncle from getting his hands on it. Lucky found out exactly how much money my father left her, and I'll bet that's the same amount he needs to market his miracle gadget."

"Lucky doesn't have to look for funding," Jonathan stated flatly.

"Then why is he hustling my mother?"

"I don't believe he is. What exactly did he tell her?"

"That his invention would make a million dollars, naturally."

"It will make a lot more than that. Which is why your story doesn't make sense. One person doesn't have the capital to back a multimillion-dollar project."

"Well, maybe he just asked her to invest. What difference does it make? Either way, she'll lose everything she has."

"Richfield Enterprises is a privately owned company. A lot of people have tried to invest in one or another of Lucky's projects, but he won't let any outsiders in, not even relatives and close friends. Are you trying to tell me he asked Evelyn for money?" Jonathan stared at her incredulously.

"It wasn't done that blatantly, from what she tells me. He pretended to discourage her. As soon as she's firmly hooked, he'll allow himself to be persuaded to take her money. I don't have to tell *you* how it's done."

Jonathan frowned. "If what you tell me is true, Lucky has more than a passing interest in her. I'd hoped he was just intrigued by a charming woman."

"Well, at least you'll admit my mother isn't all bad," Michelle remarked dryly.

"I said she was clever. I just didn't realize how much progress she'd made. But if Evelyn is really smart, she'll take Lucky up on his offer instead of going for the gold ring."

"I'd expect that kind of advice from you. You two work well together."

"It's good advice, whether you believe it or not. I realize it would be more lucrative for Evelyn to marry Lucky. She would be enormously wealthy. But I'm here to see that doesn't happen. She could win a tidy consolation prize, however, by investing whatever she can comfortably afford in Lucky's latest project."

"That sounds like a tacit admission that it's risky."

He shrugged. "Then don't invest. Go find yourselves a more promising mark."

"Anybody would be more acceptable than you and Lucky," Michelle snapped.

He smiled sardonically. "I'm crushed that you don't want to be related to me."

She gave him a startled look. "We wouldn't be related!"

"Not in any way that would be inconvenient—or against the law for us to make love." He smiled sensuously.

"In your dreams, pal!" Michelle knew he was only baiting her, but the thought of their naked bodies intertwined was disturbing.

"Don't knock it until you've tried it." He grinned.

"Who knows? We might be terrific together. All this friction between us could generate a lot of excitement."

"I could get more excitement from a pair of tight shoes," she said disparagingly.

"Are you saying you don't think I could satisfy you?" His voice was deceptively mild.

"I doubt it," she lied. "But it's a moot point because I'm not interested in finding out. You're not my type," she added unwisely.

Jonathan's hazel eyes glittered, but his voice became even softer. "I'm very adaptable. Tell me how you like to make love. Personally I prefer the lights on, so I can appreciate the perfection of your body as I undress you slowly. But caressing you in the dark has its own allure."

Michelle steeled herself not to react. "This conversation is tasteless," she said coldly. "I'm going to my room."

"You haven't seen the rest of the facilities."

"There will be lots of time for that. I'm not leaving anytime soon."

"Neither am I," he said grimly, dropping his seductive act. "It should be an interesting week."

"That isn't the adjective I'd use, but why should we agree on that when we haven't agreed on anything else?"

He stared at her moodily. "You won't win. Why don't you be realistic and go fish in another pond?"

"Because I'm going to enjoy beating you," she taunted.

"Don't count on it. I won't hesitate to play dirty if I have to."

"Is that supposed to scare me? You already have."

"You haven't seen anything yet." His smile had a dangerous quality to it. "Consider yourself warned. I don't like to lose."

"Neither do I, so we'll just have to see who blinks first."

Michelle turned away with her nose in the air and started for the door. Her impressive exit was marred when she failed to notice the jump rope coiled on the floor.

"Watch out!" Jonathan called.

But it was too late. Her high heel caught in the coil and she pitched forward onto the floor.

He raced over and knelt beside her. "Did you hurt yourself?"

"Only my dignity." She sat up.

"I tried to warn you, but it was too late." He extended a hand and helped her to stand. "They shouldn't leave all this equipment lying around on the floor."

When she was on her feet, Michelle felt a twinge of pain in one leg. It wasn't excruciating, but her face mirrored her discomfort.

"You did get hurt!" Jonathan exclaimed. "Is it your back?"

"No, I think I twisted my ankle. It will be all right."

"You'd better get off of that foot." He glanced around, but the gym had everything except a chair. Settling for the next best thing, he grasped her waist with both hands and lifted her onto the padded horse.

"Put me down," she ordered. "This thing is slippery and there's nothing to hang on to."

"I won't let you fall." He put an arm around her waist. "Which leg is it?"

"The left one, but there's nothing wrong with it," she insisted. "Just help me down."

"After I make sure you didn't break anything." He slowly flexed her leg, then gently turned her ankle back and forth. When she flinched slightly he asked, "Is that where it hurts?"

"Only slightly. Will you please stop playing doctor and get me down off this thing? I want to go to my room."

"Okay, it doesn't look like you did any serious damage." One arm was still around her waist and he hooked the other arm under her legs. But instead of setting her on her feet, he cradled her against his chest and started for the door.

"What do you think you're doing?" Michelle exclaimed. "Put me down this instant!"

"I will when we get to your room." He shifted her weight and picked up her jacket and purse.

"You're not coming to my room." She tried to wriggle out of his arms, but they only tightened, holding her more closely against his body.

"Relax, I'm not enjoying this any more than you are."

"Well, thanks a lot!" she answered indignantly.

His expression changed as he looked down at her flushed face. "Do you want me to?"

"No, of course not! But you don't have to be insulting."

"You've had enough men tell you how desirable you are. You can't expect to win 'em all."

"I have no desire to appeal to you."

"Then you got your wish. What room are you in?"

"One-o-three." She gave in reluctantly.

It was either that or prolong the uncomfortable situation. Michelle was very conscious of Jonathan's blatant masculinity. How could she help but be when she was in the man's arms? She didn't have to like him to admit that he was a very sexy fellow. Fortunately he wasn't aware of her qualified approval.

"One-o-three should be on this side of the hall. Yes, here it is." He stopped in front of a door. "Give me your key."

She fished it out of her purse and gave it to him without arguing. Anything to get rid of him. But Jonathan didn't leave after dumping her rather unceremoniously on the bed. He walked around to the other side where a telephone sat on a nightstand.

"I don't want to sound inhospitable after all your solicitude," she said acidly. "But would you mind using the phone in your own room?"

"This won't take long. Front desk? Yes, I'm calling for Miss Lacey in one-o-three. She needs a doctor. Will you please send for one immediately?"

Michelle jumped off the bed. "Are you out of your mind? There's nothing wrong with me! Tell him it was a mistake." It was too late. Jonathan had hung up.

"I'm sure you weren't really hurt," he said. "But I want a doctor to verify the fact."

She stared at him suspiciously. "Why are you so concerned about me all of a sudden?"

"Call it insurance. I want a doctor's statement that there's nothing wrong with you."

"I already told you that. Why do you need a second opinion?"

"Because I don't want you to claim tomorrow that your injuries were more serious than you thought and you'll need a lengthy recuperation—preferably at Lucky's expense."

Michelle stared at him incredulously. "You have a twisted mind, do you know that?"

"Spare me your indignation. Just get into bed," he said impatiently.

"I'll do no such thing! Get out of my room before I call the manager and have you thrown out."

"I don't think you want to do that. I'd have to give my version of what happened. It wouldn't be the gentlemanly thing to do, but what other choice would I have?"

Michelle got the picture. Jonathan would say she hurt her leg while they were having overly enthusiastic sex. And the manager would undoubtedly believe him, she thought bitterly.

"All right, I'll let the doctor examine me," she muttered, sitting back down on the bed. "But I'm not paying the bill."

Jonathan looked at her without expression. "Don't you ever think about anything but money?"

"Occasionally." Michelle forced herself to smile instead of lashing back at him. "You'd be surprised if you knew what I'm thinking about right now," she purred. Revenge! Jonathan Richfield was going to pay for what he'd put her through this evening.

Chapter Two

Jonathan was wary of Michelle's apparent change of heart toward him. "Nothing you do would surprise me," he said moodily.

"From anyone else that would be a compliment, but I know you didn't mean it that way," she remarked.

He sighed. "Just get undressed and get into bed."

"You have to be joking!"

"No, I'm serious. The doctor can scarcely examine your leg while you're wearing panty hose. What did you think I had in mind? Feeling the way we do about each other, you must know I have no ulterior motive."

Michelle was annoyed at the way he kept hammering the point home. "If I'm so distasteful to you, why don't you wait outside for the doctor? You can brief him on how tricky I am, so he'll be sure I'm faking the pain."

"Is your ankle bothering you a lot?" he asked, more gently.

"You wouldn't believe me no matter what I said."

Jonathan swore under his breath. "Where is your nightgown? I'll bring it to you. Assuming you wear one, of course."

"No, I sleep in the nude between silk sheets," she said, being deliberately provocative. "I love the sensuous feeling against my bare skin."

His expression didn't change, although the erotic description caused a surge of warmth in his midsection. He had a vivid picture of himself in bed with Michelle, her naked body as silky under his caressing hands as the sheets they'd tangled while making love.

He scowled at her in an attempt to banish the disturbing vision. "It doesn't surprise me that you sleep in the nude, but you must own a robe. You have to get out of bed sometime," he added nastily.

"I'm sure I spend less time there than you do," she snapped, dropping her seductive act. "I was just joking about the silk sheets and sleeping in the buff, but I might have known you'd take me seriously."

"There's just no pleasing you. You complain when I doubt your word, and you complain when I don't."

"You only believe me if it's something derogatory."

"There's nothing wrong with sleeping nude. I do it, myself."

"Well, *I* don't. I wear a flannel nightie that comes down to my ankles."

He looked her over consideringly. "Somehow I can't picture you in flannel."

"There's a whole world of women out there that you know nothing about," Michelle said crisply.

"I'm sure you could teach me a great deal, but it will have to wait until after the doctor leaves. Take your robe into the bathroom and get undressed."

"What part of no way don't you understand? I'm not going to do it and you can't make me," she added childishly.

"We both know I can—one way or another." He strolled over to the bed, gazing down at her. "You wouldn't be the first woman I've undressed. Although the circumstances were a lot more pleasurable," he remarked deliberately.

"It wouldn't be any great treat for me, either!" Michelle was so furious that she'd jumped off the bed to confront him, forgetting to favor her tender ankle. She winced as a twinge of pain reminded her.

Jonathan regarded her with a frown. "Does your leg really bother you?"

"No, I'm putting on an act for your benefit. Isn't that what you've decided?"

His mouth thinned in annoyance. "Get back on the bed—and stay there! I've just about had it with you."

"That doesn't begin to express how *I* feel," Michelle said, but she climbed onto the bed before he could pick her up and put her there. She'd had enough close contact with his powerful body.

The doctor arrived as they were glowering at each other. He was an older man with a calm, pleasant manner.

He pulled a chair up to the bed and gazed at Michelle with a smile. "You look pretty healthy. What seems to be the problem?"

"There isn't any," she answered. "I tripped on a coil of rope, but I didn't hurt myself. *He* was one who insisted on calling you." She shot an irritated glance at Jonathan.

"Well, it's always best to be sure there's nothing wrong. Your husband was merely concerned about you."

"He isn't my husband. We aren't even friends."

"Just let the man examine your ankle," Jonathan said curtly.

The doctor's eyebrows climbed at their hostility, but he didn't comment on it.

As he began to gently flex her ankle, Jonathan said, "Shouldn't she take off her stockings?"

"It isn't necessary. The skin isn't broken and a serious

injury would cause a lot more pain than she's experiencing," the doctor said.

When Michelle shot Jonathan a triumphant look, he gave her an annoyed one in return. "Are you sure it's nothing serious?" he insisted.

"He's afraid I'm going to claim to be an invalid," she said sweetly.

The doctor gave them a wary look, clearly reluctant to be dragged into their vendetta. "There's a little swelling, but not even enough for a sprain. Your ankle is tender because you bruised it slightly, but you didn't do any real damage. Stay off your feet tonight and prop your foot on a couple of pillows," he told Michelle. "You should feel fine in the morning."

"I was sure I would," she said. "I'm sorry for getting you up here for nothing, Doctor."

"I'm always glad when that's the case," he answered politely.

After the man had gone, she said to Jonathan, "I hope you're satisfied."

"That isn't a word I associate with you," he replied sardonically.

"Do you have to look for ways to be insulting, or does it just come naturally? I'm sorry I don't gaze at you adoringly and hang on your every word, but I—" She broke off to stare at him sharply. "What do you think you're doing *now?*"

He had opened her suitcase and was removing her clothes. "I'm unpacking for you. The doctor said to stay off your feet."

"He also said there's nothing wrong with me. Stop pawing through my things. I'll unpack in the morning."

"You'll need your toothbrush tonight, plus all those creams and lotions women consider essential."

"All I need is my toothbrush, and I'll get that myself. I don't use a lot of stuff on my face."

His gaze moved over her lovely features. "You can't tell me that perfect skin didn't get a lot of help from cosmetic companies."

"I'm sure you didn't realize that sounds like a compliment," she said mockingly.

"I never denied that you're a beautiful woman. You also have a body that could arouse any man." His golden eyes traveled over her appreciatively. "I have a feeling you'd be fantastic in bed—once you got over that attitude of yours."

Michelle had reacted to his low, sensuous voice, coupled with that lean, sexy body. It didn't take much imagination to guess how great *he would* be in bed. But his last comment reminded her of how much she disliked him.

"Learn to live with it," she told him curtly. "My feelings for you will never change."

"I'm crushed," he said mockingly. "I was looking forward to a night of wild, uninhibited lovemaking."

"Why don't you go look up your little bingo pal? She displayed the enthusiasm you admire in a woman."

"Don't knock it. That quality can make a plain woman more desirable than a raving beauty."

"If my company is so distasteful there's a simple alternative. I presume you have a room of your own. Why don't you use it and leave me alone?"

"I intend to, as soon as I finish this." He put her lingerie into a dresser drawer, then held up a short chiffon nightie. "Is this the granny gown you described? I never knew flannel was sheer and lacy."

"I'd scarcely bring a flannel gown to Florida. Put it down," she ordered. "And get out of my room right now!"

He seemed to realize he'd pushed her to the limit. "Okay, I've put away most of your things. I guess the rest can wait until morning." He walked over to the bed, holding up the fragile blue nightie. "Did someone buy you this because it's the color of your eyes?"

She snatched it out of his hands. "No, I bought it myself."

"Good choice. A man's guard would definitely be down after he saw you in that."

Michelle controlled her anger with an effort, since she knew Jonathan was trying to provoke her. "If you prefer my room to yours I'd be happy to change with you," she said pointedly.

"All right, I get the message." He grinned. "I'll see you tomorrow. Would you like me to prop some pillows under your foot before I go? No, I suppose not." The echo of his chuckle still lingered in the room after he'd left.

She stared balefully at the closed door. Michelle didn't know which irritated her more, Jonathan's coldly autocratic manner, or his periodic switch to seduction. She knew better than to believe he was really attracted to her. Jonathan would use whatever method worked to get what he wanted—and it wasn't sex. At least not from her.

Michelle had to admit he put on a good act. When he'd looked at her with that golden glow in his eyes, she had responded involuntarily. The same way she did when he cradled her in his arms earlier, even though his body was taut with anger then, rather than passion. Either way, he was potently masculine.

She got off the bed abruptly and limped into the bathroom. After washing her face and brushing her teeth, Michelle took off her clothes. Only then did she remember that her nightie was still lying on the bed.

She went back to the bedroom wearing only a pair of brief satin panties. The unexpected sight of Jonathan froze her like a marble statue.

He was equally startled, but not as immobilized. His eyes moved avidly over her pink tipped breasts, then down the length of her slender, nearly nude body.

"I knocked, but I guess you didn't hear me," he said finally.

The sound of his voice broke the spell. Michelle grabbed her gown and clutched it to her chest. The short scrap of chiffon didn't hide much. Her long bare legs were still exposed to the thighs, and the sheer fabric of the gown allowed tantalizing glimpses of her pink nipples.

"Get out of my room this instant!" she stormed. "What do I have to do to keep you out of here?"

"You could put the chain on the door," he suggested, trying to hide his amusement. Sensing that she was about to erupt, he added hastily, "I didn't realize you were undressed."

"People don't usually go to bed with their clothes on and I had a reasonable expectation of privacy. Why did you come back?"

"It suddenly occurred to me that I forgot to return your key." He held it up and started to walk toward her.

"Just put it on the table," she ordered. Michelle stood there rigidly while he did as she said, then turned to the door.

Jonathan paused with his hand on the knob, looking at her with unabashed male interest. "I apologize for walking in on you unexpectedly, but I'd be lying if I said I'm sorry it happened."

He left before she could say something withering. Which was just as well. It would only have given him more time to ogle her like a teenager with raging hormones. Although that was hardly an accurate description of Jonathan. He was an adult male who knew how to make women respond to him—even women like herself who knew what a shady character he was. A dangerous adversary, Michelle thought soberly.

She would have been surprised to hear that Jonathan was just as wary of her. A frown replaced his smile as he walked down the corridor to his own room.

He'd met a lot of scheming women—wealth seemed to

attract them like metal shavings to a magnet—but none had possessed Michelle's awesome arsenal of weapons. She had the face of an angel and a body that promised heaven on earth. What man could resist that mixture of innocence and sexuality? Worse yet, if even *he* found her irresistible, how could he convince Lucky that she and her mother were very clever fortune hunters? His uncle was in no mood to listen to warnings. He had to be presented with something concrete.

Jonathan paced up and down his room, looking for a solution. Perhaps there was something unsavory in their past. What was their source of income, for instance? He didn't buy the story of a widow with a modest inheritance and a daughter who worked for a living. It was just too pat.

After worrying the problem from every angle, Jonathan picked up the phone and punched out a number. When a man answered, he said without preamble, "I've got a job for you, Joe. Something I want you to get on right away. You can reach me at a resort called Shorehaven. I'll give you the phone number."

"Can it wait until tomorrow?" the man asked in a raspy voice indicative of time spent in a lot of smoke-filled rooms. "There's three hundred dollars in the pot and I have the first decent hand I've had all night."

Joe Henderson, a big man with a lined face, was one of the best private investigators in the business. He had almost as many informants as the police department, so there was little he couldn't find out.

"I'm sorry to interrupt your poker game, but you should be glad I'm offering you a job." Jonathan grinned. "You'll need it to pay your losses. If I got taken to the cleaners as regularly as you do, I'd give up the game."

"And put seven guys on unemployment?" Joe joked. "You could be sharing the wealth if you were here instead of lolling around some fancy resort."

Jonathan's jaw set grimly. "I'm not on vacation. I came

here to see that Lucky doesn't do anything foolish, and I met a girl who might become a problem. That's why I called you. I want you to find out everything about her and report back to me A.S.A.P.''

"What can you give me to go on?"

Jonathan repeated everything Michelle had told him about herself. "None of it is necessarily true. She does live in New York, however. I saw the airline tag on her luggage.''

"That's a starting point. Give me a description."

"She's in her mid-twenties, long black hair, big blue eyes fringed with thick lashes, classic features and a figure you don't forget.''

Joe whistled. "What more could you ask?"

Jonathan preferred to take him literally. "I want you to check on her mother, too. She *says* the woman is her mother and I can see a family resemblance, but don't take anything for granted.''

"You're talking to a pro, my friend. Gorgeous gals don't affect my judgment.''

"You've never seen this one," Jonathan commented dryly. "Get back to me when you have something. If I'm not here, leave a message and I'll return your call.''

After giving the detective his phone number, he hung up slowly. It had to be done, but Jonathan felt a curious reluctance to learn the truth.

Michelle awoke the next morning and flexed her foot gingerly. There was no pain and the slight swelling in her ankle was gone, as the doctor had predicted. That was a relief! She needed all of her faculties to deal with Jonathan.

Michelle had just gotten out of the shower when her mother phoned from her room.

"Did you have a good time last night?" Evelyn asked without giving her a chance to answer. "Isn't Jonathan the handsomest man you ever saw? The single women here have been tripping over each other trying to get him to notice them.''

"Yes, I met one of them last night. A rather plain girl with mousy brown hair. She wanted him to play bingo with her and a friend.''

"That must have been Winnie. Poor thing, she'd never have a chance with a man like Jonathan, but you'd never know it by the charming way he treats her.''

"That charm is automatic,'' Michelle said evenly. "It's programmed to kick in when any female gets in range, no matter what she looks like.''

"You don't care for Jonathan? That's a disappointment. I was hoping the four of us would have a nice time together this week. Lucky had all kinds of things planned.''

"I didn't say I don't like Jonathan,'' Michelle said quickly. If she disapproved of not only Lucky, but his whole family, her mother would think she was being unreasonable. "I just meant that a man that handsome must be used to women making a fuss over him.''

"He is rather spectacular looking. What did you two do last night?''

"We took a walk around the grounds and he showed me the exercise room.'' Michelle changed the subject abruptly. "What would you like to do today? Shall you and I check out those boutiques you mentioned?''

"The four of us can do that. Lucky wasn't just being polite. He does like to shop. I don't know about Jonathan, but if he'd prefer to do something else, the three of us can go and we'll all meet back here later for a drink.''

"That's a good idea. It would be foolish for him to spend all afternoon being bored.'' Michelle felt a lot more cheerful, knowing she wouldn't have to fence with Jonathan all day.

"Well, we'll discuss it at breakfast,'' Evelyn said. "I'll meet you in the dining room in about fifteen minutes.''

The other three were already at the table by the time Michelle arrived. Lucky greeted her pleasantly, but Jonathan looked her over critically—as usual.

"How's your ankle this morning?" he asked.

Evelyn frowned. "What was wrong with it?"

"Nothing," Michelle answered quickly.

"Then why did Jonathan ask?"

"I tripped over a coil of rope in the gym last night," Michelle explained reluctantly. "It was no big deal."

"The doctor confirmed that it wasn't anything serious," Jonathan said.

"You called a doctor?" Now Evelyn was definitely concerned.

"It was Jonathan's idea. I kept telling him I didn't need one." Michelle shot him a look of annoyance.

"I wanted to be absolutely sure," he answered smoothly.

"You did the right thing," Lucky said. "If there's a problem, it's always best to take care of it before it becomes serious."

"That's *my* philosophy." Jonathan gave Michelle a derisive smile.

She picked up a menu. "Shall we order? I'm famished."

During breakfast they discussed plans for the day. "What would you ladies like to do today?" Lucky asked.

"Why don't we just sit around the pool and relax?" Evelyn suggested.

"I thought we were going shopping," Michelle said.

"That was before I found out about your accident. You shouldn't walk around on a twisted ankle."

"It's perfectly all right. The doctor even said so. You don't have to change your plans for me."

"It doesn't matter. We can go tomorrow instead."

"Your mother is right," Lucky agreed. "We were going to stop at Pirate's Cove along the way and it might be too strenuous for you today."

"Besides, the hotel is having a dinner dance tonight," Evelyn said. "I want to have my hair done this afternoon."

"They couldn't make you look any lovelier than you already do," Lucky said gallantly.

She turned to the other two with a smile. "Now do you see why I love this man?"

Her mother was only joking, Michelle told herself, hoping it was true. Jonathan wasn't any happier about the situation. His jaw set grimly, but he didn't comment.

The day wasn't as bad as Michelle had feared. Jonathan couldn't be his usual unpleasant self in front of his uncle. He even went for long periods of time without aiming veiled barbs at her. Or maybe the warm weather made him lethargic, she thought cynically.

He didn't look sluggish. Although his long frame was relaxed on a chaise, he was like a resting tiger, capable of springing into action in an instant. Michelle had watched him in the pool, unwillingly admiring the complete coordination of his lean body.

"Why don't you put on your bathing suit and go swimming with Jonathan?" Evelyn asked her.

"I'm not in his class," Michelle answered. "He's a real pro."

"We don't have to compete at everything," he said mildly.

"Jonathan swims all year round," Lucky said. "It's natural for him to be good at it."

"You're both very fortunate," Evelyn remarked. "The weather is so beautiful here. I hate to think of going back to the ice and snow."

"Then don't go back."

"You make it sound so easy," she answered with a smile.

"It is. You're in the enviable position of being able to do anything you want."

"My father planned it that way," Michelle said evenly. "He'd be very upset if she did something risky."

"Life is a gamble, my dear," Lucky answered. "If you demand a guarantee that everything will work out, your safe little world can turn into a prison."

Evelyn slanted a glance at her daughter's tense expression. "It's much too nice a day to discuss anything more serious than what we should have to drink," she said lightly. "Although it isn't cocktail time yet."

"You know the old saying. It's five o'clock somewhere," Lucky said. "I'll join you. What would you like?"

"I'd love to have a Planter's Punch. They taste like fruit juice, but they pack such a wallop. I don't know if I should."

"Go ahead, indulge yourself. I promise not to take advantage of you." Lucky grinned.

"Would you put that in writing?" Michelle tried to make it sound like a joke.

"That's an excellent idea," Jonathan said, joining the group. "I think they should both sign an agreement, so there are no misunderstandings."

Lucky gave him a level look. "This isn't a business matter. I hope you're more diplomatic when you do talk business."

"I'm sure Jonathan is very astute," Evelyn said.

"He's been a big help to me," Lucky agreed grudgingly.

"I'll bet he has," Michelle commented.

"What exactly do you do?" Evelyn asked Jonathan. "Are you an inventor, also?"

"No, I'm an engineer," he replied. "I see that Lucky's inventions are produced cost effectively and then marketed."

"As the C.E.O. of Richfield Enterprises, Jonathan runs the company," Lucky said proudly. It was obvious that he was very fond of his nephew, in spite of a small difference of opinion now and then. "He started to work for me when he got out of college. It was his first and only job."

Michelle looked at Jonathan with only partially concealed scorn. "So you never even tried to get a conventional job."

Lucky gave her a puzzled frown. "I don't understand what you mean by conventional."

"She means working for someone other than family," Jonathan explained.

"I can assure you that he earned every promotion he got," Lucky said. "Jonathan started at the bottom and learned the business thoroughly before advancing to his present position. As a matter of fact, I've had one devil of a time keeping him. Other companies try to steal him away regularly. When money and stock options aren't enough, I appeal to his family loyalty," Lucky joked.

"He certainly must be a valuable asset," Michelle commented.

Evelyn detected the derisive note in her voice. "People shouldn't automatically assume it's nepotism when someone rises to the top of a family company," she told her daughter reprovingly.

"The ones who know him intimately are aware of his capabilities," Lucky said.

Jonathan's eyes glinted mischievously. "I tried to convince her of that, but she's a hard sell."

"The consensus seems to be that I'm wrong," Michelle remarked lightly.

"But you're not ready to admit it yet. That's okay. I like a worthy opponent."

"I hope you don't consider yourselves adversaries," Evelyn protested.

"Only in the ongoing battle of the sexes," Jonathan answered smoothly.

"That's utter nonsense!" Lucky stated. "Why shouldn't

men and women be able to get along? I don't understand you young people today.''

Jonathan laughed. ''I believe Socrates said something like that around 400 B.C.''

''And if it's any consolation to you, we'll be saying the same thing to *our* children,'' Michelle agreed with a grin.

''If you ever have any,'' Evelyn remarked. ''When I was your age I'd been married for five years.''

''That's another thing that's different today,'' Lucky said. ''The kids don't get married young and settle down like we did.''

Jonathan swung his long legs off the chaise and stood. ''I think this is a good time for me to go for another swim. I've heard this lecture before.''

''Me, too.'' Michelle picked up her tote bag and sunglasses. ''I'm going to my room and read a book.''

''I didn't mean to drive them away,'' Lucky said as he watched the young couple go in opposite directions. ''I suppose I shouldn't be so outspoken, but I worry about Jonathan. He's like a son to me.''

''It's too bad you didn't adopt children when you discovered you and Agatha couldn't have any of your own,'' Evelyn commented.

''We probably would have if Jonathan and his sister hadn't come to live with us after their parents were killed so tragically in that car crash. The children were young and confused. They couldn't understand why their mother and father had left them. We tried to make them feel secure by giving them all the love and attention they missed.''

''You did a good job. Jonathan is a fine young man and he obviously adores you. Do you have as good a relationship with his sister?''

''Shelley couldn't be more devoted if she were my own daughter. She married a dashing Frenchman and lives in Paris, but she phones me at least once a week. You're very fortunate, too. Michelle seems quite concerned about you.''

"Sometimes too much so," Evelyn answered dryly.

Lucky smiled. "They do have a tendency to think we need looking after."

"As though good judgment evaporates with age," she agreed with a touch of annoyance. "Suddenly your children think they're your parents."

"It's easier than raising their own children." Lucky laughed. "I'm surprised Michelle isn't married by now. A beautiful girl like that must have had lots of proposals."

Evelyn nodded. "She has, but something was always wrong with them, according to her. Still, I'd rather she waited and found just the right man."

"It seemed like a good omen when Michelle and Jonathan both came to Shorehaven at the same time. I thought something might develop between them, but they don't seem to like each other much."

Evelyn smiled. "They're like two strange dogs circling each other warily."

"Exactly," Lucky agreed. "Not a very good sign."

"I wouldn't say that. I sense a definite chemistry between them."

"Something like the components of T.N.T.?"

"Possibly. We'll just have to wait and find out."

He reached over and took her hand. "That's what I like about our relationship. We don't have to play games."

"Yes, it's nice that we're so comfortable with each other."

"That isn't the word I'd use to describe my feelings," he said in a deepened voice.

Michelle stretched out on her bed and propped a couple of pillows behind her head before opening her novel. It was an unaccustomed luxury. Usually at this time of day she'd be fighting her way through rush hour crowds, on her way home to fix dinner for herself.

The book was engrossing, but after a short time, her eyelids began to droop. She hadn't gotten much sleep the night before, thanks to Jonathan. Long after he finally left her room, she was still awake, staring up at the ceiling and thinking of cutting remarks she could have made. Gradually her eyes closed and she fell asleep.

It was late when Michelle awoke. She had to rush in order to change clothes and meet the others at the time they'd agreed upon. Instead of a nice relaxing bath she took a quick shower, then applied makeup sparingly. Only lipstick, and a touch of mascara on her long, naturally thick lashes.

Deciding what to wear took almost as long, although she didn't have much choice. Michelle hadn't planned to do anything more exciting than go to the movies, so she'd brought only casual clothes—and not very many of those. Certainly nothing fancy enough for a dinner dance. It didn't matter, she told herself. She wasn't trying to impress anyone.

The others had already ordered a drink when she joined them in the bar.

"I was just about to call your room," Evelyn told her. "What kept you so long?" She looked disapprovingly at her daughter's printed cotton skirt and sleeveless blouse. "It certainly didn't take all this time to put on that outfit."

"I think she looks charming," Lucky said gallantly.

"For a backyard picnic, perhaps. I told you it was a dinner dance," Evelyn said to her.

"I didn't expect to need anything dressy," Michelle explained. "It was either this, or pants and a T-shirt."

"Well, never mind. We'll go shopping tomorrow and buy you a suitable wardrobe."

"It's the middle of winter in New York, Mother! I'm not going to buy a lot of warm weather things that I don't need. We'll be going home soon."

"*You* will," Evelyn said pointedly. "I'm thinking about staying longer."

As Michelle's face expressed her dismay, Lucky said soothingly, "It won't hurt to go shopping. You don't have to buy anything." Before she could answer, he said to his nephew, "Go to the bar and get Michelle a drink, Jonathan. The service is very slow here tonight."

"What can I get for you?" Jonathan asked her.

"Something very strong," she muttered.

Michelle was conscious of being woefully underdressed. She hadn't realized Shorehaven was such an upscale resort. Most of the guests had on expensive gowns and a lot of jewelry. Even Jonathan's bingo playing admirers were decked out in their party best.

He touched her hand briefly. "Don't worry about your outfit. All the women here would like to be as beautiful as you are."

It was a nice thing to say—and completely out of character. Michelle gazed at him uncertainly, but his expression wasn't mocking. She didn't know what to think.

"Jonathan is right," Lucky said, saving her from having to reply. "You'd be gorgeous no matter what you were wearing."

Michelle knew they were buttering her up, but she couldn't work up any indignation over it.

"You should see her when she's really dressed," Evelyn said proudly.

"Even when she isn't your daughter is enchanting." Jonathan's eyes sparkled with mischief.

Michelle's body warmed as she remembered last night's embarrassing incident. He was taking great delight in taunting her with it. She should have known better than to think Jonathan had changed his attitude toward her.

"About that drink," she said pointedly. "I'll have a martini, straight up."

His eyebrows climbed, but he merely said, "I'll be right back with it."

Michelle could tell that Jonathan thought she was a serious drinker. Well, let him! It fit in with the rest of his image of her. Actually she drank sparingly and didn't even like martinis. But she was glad now that she'd ordered one, Michelle thought sulkily.

To her surprise, the evening got better from then on. Either Jonathan felt he'd pushed her to the limit, or he was on his good behavior in front of his uncle. For whatever reason, he worked at being excellent company.

Michelle didn't trust his motives, but it was nice not to have to fence with him, if only for one evening.

After a pleasant cocktail hour, they went into the dining room. It looked very festive, with pink tablecloths, flowers and soft lighting. The tables were all arranged around a portable dance floor, and a small combo was tuning up on a makeshift bandstand.

The dinner was excellent and so was the wine Lucky ordered. When Michelle complimented his taste, he kept refilling her glass, even before it was empty. By the middle of dinner she was her normal, bubbly self rather than the reserved, wary woman she'd been since coming to Shorehaven. Jonathan watched with amusement as she entertained them with funny stories about other vacations she'd been on that weren't nearly as luxurious.

"I'll be thoroughly spoiled by the time I get home."

"It's nice to see you enjoying yourself," Evelyn told her fondly. "You needed some relaxation."

Jonathan exchanged a mischievous glance with his uncle. "I think she'll sleep well tonight."

While the waiter was clearing away their dinner plates, Jonathan asked Michelle to dance. She agreed without hesitation and they joined the crowd on the small dance floor.

When Jonathan's arms closed around her and their bodies merged, she made a small, involuntary sound of contentment. This was different from last night. They'd both been taut with anger when he carried her to her room. His embrace was seductive now, bringing a languorous response.

It intensified when his lips brushed lightly across her temple. "You're very lovely," he murmured.

She gazed up at him uncertainly. "Why are you being so nice to me?"

He smiled. "You make it very easy."

"You never felt that way before. What's different about me tonight?"

"Just about everything. You're utterly enchanting. I'd like to make love to you until the sun comes up."

His sensuous voice was compelling. Michelle had a sudden, vivid picture of their naked bodies joined and vibrating with passion. Jonathan would be a superb lover, she was sure. He would arouse her unbearably, then satisfy her completely.

Shaking off the disturbing image, she said lightly, "If that's a proposition, I'll have to decline."

"It wasn't. I was merely telling you what I'd *like* to do, but don't let it trouble you. I never take unfair advantage."

"What do you mean?"

"Let's just say, I don't think you have a high tolerance for alcohol."

"Are you insinuating that I'm drunk?" she demanded.

"Not at all. Just happy and relaxed." He grinned.

Michelle couldn't very well get indignant when it was the truth. She never drank this much. "Now that the effects are starting to wear off, I guess I'll have to admit I did lose some of my inhibitions."

"Would another martini help?" he asked mischievously.

"That depends on which one of us you expect it to help."

Her laughter died as their eyes met and Jonathan's expression changed. His desire was unmistakable, but it only mirrored her own emotions. Michelle's lips parted as her gaze shifted to his firm mouth, wanting to feel it move over hers.

Jonathan drew in his breath sharply. His embrace tightened for a moment, then he drew back. "Sweet, lovely Michelle, if you don't sober up soon, I'm going to lose my reputation as an honorable man."

She glanced away, grateful that he thought she was still a little tipsy. It wasn't true, but Jonathan mustn't know her response to him had nothing to do with wine. He had awakened a deep, sensuous tide of feeling she never even knew she was capable of.

"We, uh, we should go back to the table," she said haltingly.

"In a few minutes." He smoothed her hair gently. "I might never catch you with your guard down again. Tomorrow we'll be back to sniping and snarling at each other."

"I suppose so." She sighed unconsciously.

They were unaware of being observed. Lucky and Evelyn had been watching them with interest.

"It seems you were right about the chemistry between them," he remarked.

"I could tell they were attracted to each other. It was just a matter of time until they admitted it to themselves."

"It would be nice if something developed between them."

"I don't know about that, but they'll be company for each other while they're here."

"And perhaps leave *us* alone." Lucky chuckled.

"That would be a pleasant bonus." Evelyn smiled. "But I wouldn't count on it. Young people seem to be suspicious of a relationship that runs smoothly. They have to examine every word and gesture until they find something to argue about. It almost makes me glad I'm not young anymore."

Lucky covered her hand with his. "You're just the right age. I wouldn't change a single thing about you."

Chapter Three

At the end of the evening Jonathan walked Michelle to her room, ignoring her protests that it wasn't necessary.

"A gentleman always sees a lady to her door," he said lightly.

She didn't want to make an issue of it, but she couldn't help wondering if he intended to kiss her good-night. It seemed likely for a moment. Something flickered in his eyes as they paused outside her room. The moment passed and he said a pleasant good-night and walked away.

Michelle closed her bedroom door, torn between regret and relief. She had no doubt that Jonathan's kiss would have been enjoyable—perhaps too much so. She'd already had trouble tonight remembering that he was the enemy.

Jonathan's apparent indifference vanished when he reached his room. He was as disturbed as Michelle by his inexplicable emotions.

Pacing the floor restlessly, he muttered, "Okay, so she's

beautiful, big deal! The world is full of gorgeous women—a lot more glamorous than this one.''

It was true, but Michelle was a natural beauty. She didn't need cosmetics or fancy clothes. She was incredibly sexy without them. Jonathan's blood ran hot when he remembered the glimpse he'd had of just how perfect her body was.

All right, he'd admit he was sexually attracted to her. What able-bodied man wouldn't be? That didn't mean he should lose sight of why they were both here. Michelle and her mother were unscrupulous women, but he could scarcely blame Lucky for being taken in. Too often tonight, Jonathan had found himself wishing he was wrong about Michelle.

His jaw firmed and he strode to the telephone. When Joe Henderson's answering machine clicked on, Jonathan left a message. ''I need that information I requested as soon as possible. Call me and tell me what you have so far.''

The next morning at breakfast, Jonathan was his usual distant self. Michelle could hardly believe he was the same charming man who'd given her such nice compliments the night before and pretended to be attracted to her.

It shouldn't surprise her, she thought cynically. Jonathan was an opportunist. He'd try whatever he thought would distract her. She could have told him it wouldn't work.

In contrast to the young people, Evelyn and Lucky were all smiles. ''Wasn't it a lovely party last night?'' she asked, expecting universal agreement.

Lucky was the only one who concurred. ''I thought the music was especially good, considering it was such a small combo. Wouldn't you say so, Jonathan?''

''I suppose.'' He handed his menu to the waiter and said, ''I'll just have toast and coffee.''

''You enjoyed the evening, didn't you, Michelle?'' Evelyn asked.

"It was nice," she answered tepidly. "Just coffee for me," Michelle told the waiter.

Evelyn and Lucky exchanged a glance. "Well, what does everybody feel like doing today?" she asked brightly.

"Whatever you like." Michelle's lack of enthusiasm was evident.

"How about you, Jonathan?" Lucky asked. "Do you have any suggestions?"

He shrugged. "Whatever you say."

A look of annoyance crossed the older man's face. "If you really want to know, Evie and I would prefer to be alone. Neither you nor Michelle are a great joy to be around. Sorry, Evie."

"Don't apologize, it's true," she said. "If Shorehaven isn't what you expected, perhaps you'd prefer to go home," Evelyn told her daughter.

Michelle sat up straighter in her chair and forced a smile. "I'm having a lovely time. I guess I had a little too much wine last night and it left me with a slight headache, but I'll be fine after I have coffee." She wanted to ask Jonathan what *his* excuse was, but she managed to resist.

"I'm sorry if I seemed withdrawn," he said. "I'm afraid I was thinking about an important phone call I'm expecting."

"Then maybe you should stick around here," Michelle said sweetly. "Weren't we going to Pirate's Cove and then on to the shops?" she asked the others.

"That sounds good to me," Jonathan said quickly. "The hotel can take a message for me."

"Then Pirate's Cove it is," Lucky said. "Wear your bathing suits under your clothes. It's supposed to have a beautiful beach."

The road to Pirate's Cove was very scenic. It wove through tropical vegetation with occasional views of the ocean sparkling under bright sunshine.

Lucky was driving, with Evelyn beside him and Michelle and Jonathan in the back seat. The younger couple made a great effort to be pleasant to each other, but their conversation was forced.

Their differences were forgotten, however, when Lucky pulled off the highway into a parking area and they all got out of the car. Pirate's Cove was idyllically beautiful. It was located at the foot of a cliff, protected from the wind by large boulders on both sides. The small strip of white sand between them was lapped by little white-capped wavelets that foamed briefly on the shore before rushing back to sea.

"What a heavenly little beach!" Michelle exclaimed.

"If you could get down there," Evelyn said doubtfully, gazing at the rocky path.

"I'll hold onto you," Lucky said. "It isn't as steep as it looks."

"I'm so glad you told us to wear our bathing suits," Michelle said. "I can't wait to get in that water."

"It does look great," Jonathan agreed.

They scrambled down the path together. When they got to the beach he spread out the large towels he was carrying and began to strip off his T-shirt and jeans. Michelle was wearing a short sundress over her fairly modest bikini.

While Jonathan searched for some rocks to anchor their clothes so they wouldn't blow away, Michelle glanced around for her mother. She spotted the older couple, still standing at the top of the cliff.

"What are you waiting for?" she called. "It's fantastic down here."

"Evie thinks it's too steep a climb," Lucky called back. "We're going to go for a little ride and maybe stop someplace for coffee, but you two can stay here. Take a swim and we'll come back for you in an hour or so."

"No, wait!" Michelle shouted. "We'll come with you."

"Just give us a minute to put our clothes on," Jonathan called.

"That would be foolish." Lucky waved his hand. "Have fun." Before they could argue further, he and Evelyn got in the car and drove away.

Michelle and Jonathan stared at the top of the bluff in frustration.

Finally he said, "Your mother was very clever at getting rid of us."

"It was *your* uncle who left us here!"

"Guess who put the idea in his head. I'll bet this is what she had planned all along."

"Unlike you, my mother isn't devious. I'm sure it was Lucky's idea to get her alone so he could pitch his fabulous invention to her without my interference. You probably suggested it to him."

"Knowing I'd be stranded alone on a beach with you?" Jonathan asked derisively. "Think about it."

Michelle's temper flared. "It isn't any great treat for me, either. You're rude and bad tempered and I dislike you intensely."

He started to answer, then threw up his hands. "This is pointless. I don't intend to spend the next hour trading insults with you. Think whatever you like. I'm going swimming." He loped across the sand and dived into the surf.

She watched moodily as he cut through the water with powerful strokes. How could such a perfect physical specimen be so defective in every other way? After brooding for long minutes, she decided to ignore him. It was foolish to let Jonathan spoil her day.

Michelle's spirits rose as she frolicked in the lovely lagoon. The water was refreshingly cool and crystal clear. She could see shells on the ocean bottom and darting little tropical fish that made bright streaks in the blue water. Michelle was enchanted by this tropical wonderland. She surface dived for a better look.

Suddenly a long dark shape appeared. Her heart started to pound and she scrambled for the surface. Before she could strike out for shore, Jonathan's head appeared only a few feet away.

"You scared the life out of me!" she exclaimed. "I thought you were a shark."

He grinned, showing a blaze of even white teeth. "Isn't that the way you always think?"

She decided to let that pass. "Isn't this glorious? It's like swimming in an aquarium. I just wish I could stay down longer."

"We should have rented snorkel equipment. Next time we will."

"That would be nice if I knew how to snorkel. It must be a lot of fun."

"I can see your education has been sadly neglected." He smiled. "There are a lot of things I could teach you." Jonathan had evidently decided to be civil.

Michelle was relieved—it would make the day easier—but she didn't want any more than that from him. Certainly not a return to seduction. Peering down into the water she said, "Look at those little striped fish. Aren't they beautiful?"

"They're very common in these waters, but that small blue one isn't. Let's see if we can get a better look."

Michelle stayed underwater until her lungs were bursting. Then she surfaced for air and went back down. She and Jonathan were like two children at play, completely at ease with each other for the first time.

When they finally got out of the water she said, "That was wonderful. You're so fortunate to live in Florida where you can swim all year long."

Jonathan didn't look up from where he was brushing sand off the beach towels. "Your mother seems to like it here, too," he remarked casually.

"I was hoping she would. She didn't want to come on

this trip, but I insisted. I was really worried about her. Mother hasn't taken an interest in anything since Dad died.''

"She doesn't act like a recent widow."

Michelle stopped towel-drying her hair and gave him a level look. "Our truce didn't last long, did it? I should have known."

"You're the one who's looking for an argument. I just made a simple observation."

"You'd better get rid of the attitude, or the next time they strand us somewhere they won't come back for us," Michelle said dryly.

Jonathan grinned unexpectedly. "I have to admire the way they waited until we got down to the beach, knowing we couldn't get back up in time. That was a Machiavellian touch."

"I guess I can't blame them. We weren't exactly sparkling company."

"It looks like we'll have to pretend to like each other," he joked.

Jonathan gazed at her in silent appreciation. As the warm breeze dried Michelle's long hair, her piquant face was framed with tousled curls. It gave her a seductive look, as though she'd just made love. After a quick glance at her curved body, he looked away.

"We can try, anyway," she said carelessly.

Michelle's air of unconcern was deceiving. She was as conscious of him as he was of her. It was difficult not to be. His brief white trunks concealed very little of his splendid body. Jonathan had the lean, muscled physique of a healthy male in his prime.

After stretching out on one of the beach towels he sighed happily. "This is nice. I haven't been this relaxed in a long time."

"Aren't you afraid Mother is seducing your uncle?" Michelle asked mischievously.

"I doubt if she'd meet much resistance. Your mother is a very attractive woman." He turned his head to look at Michelle. The sun had colored her cheeks a delicate pink and her long lashes were still star-pointed from her swim. "It runs in the family."

"That's not exactly an extravagant compliment, but it's better than nothing."

"You get angry when I'm more explicit. What can I do to please you?"

"You're doing fine," she assured him. "I'm enjoying this lull in the hostilities. Too bad it won't last."

"You never know. If you win our private contest, we might be relatives someday, as I pointed out."

"That's a frightening thought!"

"Not necessarily. Think about it. We wouldn't need to argue anymore and I could give you advice on the men in your life. There must be a lot of them," he remarked casually.

She shook her head. "I have poor judgment when it comes to choosing men."

"What kind of men are you attracted to?"

"The wrong kind," she said briefly. Michelle didn't want to talk about Stuart, her latest disappointment. He'd been handsome like Jonathan, and they'd been unofficially engaged, until she found out he'd been cheating on her. "What sort of woman interests *you?* I suppose they're all glamorous and sophisticated."

"That isn't a requirement. Intelligence and a sense of humor are more important to me."

"I'll bet! What does your current girlfriend look like?"

"There's nobody special in my life right now."

"I'm sure you have many women, but isn't there one you date more often than the others?" Michelle persisted.

"I suppose so. You feel comfortable with certain people. They get to be sort of a habit."

"What does your current 'habit' look like?" she asked ironically.

"Why do you want to know?"

"I just do. Humor me." He was clearly reluctant to talk about her, which made Michelle even more curious. "What's her name?"

"I guess that would be Ashleigh Grant. She's blond, a little taller than you and more…voluptuous," he said delicately.

Michelle got the picture. Ashleigh was a showgirl type with big breasts and long legs. Exactly the sort of woman he denied being attracted to.

"I can see why she'd become a habit," Michelle remarked.

"I knew you'd jump to that conclusion. Ashleigh and I have been friends for years. She crews for me sometimes when we go sailing. We know all the same people, so naturally we spend a lot of time together."

Michelle wondered cynically if Ashleigh viewed their relationship in the same light. Before she could pursue the subject, Lucky and Evelyn appeared at the brow of the hill.

"We're back," Evelyn called. "Did you have a nice swim?"

"The water was marvelous." Michelle stood and brushed the sand off her bikini. "You should have joined us."

"Would you like to stay longer? We can come back for you later this afternoon."

"No, we're ready to go." Michelle didn't have to consult Jonathan. She knew he felt the same way.

"Just give us a couple of minutes to get dressed." He started to gather up the beach towels.

"We'll wait for you in the car," Lucky called.

"I'll go in back of this rock to change and you can take that one," Jonathan told Michelle, indicating a large boulder on the left. "And don't dawdle. They might leave us here again."

"I'll be ready before you are." She grabbed her dress and went behind the rock.

The strings that tied her bikini bra had become knotted. She needed two hands to untie them so she slung her dress over the top of the boulder. It took long minutes to loosen the knot because the salt water had made the strings stiff and she couldn't see what she was doing.

Michelle was gritting her teeth in frustration by the time she finally got her bra untied. She threw it on the sand and reached for her dress, just as a puff of wind blew it off the rock in the direction of the water. Without thinking, she ran after it—and collided with Jonathan.

As his arms closed around her automatically, her breasts were pressed against his bare chest. The tips hardened instantly at the erotic contact and a flash of desire rocketed through her. She had an insane impulse to twine her arms around his neck and pull his head down for a deep, satisfying kiss.

Jonathan's embrace tightened, almost as if he'd read her mind. His hands moved seductively over her body, stroking her hips and the rounded curves of her bottom, heightening her desire for him. When he lowered his head, she lifted her face in anticipation, vibrantly aware of every hard muscle in his taut frame.

"Sweet Michelle," he murmured. "You're so exquisite."

His velvety voice brought her to her senses. She pushed him away and ran behind the rock. "Get my dress and throw it to me," she ordered.

While he was following instructions he called, "I didn't know you weren't dressed yet. You said you'd be ready first."

"You might at least have asked before you barged in on me," she answered stiffly.

"I didn't! You came charging out. I was coming over to put your tote bag on top of the rock. I thought you might need it." Jonathan had retrieved her dress. He tossed it over the boulder along with her tote bag.

"Go up to the car and tell them I'll be along in a minute." Her voice was muffled as she hurriedly pulled the sundress over her head.

"I'll wait for you. I still have to put on my shoes and T-shirt. Jonathan had been wearing only his jeans when they collided.

"I don't want you to wait for me!"

"Aren't you being a little foolish? I realize you're embarrassed, but I can't imagine why. You have a beautiful body."

"I'm not in the habit of parading around half naked in front of virtual strangers. Forgive me if I'm not as sophisticated as you," she said witheringly.

He sighed. "Okay, I'll meet you up top."

Michelle knew she was overreacting. With anyone else it would have been a mildly embarrassing incident. What really disturbed her was her reaction to Jonathan. She lost all of her inhibitions in his arms. No other man had ever aroused her this powerfully. It was baffling because she disapproved of everything about him.

After hurriedly pulling on a pair of panties from her tote bag, she grabbed her sandals and ran across the beach. When Michelle reached the car, her mother looked at her critically. "Jonathan said you were combing your hair. Is that the best you could do?"

"I think she looks charming," Lucky said. "I like that natural look. It's very refreshing."

Evelyn surveyed her daughter critically. "It does make her look rather young and innocent."

Michelle was acutely aware of Jonathan's struggle to contain his amusement. She'd displayed neither innocence nor inexperience in his arms a few minutes ago.

"There's nothing I can do about my hair right now, so can we just drop the subject?" Her voice was sharper than she intended. Modifying it, she asked, "Where did you two go all this time? You were gone for quite a while."

"Did it seem like that to you? I thought the time just flew by," Jonathan flicked a laughing glance at Michelle, which she failed to return.

"We had coffee in a little restaurant overlooking the water," Lucky said, in answer to Michelle's question. "We had intended to drive to one of the seaside towns around here and go window-shopping."

"But we got so engrossed in conversation that we never got any farther than the café," Evelyn finished for him.

"We always find so much to talk about," Lucky marveled.

Jonathan's laughter had vanished. "Where are we going now?" he asked abruptly.

"Wherever the three of you would like," Lucky answered cheerfully. "I'm just the chauffeur."

"Perhaps you'd prefer to let Jonathan drive," Evelyn suggested.

"That's an idea. Then you and I could make out in the back seat." Lucky grinned.

"Aren't you a little old for that?" Jonathan asked evenly.

"I'll leave that up to Evie," he replied.

"Age is a state of mind," she said dismissively. "I think of Lucky as a vital, interesting man. His age doesn't matter."

"We both have a lot of living left to do." He reached over and squeezed her hand.

Michelle's heart sank. She was losing ground rapidly. Her mother was completely taken in by Lucky. "I wish you'd decide who's going to drive," she said, to change the subject. "I want to go shopping."

"As long as Jonathan frowns on my having any fun, I'll drive," Lucky said.

Michelle and Jonathan were very quiet in the back seat, ignoring the beautiful scenery that unwound on both sides of the road. Jonathan seemed to be brooding over the situation, as she was, but Michelle knew his opposition was as phony as everything else about him. It was all part of the act.

Her mother and Lucky carried on an animated conversation in the front seat, oblivious to any disapproval. When they parked on a street lined with small shops she said, "I want to take Michelle into Chez Doreen. They're supposed to have darling things. You two might want to look for a men's store."

"I don't need anything," Lucky said. "Do you?" he asked his nephew.

"No, I'm just along to see that you don't do anything foolish." Jonathan's smile didn't reach his eyes. "My uncle has a tendency to want everything he sees," he told the two women.

"What's wrong with that?" Lucky asked. "That old saying might be trite, but it's also true. You can't take it with you."

"Come along, then," Evelyn said. "You can help Michelle pick out some suitable outfits."

"I don't intend to buy things I have no use for, Mother. I already told you that." Michelle protested all the way into the shop.

"I know you did, dear, but it won't hurt to browse. Oh, look, isn't this stunning? And your favorite color, too."

A lavender piqué suit was artfully draped on a mannequin. Under the short jacket was a lavender-and-white striped T-shirt.

"You could wear it with the T-shirt for casual affairs, and dress it up with a silk blouse for more important occasions," Evelyn said. "It's really quite practical."

"Not for New York in the winter," Michelle said.

"Honestly, Michelle! You sound as if you never take a summer vacation," Evelyn exclaimed impatiently.

"I won't be able to afford one after my stay here."

"All right, I'll pay for it. You need to have something to wear while you're here."

When Michelle refused the offer, Lucky said to her, "I have a solution. Your mother wants you to have some pretty things, so why don't I make you a little loan. You can take your time paying me back."

"Now see what you've done," Evelyn scolded her.

Michelle sighed, knowing neither of them would let the matter drop. "That's very nice of you," she told Lucky. "But it won't be necessary. I can afford to buy my own clothes. Every now and then I just have a tendency to get frugal."

Jonathan had been watching the entire exchange with a sardonic look on his face. Did he think she would have accepted a loan from Lucky if he hadn't been there? Undoubtedly. He always thought the worst of her.

Michelle was so annoyed that she didn't object when her mother kept urging her to try on various other outfits. By the time they left the shop, Michelle had bought much more than she intended. This trip would end up costing her a fortune, but it couldn't be helped. Lucky's designs on her mother had to be thwarted at any price.

When they returned to the hotel, Jonathan left them to take a swim in the pool.

"Why don't you join him?" Lucky asked Michelle casually.

"I swam enough today," she answered. "I'm going to take my packages to my room and then read for an hour or so. Unless you want me for something." She looked at her mother inquiringly.

"No, that's what a vacation is for, dear, doing whatever

you feel like. I think Lucky and I will take a little stroll along the beach.''

''Oh…that sounds like fun.'' Michelle managed a bright smile. ''Wait till I dump these packages off and I'll join you.'' Before her mother could object, she hurried off.

Lucky looked at Evelyn with a wry expression. ''It's pretty obvious that your daughter thinks I'm a threat.''

''You know how overly protective children can be,'' she answered dismissively.

''I suppose it's understandable. You haven't been widowed for very long. She feels that by showing an interest in me, you're being disloyal to her father's memory.''

That might have been part of the problem, but Evelyn knew it wasn't the major one. She could hardly tell Lucky the truth, however. That her daughter thought he was a con man.

''You could be right about Michelle. She was very close to her father.''

''I hope that means she doesn't have anything against me, personally.''

''How could she when she doesn't even know you?'' Evelyn couldn't conceal her indignation. ''I wouldn't worry about it,'' she said, modifying her tone. ''Michelle will get over whatever is bothering her.''

''I certainly hope so, because I plan to see a great deal of you,'' Lucky said warmly.

After trying to work off his pent-up emotions by swimming rapid laps in the hotel pool, Jonathan went to his room and put in a long-distance call to his private detective friend. That only added to his frustration because he reached the man's answering machine again.

He went to take a shower, telling himself to face the facts instead of looking for a way around them. Michelle was a bewitching woman with the face of an angel and a body that promised unlimited pleasure. But she was also a con artist, adept at fooling people—especially men. The attraction she occasionally exhibited toward him was undoubtedly feigned. The men who believed her must have gotten badly burned.

Michelle could tell by Jonathan's face that he was in a bad mood when he joined them for cocktails before dinner. So, what else was new, she asked herself derisively? It promised to be another difficult evening.

She would have excused herself after dinner if it hadn't meant leaving her mother alone with the Richfields. That was a risk she couldn't afford to take, even for one night. Evelyn was already much too vulnerable to Lucky. When Michelle had joined them for a walk along the beach that afternoon, neither could hide the fact that her presence wasn't exactly welcome.

As they were finishing their coffee, Michelle remarked, "It's been a very eventful day. I guess we're all looking forward to turning in early."

Lucky looked at her with concealed amusement. "You young people today don't have our stamina. The evening has barely begun. Evie and I planned to take in a movie and then go to one of those clubs in town that have dancing until all hours." His eyes gleamed with mischief at the look of dismay she couldn't hide.

Jonathan wasn't any happier at the prospect than Michelle. "Don't you think we should save something to do tomorrow night?" he asked.

"You two don't have to come with us," Lucky replied blandly.

"No, it's okay. Now that I think about it, it sounds like fun."

Evelyn and Lucky exchanged a look of shared amusement before she took pity on the young couple. "Actually, it *has* been a busy day. I believe I'd rather stay in tonight and go to that lecture they're giving on tropical islands.

You and Jonathan are welcome to join us," she told her daughter.

"Thanks, but I think I'll just hang out in the lounge for a while," Michelle said. It was safe to leave them alone, since Lucky could scarcely get amorous at a lecture.

"Whatever you prefer. You know where we'll be if you want to check on us," Evelyn added dryly.

"Why would I want to do that?" Michelle tried to sound puzzled.

"It would be foolish, I agree. I'm a mature adult in possession of all my faculties." After giving her a level look, Evelyn turned to Lucky. "I'm ready when you are."

"Another fun evening at Shorehaven," Jonathan commented, after the older couple left. "What would you like to do for excitement?"

"There isn't anything here that excites me," she answered coolly.

His eyes narrowed in annoyance for a moment. Then he smiled seductively and sauntered toward her. "I'll have to see what I can do to change that."

Michelle stood her ground until he was close enough to set her nerves jangling. Who knew what he would do? The dining room was deserted except for a busboy clearing the last few tables, but that wouldn't deter Jonathan. He was looking sensuously at her.

"Don't bother. I'm going to the bar." She left the room quickly, without asking him to join her.

It didn't prevent him from following her, but two women at one of the tables in the bar stopped him, waving eagerly.

"Come and have a drink with us, Jonathan," the slightly plump one called. She was the woman who'd wanted him to play bingo the night Michelle arrived. "We got our snapshots back this afternoon and there's a great one of you and Ruth."

After hesitating for a moment, he went over to join them. Winnie's companion was an attractive young woman, pretty without being glamorous. From the look on her face as she gazed at Jonathan, it was evident that she shared her friend's admiration for him.

He was loving every minute of it, Michelle thought sourly. She slid onto a bar stool and ordered an after dinner drink she didn't want. It promised to be a long evening.

The sound of Jonathan's low, amused voice and the excited chatter of his companions irritated Michelle even further. They were too far away for her to hear their conversation, but his enjoyment was evident—quite different from his behavior toward *her*.

Jonathan wasn't as indifferent to Michelle as she thought. He was very conscious of her sitting alone at the bar. Should he ask her to join them? What for, he asked himself? She'd made it quite clear that his company was unwelcome. Let her sulk, if that's what she wanted.

"So, how about it, Jonathan?" Winnie was looking at him hopefully. "Will you go with us?"

He stared at her blankly, trying to recall his wandering attention. "Uh, where was that again?"

"Pirate's Cove. I just told you! They say the beach is gorgeous, so picturesque and secluded."

Jonathan's mind flashed back to that erotic moment at the cove when he'd held Michelle's nearly nude body in his arms. He would never forget the feeling of her breasts pressed against his bare chest, or the satiny smoothness of her thighs against his rougher, more muscular ones.

Ruth added more incentives. "We can swim and lie on the beach afterward."

"No!" Jonathan quickly softened his first, explosive reaction. "I mean, my uncle has something planned for tomorrow. He expects me to be with him, since that's the reason I came."

"He doesn't look lonesome to me," Winnie remarked.

"I'll bet he'd welcome some time alone with that nice-looking, older lady."

"They hit it off immediately," Ruth agreed. "I wouldn't be surprised if something developed there."

Not if I can help it, Jonathan replied silently. It was a timely reminder not to let himself get sidetracked by a beautiful face and an alluring body.

Michelle was unaware of his dark thoughts. She was staring broodingly at the mirror in back of the bar when a man appeared next to her. He was tall, blond and broad shouldered, the athletic type male who was always cast as a lifeguard in a movie.

"Do you mind if I join you?" he asked pleasantly.

"Not at all," she answered. "I was getting tired of my own company."

"I'm sure nobody else would." He gave her an admiring, but respectful glance. "My name is Roger Kirkenhoff. May I buy you another drink?"

After supplying her own name, Michelle declined his offer. "I didn't really want this one, but I couldn't think of anything else to do after dinner."

"Shorehaven offers a lot of activities. I believe there was a lecture tonight, and if that didn't interest you there's a well-stocked library and a card room."

"You sound like a social director. They should give you a job here."

"Actually, I do take a special interest." He smiled. "My father owns the hotel."

"Do you work here? I haven't seen you around."

"No, I live in Atlanta. I'm just here for a few days. Dad is thinking of putting an addition on the hotel, and he wanted my input. I'm an architect."

She looked at him with unfeigned interest. "You probably don't have anything to do with it but I've always wanted to ask someone in the hotel business, why they provide those clothes hangers that you can't take off the rod.''

"I agree with you that they're an abomination, but you'd be surprised at the things guests walk off with if they're not fastened down. People take pictures off the wall and blankets. I even heard of someone carting away a television set, although thankfully that's never happened to us." He laughed.

Roger was so easy to talk to that Michelle shelved her problems for the time being. He was just what she needed after her trying day. For the first time that evening, she was enjoying herself.

After a while he suggested they move to a booth. "I'll have to tell Dad these bar stools could be more comfortable."

"I was so interested in what you were saying that I didn't even notice," Michelle remarked as they strolled past Jonathan's table.

Jonathan ignored her as studiously as she was ignoring him, but his firm jawline got even tighter.

"I'm glad I'm not boring you too badly—or perhaps you're just being polite." Roger smiled at her.

"Not at all," she assured him. "This is the nicest time I've had since I got to Shorehaven."

As they slid into a booth, he said, "I appreciate the compliment, but if that's true, you're not having nearly enough fun here. As the owner's representative, I'd like to do something about that. Will you have dinner with me tomorrow night? There's a little seafood place in town that's known for their baked pompano. We can have dinner and perhaps go to a movie."

"I wish I could," Michelle said with genuine regret.

Roger didn't make her nerves skitter or her pulse accelerate, but that was part of his charm. He was almost as handsome as Jonathan, in a different way, and a lot easier to be with. This was the kind of man she should be looking for, not some glamorous rogue with a wickedly irresistible smile and a line to match.

"If you have a date for dinner, how about lunch?" Roger asked. "I don't mean to be pushy, but I'm only going to be here for a couple of more days and I'd like to spend at least a little time with you before I leave."

"I'd like that, too." Michelle sighed. "The problem is my mother. I came down here to, uh, sort of watch over her. That means my time isn't my own."

"Does she have some kind of disability?" he asked delicately.

"Nothing that shows," Michelle answered grimly. "Actually it's emotional. Mother is a fairly recent widow."

"I'm sorry to hear that. It's always—" He paused as Jonathan appeared at their table.

"I just wanted to tell you the lecture appears to be over," Jonathan said to Michelle. "You can stay here and enjoy yourself, however. I'll keep an eye on them."

She was instantly on the alert. "No, I'm coming, too." She turned to Roger. "It was so nice meeting you. I hope I'll see you again before you leave."

"I'm available whenever you have some free time," he replied. "Just give me a call. I'm in room 107."

"That's just down the hall from me. I'm in 103."

Jonathan's expression had gotten chillier by the moment. "I can tell I'm inhibiting you two," he said sarcastically. "Perhaps I'd better leave."

Roger slid out of the booth and stood, extending his hand. "Sorry, I should have introduced myself sooner. I'm Roger Kirkenhoff."

Jonathan shook his hand briefly, supplying his own name while giving the other man a thorough scrutiny. "Did you just arrive?" he asked.

"Yes, I got here yesterday, but only for a brief visit. I'm leaving quite soon."

"Lucky you," Jonathan muttered. "I wish *I* could."

Roger frowned slightly. "You don't like Shorehaven?"

"He had different expectations for this vacation," Michelle said sweetly.

"I'm sorry to hear that," Roger said. "Perhaps you aren't taking advantage of all the opportunities here."

She snorted in a decidedly unladylike manner. "It certainly isn't for lack of trying."

As Jonathan's eyes narrowed angrily, Evelyn called to them from the doorway. "We're back." She and Lucky walked over to the booth. "You really should have come to the lecture, Michelle. You, too, Jonathan. They showed slides of these incredibly beautiful tropical islands."

"I asked Evie to run away with me to one of them and she's considering it." Lucky chuckled.

"Is this your mother?" Roger gave Michelle a surprised look.

She could see why he'd be confused. Evelyn wasn't acting like a woman suffering from depression. She looked animated and happy. It was Michelle who was depressed at the way things were going. Lucky was gaining ground with every hour he and her mother spent alone together. From now on she had to stick to them like glue, Michelle decided, as she introduced Roger.

After Evelyn and Lucky both told him how much they liked the hotel, Roger said, "I'm delighted to hear it. I'm just sorry Jonathan isn't having a better time."

"I didn't realize he wasn't." Lucky frowned at his nephew. "What's wrong? Are you afraid the business will fall apart with both of us gone? That's nonsense. Young Helmsley is working out very well. He can handle things."

"I agree with you. I wouldn't have left otherwise," Jonathan said. "I'm sorry if Roger got the wrong impression. I'm having a fine time."

Roger was unconvinced, but he didn't press the point. "Well, if there's anything we can do to make your stay more enjoyable, please don't hesitate to ask." He looked at his watch. "If you'll all excuse me, I have some paper-work to do."

After he left, Evelyn remarked, "What a nice young man."

"He's very interesting, too," Michelle said. "Roger is an architect, quite a good one, I imagine. His father values his opinion highly. I think it's admirable when a man works at a career instead of expecting everything to be handed to him."

"Or *her*," Jonathan said ironically. "The same thing applies to women."

"You seem to be in complete accord, so what's the argument?" Lucky asked impatiently. "Would you like a drink, Evie?"

"No, thanks," she replied. "I think I'll turn in early tonight. But first I'd like to take a last stroll along the beach. Just the two of us," she added, looking Michelle squarely in the eye.

After the older couple had gone, Jonathan said, "You and your mother won this round. I didn't have to bother hanging around here all night."

"It wasn't a wasted evening," Michelle said. "You had your mini-harem to boost your ego. From the way they were hanging on your words, anybody would think you invented the wheel."

"Hardly, but I'll admit their unjudgmental attitude was a pleasant change."

"They don't know as much about you as I do."

"I could say the same about you and your new conquest, the fair-haired architect who works for a living."

"That isn't his only attraction. He's witty and charming, and he's a gentleman." She stressed the pronoun slightly.

"Are you intimating that I'm not?" Jonathan asked ominously.

"You've had some lapses."

"Considering the provocation I've had, you're lucky I

am a gentleman. You've done everything you can to distract me, including that provocative encounter on the beach today. I'm beginning to wonder if it really was accidental.''

"You were the one who made a pass at *me!*" she gasped.

"When you throw yourself half nude into a man's arms, you shouldn't be surprised if he reacts. Even a gentleman like your architect friend—if he has any red blood in his veins, that is," Jonathan drawled.

"I consider this conversation in very bad taste—like the rest of your conduct." Michelle lifted her chin and stalked out the door.

His expression was moody as he watched her go. If she wasn't the world's most aggravating woman, she was right up there with the contenders!

Chapter Four

The red light was glowing on Jonathan's telephone when he reached his room, telling him he had a message waiting. It couldn't be anything pertaining to business at this hour, and his friends at home didn't know where to reach him. Joe Henderson must have completed his report on Michelle.

That was good news, Jonathan told himself. If Joe found out something really damaging, Michelle and her mother would have to give up on Lucky. They'd undoubtedly leave Shorehaven immediately, after inventing some emergency at home. The game was very likely over, and he wouldn't have to see either of them again.

Jonathan's face wasn't as happy as it should have been. He gazed out at the starry night for long minutes before his expression hardened and he picked up the phone.

"What do you have for me?" he asked curtly when the private detective answered a few moments later.

"You were in such a flaming hurry that I couldn't be as

thorough as I usually am,'' Joe complained. ''I really moved my tail on this one.''

''Never mind the buildup, I'm not going to quibble about your bill. What did you find out?''

''Not what I expected. I don't imagine you did, either.''

''I didn't think she was a choir girl,'' Jonathan commented ironically. ''How bad is it? Has she ever been arrested? Or should I ask, how many times?''

''That's what I mean. She's squeaky clean.''

Jonathan wasn't sure he'd heard correctly. ''What did you say?''

''Miss Wholesome. Susie cream cheese. She never even got a speeding ticket. If everybody was that straight arrow I'd be out of business.''

''Are you sure you dug deep enough?'' Jonathan persisted. ''I know she puts up a good front. Maybe the people you talked to were deceived.''

''I don't rely on hearsay. I deal in facts. Subject is twenty-six years old, the only child of Richard and Evelyn Lacey.'' Joe was evidently reading from his notebook. ''Father, Richard, died one year, six weeks ago. Mother, Evelyn, still lives in family home in Roslyn, Long Island. Mother doesn't work. Was evidently left enough to live on. I didn't have time to find out how much, but I can if you're interested.''

''I'm not,'' Jonathan said. ''Go on about Michelle. Does she hold down a regular job?''

''She's a buyer at Barrington's. Started as a stock girl originally. It's an upscale women's shop on Fifth Avenue.''

''Yes, I've been there.''

''Buying fancy lingerie for your girlfriends?'' Joe joked.

''Get on with it,'' Jonathan answered curtly. ''What about men in her life?''

''I didn't have time to go too far back, but I found out she just broke up with a guy. He was tall, dark and handsome, even had a good job. They were unofficially engaged—whatever that means—but lover boy wasn't too particular about whose bed he slept in. When your friend found out, everything hit the fan. She broke up with him.''

''How long ago was this?''

''Not long, maybe a month. He's been trying to get her back, but she won't give him the time of day. Everybody says she's a terrific gal, beautiful, smart, great personality. Everything but forgiving, evidently. So don't try to put anything over on her.'' Joe laughed.

''There's nothing personal between us. I wanted to find out about her for business reasons.''

''Okay, if you say so. There's some more in the report about what schools she went to and who her friends are, things like that. I can find out more details if you want me to continue the investigation, but this pretty much gives you the picture. Do you want me to stay on the job?''

''No, I've heard enough. Mail me a copy of your report along with the bill.''

Jonathan hung up with dawning excitement as the full impact of the information hit him. He didn't have to fight against his attraction to Michelle. She was exactly who she said she was!

His elation was tempered momentarily when he remembered the present, rocky state of their relationship. But that was his fault for being a jerk. He should have known Michelle wasn't the devious person he suspected. She was too honest and direct. And her emotions were mirrored on her lovely, expressive face.

That was the thing that gave him hope for the future. There was a potent attraction between them, and it wasn't one-sided. Michelle couldn't hide her feelings, even though she tried. Once he stopped antagonizing her, they should be able to put their differences behind them.

Jonathan went to bed feeling a lot more cheerful than he'd been when he got up that morning.

* * *

Michelle didn't share his mood. She felt cranky and put upon as she got undressed. Why couldn't her mother act her age—or at least find a suitable gentleman friend. Michelle would have been delighted for her if she'd met a nice, respectable man.

But Evelyn seemed perfectly happy with the one she had. She and Lucky couldn't stop smiling at each other. Jonathan was another annoyance. He'd broken his own record for acting disagreeable that night!

Michelle was wary of him the next morning, but he caught her off base by being exceedingly pleasant. She wasn't impressed. His new attitude aggravated her even more because her mother fell for his phony act. Evelyn was utterly charmed by him.

When Jonathan suggested they all go to the races that day, Michelle said quickly, "Mother has never been interested in horse racing. Why don't you and Lucky go?"

"I wish you wouldn't answer for me, Michelle," Evelyn said with a trace of irritation. "I don't know whether I like horse racing or not. I've never been to a racetrack."

"I can't believe it!" Lucky exclaimed. "We'll have to do something about that. You don't know what you're missing."

"Do you go to the track often, or do you bet with bookies?" Michelle asked with an innocent expression.

"Betting with a bookie is like playing the stock market. You might make money, but it's no fun," he said deprecatingly. "The excitement comes from watching your horse romp home a winner, not from collecting on an exacta."

"What's that?" Evelyn asked.

Lucky explained the system of picking a series of horses in their winning positions.

"It sounds so complicated," she protested.

"I guess you have to be a gambler to understand it," Michelle said ingenuously.

"A person who enjoys going to the track isn't necessarily a gambler." Jonathan corrected her mildly. "It's the same as watching any other sporting event, like a football game, for instance. People bet on those, too."

Michelle didn't argue. She was content to have planted the seed in her mother's mind. Sooner or later, Evelyn had to see Lucky for what he really was.

"It sounds like a great deal of fun." Evelyn's face was animated. "What time shall we leave?"

"Well, let's see. It will take about half an hour to get there," Lucky said. "Let's plan on leaving here at eleven-thirty. We can have lunch in the clubhouse and look over the racing form to see who's running today."

Evelyn looked at him in surprise. "You know the horses by name?"

"A few, but I'm more familiar with the jockeys. They're the ones who can tip the odds in your favor." Lucky proceeded to explain the intricacies of horse racing.

"You certainly are knowledgeable about the sport," Evelyn remarked, but she said it admiringly.

Michelle wasn't discouraged, though. Lucky didn't know it yet, but he was wasting his time. Then she noticed Jonathan watching her, and she wasn't as sure. The amused look on his face seemed to indicate he knew something she didn't.

Under different circumstances, Michelle would have enjoyed the ride. The air was perfumed with the scent of orange blossoms from the groves that lined both sides of the winding highway. The road also ran along fields of pineapple before curving toward the ocean.

"Isn't this scenery just awesome?" Evelyn asked from the back seat. Jonathan was driving that day. "I love the way the coconut palms grow right up in the sand, with the blue water beyond. It's like a painting."

"That's the view I look out on at home when I pull open the drapes in the morning," Lucky said.

"Aren't you fortunate? All I see are bare trees and overcast skies," Evelyn said.

"Only in the winter, Mother," Michelle protested. "Long Island is beautiful in the spring and summer months."

"It's a shame to have to suffer through an entire season of dreariness, though. Have you ever thought of moving down South?" Lucky asked casually.

"Not really," Evelyn replied. "All of my friends live in the New York area."

"You can make new friends," he said, taking her hand.

After a quick glance at the couple in the back seat, Michelle asked abruptly, "Aren't we almost there?"

"About another five minutes," Jonathan assured her.

Michelle's personal problems were temporarily shelved when they reached their destination. The high spirits of the crowd were catching. People milled around the oval track, clutching racing forms and watching jockeys in colorful silks leading their sleek, prancing mounts. Food vendors hawked their wares in the grandstand and there were long lines in front of the betting windows.

"I've never seen so much activity!" Evelyn exclaimed. "Doesn't anybody ever sit down?"

"Rarely." Lucky chuckled, guiding their little group to an elevator.

The atmosphere in the clubhouse was less hectic. Groups of people were clustered around the bar chatting, or seated at tables having lunch. A wide glass window across one end of the room gave a view of the racetrack and the activity below, but the noise was muted.

When the two couples were seated at a table by the window, Lucky ordered champagne. After it arrived he raised his glass. "This is a special occasion, so I want to propose a toast." As Michelle caught her breath he continued, "To Evie's first horse race."

"You really have to stop expecting the worst," Jonathan told Michelle in a low, amused voice.

"You haven't won yet," she muttered.

"No, but hope springs eternal," he murmured, draping an arm casually across the back of her chair.

While they were sipping their champagne, Lucky produced two racing forms. They had columns of statistics on all the horses running that day, their past performance, the length of the race, if they were moving up or down in class.

"That's much too complicated," Evelyn complained. "What would happen if I just picked out a name that appealed to me?"

"You'd probably stand as much chance of winning as the experts." Jonathan laughed.

"Oh, look, here's one I simply have to bet on," she exclaimed. "Sun and Fun."

"That definitely sounds like a winner," Lucky said fondly.

"What's your choice?" Jonathan asked Michelle. "I don't think they have a horse named Gloom and Doom," he teased.

"I'm looking for one called Victory," she answered coolly.

"There's a horse called Sir Prize. Will that do?" Lucky asked. "His odds are long, but he just might go all the way."

"The uncertainty is what makes it interesting." Jonathan gave Michelle a mischievous look.

"Hadn't we better order?" Evelyn asked. "If we don't hurry up and have lunch we'll miss the first race."

"We can see it from up here. There are betting windows, or an attendant will come over to the table to take our bets," Lucky explained.

They made their selections for the first race while they were having lunch. As they were drinking coffee, the horses were herded into the gate. Some of the horses reared or danced around, reluctant to enter the narrow stalls.

"Oh, no!" Michelle exclaimed. "Look at number six, he doesn't want to race. I should have bet on the one in purple and white. I like those colors better anyway."

"Your horse is just spirited," Jonathan soothed. "That's a good sign."

"He's twenty to one," Lucky said in an undertone.

"Long shots sometimes pay off." Jonathan smiled.

The gate opened and the horses thundered out. Michelle watched anxiously as her choice, Fashion's Pride, was caught in the middle of the pack. At the first turn he pulled away, but he was still trailing three other horses. She leaped to her feet when Fashion's Pride closed the gap and overtook all but the leader.

Coming down the stretch the two horses were neck and neck. Michelle was jumping up and down, shouting, "Come on, Fashion's Pride!" as the horses crossed the wire. "Did I win?" she asked when some words flashed on the announcement board. "They were so close I couldn't tell."

"It's a photo finish," Jonathan said. "We'll know in a minute."

After Fashion's Pride was declared the winner, and Michelle discovered he'd pay forty dollars for her two-dollar bet, she was so excited she threw her arms around Jonathan's neck.

"I won! I won!" she exclaimed.

He held her close, kissing her temple so lightly she wasn't aware of it. "Congratulations," he said huskily. "I'm happy for you."

"I'll have to follow your system," Lucky joked. "You were the only one in the group with a winning ticket."

"It's beginner's luck," Evelyn said. "I'm not sure if she's ever been to the races, either. Have you, Michelle?"

She was abruptly aware of being in Jonathan's arms.

Michelle's cheeks were flushed as she drew away and mumbled, "Sorry. I guess I got carried away."

"Don't apologize. It was an exciting race. The close ones always are," he said.

She looked at him narrowly, but there didn't seem to be any hidden meaning in his remark. "Yes, well, I'll try to restrain myself after this."

"Why? You're charming when you allow yourself to act naturally. It's normal to be exuberant." He grinned suddenly. "I hope you have a lot of winners today."

Michelle wasn't as lucky after that, but it didn't dampen her enthusiasm. She and her mother pored over the racing form, sometimes relying on its recommendation, but usually picking a horse because they liked the name.

They would have been better off it they'd taken Lucky's advice. He won more often than not, large sums because he was betting a hundred dollars each time.

"Isn't that an awful lot of money?" Evelyn asked.

"Only if you lose," he said.

"I'd be very nervous if I had that much money riding on a horse race," she said.

"Then you shouldn't risk it," he answered. "Betting is only fun if you don't wager more than you can comfortably afford to lose."

Michelle was glad her mother was starting to question Lucky's life-style, but she had to admit to herself that it was enjoyable. She wouldn't complain if he'd worked for the money he was flinging around, instead of bilking someone else out of it.

After a few races, Jonathan asked if she'd like to go down to the paddock and inspect the horses. Her mother and Lucky declined to join them, so they went alone.

"It must be fun to own a racehorse," Michelle remarked as they strolled toward the paddock. "You have all the excitement of seeing it run, and you can win thousands of dollars, too."

"Racing stables are rarely profitable," Jonathan told her. "They're enormously expensive to run."

"How much can oats cost?" she joked.

"More than you'd imagine. There are also veterinary bills, stable help, entrance fees and on and on. You have to be rich and preferably retired. That's why I sold my horses. I didn't have time to travel around the country to watch them run."

"You owned racehorses?" she asked in disbelief.

"Lucky and I owned a stable briefly."

"You must have made a good score that year," she observed sardonically.

Jonathan sighed. "We have to talk, Michelle."

"Not now. It won't change either of our minds and we'll only wind up angry again. Can't we suspend hostilities for just this one afternoon?" When he hesitated she said coaxingly, "I'm having a really good time."

"All right, it's a deal—but only if we extend our truce to this evening as well."

"I don't know if we can go twenty-four hours without arguing."

"We've never tried before. How about it? We'll go out to dinner, just the two of us, and perhaps finally get to know each other."

She looked up at him doubtfully. "Maybe we'd better not push our luck."

"What's the matter, Michelle? Are you afraid you might grow to like me?" he asked softly.

It was a distinct possibility. Jonathan's charisma was awesome. If he continued to be as charming as he'd been all day, she couldn't guarantee her own immunity. But she didn't want him to know that.

Feigning indifference, she said, "I think it's going to be a short evening, but I'm willing to go along with you."

"That's all I ask." He put his arm around her and led

her toward the paddock, hiding his jubilation. "Come on, let's go pick ourselves a winner."

By the end of the day, Evelyn declared she was exhausted. "All I want to do tonight is have dinner and go to bed early."

"How about a movie?" Lucky suggested. "That's not too strenuous."

"I might consider it if we go to an early one."

"How does that sound to you kids?" Lucky asked.

"Don't worry about us. Michelle and I are going out to dinner," Jonathan answered.

"That's nice," Evelyn said approvingly. "Wear the lavender suit you bought yesterday," she told Michelle. "With the ivory silk blouse."

"We're not going anyplace special," Michelle protested.

"You'll make it special," Jonathan said with a melting smile.

Jonathan was waiting in the bar at seven-thirty that evening. When Michelle saw the admiring expression on his face, she was glad she'd worn the lavender suit and taken pains with her hair and makeup.

It was what she would do for any date, she'd told herself as she used eyeliner, shaded her high cheekbones with blush and lengthened her thick lashes with mascara. She'd also used a curling iron to make her hair as picture perfect as a shampoo ad.

If Michelle realized she was inviting a response from Jonathan, she dismissed the fact as irrelevant. He would try to romance her, anyway.

Jonathan couldn't stop staring at her. "You look ravishing!"

"You sound surprised," she teased. "Were you expecting me to appear in jeans?"

"You'd look beautiful no matter what you had on, but

I'm glad you listened to your mother. That outfit is smashing.''

"This old thing?" She laughed.

The evening was starting out well. Michelle only hoped it would continue that way. She didn't mind a few compliments—if he just kept it at that.

They drove to the nearby town of Olaca where Jonathan had made a dinner reservation at a restaurant called the Sea Vista.

"I hope the food is good," he said. "The manager at the hotel recommended it, but you never know."

"I'm sure it will be fine," she answered.

The Sea Vista was more than just nice. It was a surprisingly elegant restaurant for a small town. The tables were covered with crisp linen tablecloths centered by a spray of tiny orchids in a bud vase, and wineglasses were lined up at each place setting.

Michelle and Jonathan were seated at a choice table near the picture window. Since he'd never been there before, he couldn't be a favored customer. The maître d' simply assumed from Jonathan's expensive clothes and impeccable grooming that he was used to preferential treatment.

Michelle had to admit that Jonathan acted the part. It wasn't only the clothes, although he looked especially handsome that night in a lightweight beige sport jacket and darker beige slacks, both perfectly tailored to his lithe frame. His shirt looked custom made, also. It had a tiny, unobtrusive monogram on the cuff. The white linen contrasting with his tanned face was very effective. He was a dazzlingly attractive man, much more virile than Stuart. And look how that turned out, Michelle reminded herself.

"What does the *A* stand for," she asked, pointing to the monogram on his cuff, *JAR*.

He groaned. "Do you really have to know?"

"Now, I do. You've piqued my curiosity."

"I should have lied and said Adam or Al."

"Come on and tell me," she coaxed. "How bad can it be?"

"Pretty bad. It's Artemis. I was named after my paternal grandfather, who probably got into innumerable fights over his name when he was a boy. Fortunately he was a big strapping kid, I'm told. He could hold his own."

"I'll bet you can, too." Michelle glanced at Jonathan's broad shoulders.

"If I have to, but I'm a lover, not a fighter." He grinned.

"I already figured that out," she answered dryly.

"That isn't fair," he protested. "I haven't made a pass at you all night."

"The evening's young."

His eyes were more golden than green as he gazed at her with a little smile. "If you're expecting one, I'd be happy to oblige."

"But it doesn't matter to you one way or the other? That's not very flattering," she joked.

"Dear little Michelle," he said in a throaty voice. "I'd be ecstatic at the opportunity to make love to you. I want to hold you in my arms again and feel you respond with all the passion I know you're capable of."

She realized he was referring to their erotic encounter on the beach. Her entire body heated at the recollection of the searing desire that had flared so instantly between them.

Trying to defuse the moment, she managed a little laugh. "You said we should get to know each other better, but I didn't realize you meant that well."

"Whether you choose to admit it or not, there is a very real attraction between us. It would be nice if we could cut through all the stylized games men and women play, but I don't expect it to happen."

"That's a relief," she said lightly.

"Is it really?" he asked softly. "I think our lovemaking would be like nothing either of us has ever experienced. Don't you wonder if I'm right?"

Michelle didn't have to wonder. She'd felt the seductiveness of his hard body, the sensuous allure of his smooth, supple skin. Jonathan would raise her passion to a fever pitch before satisfying her with superb male expertise.

She moistened her dry lips. "This is why I didn't want to go out with you. You're a very experienced man. You know exactly what buttons to push to make me respond to you."

He reached across the table and covered her hand with his. "I'm not trying to seduce you, Michelle. When we make love it will be because you want me as much as I want you. That's the only way it would be good for both of us." He leaned back in his chair, smiled and signaled the waiter to bring more wine. "Don't look so serious, honey. I always take no for an answer."

The rest of the evening was pure pleasure. Michelle almost forgot this wasn't an ordinary date. Although when he suggested going somewhere to dance after dinner, she knew it wasn't a good idea. Her judgment was always affected when Jonathan held her in his arms—for whatever reason.

"It's been a full day," she said. "I think I'd like to go back to the hotel."

He didn't try to persuade her, but when they arrived back at Shorehaven he suggested having a nightcap in the bar before turning in.

Michelle declined that offer, too. "I've had enough to drink tonight. I don't want to disgrace myself again the way I did at the dinner dance the other night."

"I thought you were charming. It was the first time I caught a glimpse of what you're really like when you're not on your guard."

"That's a good reason for not drinking. I need to be alert when I'm around you."

"Because you might do what you want to do, instead of what you think you should?" he asked softly.

"No, because you're a very clever man. You almost made me forget tonight what you're after."

"I thought that was obvious." His even teeth gleamed whitely in his tanned face as he grinned mischievously.

"Sex would be a pleasant bonus you wouldn't turn down, but it isn't your real objective. Your primary aim is to convince me that you and Lucky are legitimate. I realize that."

"I thought I was making progress," he teased. "How about letting me make love to you, anyway? You can call it a consolation prize."

"That would mean you were giving up—and I know you aren't."

"If I did, I wouldn't see you anymore." He stroked her cheek gently. "A lot of the color would go out of my life."

His long fingers felt sensuous, although the gesture wasn't intimate enough to object to. Michelle tried to ignore it. "I can scarcely believe I mean that much to you. We haven't known each other very long, and most of our time together has been unpleasant."

"I remember it differently."

"You have a selective memory," she said curtly, although she remembered the same things he did.

"Every relationship has its ups and downs. I prefer to dwell on the positive moments."

"We don't have a relationship," she stated.

"Not yet, but I'm optimistic." His eyes danced with merriment at the stormy look on her face. Before she could answer, he said, "If you're sure you won't change your mind about that drink, I'll walk you to your room. It's been too nice a day to spoil it now with an argument."

Michelle couldn't help agreeing with him. When they reached her room she said, "Thank you for a lovely evening. I really enjoyed it."

"I did, too." He smiled. "We'll have to do it again."

She hesitated, but there was no point in telling him this

was a one-time event. It might lead to a quarrel and she didn't want the evening to end on that note.

Jonathan leaned down to kiss her cheek. That would have been the end of it if Michelle hadn't turned her face toward him at the same time. Their lips touched and both were too bemused to draw away. After an instant his arms closed around her and the pressure of his mouth increased.

Michelle stiffened in his arms, but when Jonathan parted her lips and probed the moist warmth inside, her resistance was washed away in a flood of desire. She'd known it would be like this. His mouth lit a fire inside her, and his hands fed the flames. As they moved over her back sensuously, she couldn't hold back a tiny cry of pleasure.

Jonathan's embrace tightened and he buried his face in the scented, midnight cloud of her hair. "Darling Michelle," he murmured. "You're so sweet, so incredibly open and honest."

Her heated body didn't want to hear any warnings, but her drugged brain was starting to function again. Jonathan knew exactly how to make her respond, but he'd gotten overconfident. Her reaction *was* uncalculated—too bad his actions weren't.

She drew away and fumbled in her purse for her key. "It's late," she said without looking at him.

"Let me do that for you," he offered, when she had trouble fitting her key in the lock.

She pulled her hand away so quickly when his hand touched hers that the key fell to the floor.

He picked it up, then cradled her chin in his palm and tilted her face up to his. "One of these days you're going to trust me and we're going to make glorious, fulfilling love. But I won't rush you." He unlocked the door and kissed the top of her head. "Get a good night's sleep, angel. I'll see you in the morning."

As if she could sleep when her entire body was clamoring for him! Michelle got undressed slowly, deeply troubled by Jonathan's powerful hold over her. Was it more than just sexual attraction? Stuart had been handsome and sexy, but that hadn't blinded her to his faults. Even before she found out about his womanizing. Could she possibly be falling in love with Jonathan?

Michelle rejected the idea violently! He was simply a very experienced man who knew how to get what he wanted. And yet…she admired everything about him except his profession. Jonathan was intelligent and thoughtful. He was warm and kind—when they weren't arguing. He was every woman's dream.

He was also helping his uncle fleece her mother out of her life savings, Michelle reminded herself. She got into bed and punched up the pillow savagely. Tomorrow she needed to have a serious talk with Evelyn. It was time they went home where they belonged.

Michelle went to her mother's room early the next morning, to catch her before she went down to breakfast. Evelyn was still in her bathrobe and slippers.

"You're up early," she commented. Looking at her daughter more closely she said, "You should have stayed in bed longer. You look tired. Did you get in late last night?"

"No, we got back fairly early," Michelle said.

"How was your dinner? Where did you go?"

"To a restaurant in Olaca called the Sea Vista."

"I heard some people at the pool talking about it," Evelyn remarked. "They said the food is excellent."

"It was, but that's not what—"

"Is it a seafood restaurant? The fish is wonderful down here, but frankly I'm getting a little tired of seafood. What did you have for dinner?"

"I had stone crab, and Jonathan had a steak," Michelle added, anticipating her mother's next question.

"Isn't he a gorgeous man? I hope you know you're the

envy of every single woman here. He doesn't look at anyone but you."

"Men like Jonathan know how to put on a good act," Michelle answered grimly.

"Really, Michelle, I'm losing patience with you!" Evelyn exclaimed. "A handsome man goes out of his way to be attentive to you and you can't even say a nice word about him."

"You're taken in by his surface charm. I'm not."

"It isn't superficial. Jonathan is a genuinely nice man." Evelyn looked narrowly at her daughter. "Surely you don't think he's like that Stuart fellow?"

"He has nothing to do with the way I feel about Jonathan."

"I wonder. Stuart was handsome, too, although he couldn't compare to Jonathan. I was glad when you stopped seeing him. I never did trust that man."

"You were more perceptive than I was. I don't have any faith in my own judgment anymore." Michelle sighed.

"Anyone can make a mistake. You can't let it ruin all your future relationships."

"I assume you're referring to Jonathan, but even if I was attracted to him, nothing is going to develop there. In a couple of days I'll be going home and I'll never see him again."

Michelle decided it would be better not to tell her mother what Jonathan's real motive was for being so affable. All she wanted to do was get her away from him and his uncle. She hoped to accomplish that without an argument.

"You just got here a couple of days ago," Evelyn said. "You can't be thinking of going home so soon."

"I just wanted to escape from the cold and spend some time with you. I'm ready to leave whenever you are."

"I have nothing special to go home for, and I'm paid up here until the end of the week."

Michelle suppressed a groan. That was four more days!

"Maybe they'd give you a refund. This is the height of the season, so I'm sure they could rent your room."

"I don't doubt it, but I'm staying right here. You talked me into this vacation and I'm grateful to you. I'm having a wonderful time. I have no intention of leaving. As a matter of fact, I'm considering staying longer."

"Does Lucky have anything to do with that decision?" Michelle realized there was no hope of avoiding a quarrel.

"He's made my stay here very enjoyable," Evelyn answered evasively.

"Can't you see what he is, Mother? Didn't yesterday at the track open your eyes? He's a gambler!"

"I seem to remember we both bet on the races, too."

"A few dollars. He bet hundreds!"

"Why not? He can afford to. He's a very wealthy man."

"Because he told you so? You have only his word for it. I'm telling you, Lucky and Jonathan are con men. They hang around expensive resorts like Shorehaven looking for pigeons. You happened to be the one they picked."

"Thank you very much," Evelyn said indignantly. "It's nice to know you think no man could be attracted to me for myself alone."

"That's not what I meant at all. You're a very attractive woman, and I'm sure in time you'll meet a nice man—not one like Lucky who is only after your money."

"You talk as if I'm an heiress, for heaven's sake! Your father left me comfortably provided for, but I'm certainly not rich."

"It's a mistake to think that con men don't go after ordinary people. They're probably easier marks. Millionaires have lawyers and financial advisers to protect them. You obviously have enough money to make it worth Lucky's while."

"When did you get so knowledgeable about con men?" Evelyn asked.

"It doesn't take a genius to figure it out. He found out

how much Dad left you, and then got you interested in some vague invention you can't even describe. If I told you *I* intended to invest in a pie-in-the-sky deal like that, you'd tell me to have my head examined!''

"Just to set the record straight, Lucky didn't ask me to invest, I asked *him*. And after agreeing initially, he's evidently having second thoughts. I've mentioned it to him several times and he keeps putting me off.''

"Don't you see? That's a classic come-on to make you so eager you won't ask for details. He's probably hoping for a blank check.''

"I'm disappointed in you, Michelle. You have a completely closed mind. You won't even admit the possibility that you might be wrong about Lucky.''

"Have you ever considered the fact that I might be right?''

"You're not,'' Evelyn said, calmly but firmly. "You have many admirable qualities, but you aren't a very good judge of character, as you yourself admitted. I hoped you would like Lucky once you got to know him, but I'm afraid that isn't going to happen. It's too bad, because I intend to go on seeing him.''

Michelle's heart sank as she realized she was fighting a losing battle. The knowledge forced her to change tactics. "He's a very charming man, I'll admit that.''

"Well, it's a start,'' Evelyn said dryly.

"Maybe you're right about my not giving Lucky a chance. I guess I jumped to conclusions when you told me you'd discussed your finances with a man you'd just met. It was so unlike you.''

"That wasn't the way it happened. Lucky and I had an instant rapport. We discussed our mates and what good marriages we'd had. I told him how concerned your father had always been about his family, how he'd provided for me if anything should happen to him, as it did so unexpectedly. Lucky didn't pump me for the information.''

Michelle groaned inwardly at the way her mother had been manipulated without even realizing it. Trying to sound sincere, she said, "That makes a lot of difference. I was worried because you're usually such a private person."

"I always used to be. I even surprised myself, but Lucky is so easy to talk to. That's one of the things I love about him. It's nice to have a man's viewpoint. I've missed that since your father died."

"It's certainly understandable. Friendships are important. And since you enjoy this one so much, you should be careful not to have any business dealings with Lucky," Michelle said artlessly. "Nothing can fracture a friendship faster."

Evelyn gave her an outraged look. "You haven't changed your mind about him, just your tactics! Did you really think I'd be fooled by such a transparent ploy?"

It was useless for Michelle to pretend innocence. "I'm desperate enough to try anything. I don't want to see you wind up penniless, which is what will happen if you continue to think Lucky is just a charming southern gentleman. Enjoy his company. Have a ball. Just promise me you won't give him any money."

"I don't have to promise you anything! It's my money and I'll do whatever I like with it." Evelyn's anger caused her to overreact. When she saw her daughter's stricken face she was sorry. "I know you're concerned about me, darling. I wish there were some way to assure you that I'm neither gullible nor stupid, but I guess you'll simply have to take my word for it."

"I know you're not stupid, Mother," Michelle said miserably. "I just want you to have a good life and be happy."

"Then trust me." Evelyn smoothed her daughter's hair lovingly. "You're much too serious for such a pretty girl. What is it you young people say? Lighten up."

"I'll try." Michelle forced a smile.

"Good. Now run along and have breakfast with Lucky

and Jonathan. They'll be waiting. Tell them I'll be down in a few minutes.''

Michelle left her mother reluctantly, yet what else was there to do? She'd just have to bide her time and hope Lucky made a serious mistake. It was a long shot, considering the fact that he had Jonathan to do damage control. Those two were formidable opponents.

Chapter Five

Michelle knew she had to be cordial to Jonathan and Lucky from then on or risk alienating her mother, which could have tragic results. Starting immediately, Michelle worked hard at being pleasant. She agreed to everything any of them suggested, and then pretended to be having a fine time. Jonathan was puzzled at first, especially by her failure to give as good as she got when he baited her. Then he figured it out.

He had asked her to go for a drive after dinner. She made some excuse to get out of it, but Evelyn and Lucky urged her to go. Instead of arguing as she would have before, Michelle forced a smile and gave in immediately.

Jonathan didn't comment on her changed attitude until they were driving along the ocean. It was a beautiful night. Moonlight had dusted a sparkling path across the calm water, and the palm trees were fluttering in a soft breeze that also ruffled Jonathan's dark brown hair. It was all so lovely that Michelle felt relaxed and curiously happy. Until he turned his head and gave her a sardonic smile.

"I'm glad you allowed yourself to be persuaded, even though you didn't really want to be alone with me. What happened? Did your mother tell you to make nice?"

"I don't know what you're talking about." Realizing her tone was too curt, Michelle modified it. "We might not agree on most things, but that doesn't mean we can't be friends."

"I'm delighted to hear that. I just wish you meant it."

She slanted a watchful look at him. "Why would you doubt it?"

"Because you have such a wonderfully expressive face. You'd like to tell me to get lost, but you're forcing yourself not to." He chuckled. "Don't ever play poker, honey. You'd lose your shirt."

"You would know more about that than I would," she said tartly.

"There, that's better." He grinned. "That's the Michelle I've grown accustomed to."

"You complain when I snap at you, and you complain when I don't," she said lightly. "I don't know what you want from me."

"I haven't made any secret of it." Jonathan pulled off the road and cut the engine.

Michelle stiffened warily, but she kept her voice casual. "I'll say one thing for you, you don't quit. But you should know by now that meaningless affairs don't interest me."

He reached out and stroked her cheek sensuously. "It would be very important to *me*. Making love to you would be an experience no man could ever forget."

When he linked his arms around her waist and urged her toward him, Michelle braced her palms against his chest. "Don't spoil things, Jonathan. We've been getting along so well the last couple of days."

He smiled charmingly. "That's what gives me hope."

He dipped his head until his mouth was just barely touching hers. "You seem like an entirely different person lately." The tip of his tongue traced the line of her closed lips, teasing them apart.

Michelle tried to shake off his hypnotic spell, but when he was this close it was difficult to remember why she had to. Jonathan was so irresistibly male. She wanted to lie in his arms in the moonlight and let him fill her with joy.

"You want me, too, don't you, darling?" he crooned.

He must never know how much! The intensity of her desire frightened Michelle. It gave her the strength to push him away, but it also made her incautious.

"I know exactly what you're trying to do," she said angrily. "You're completely without scruples. You'd make love to me just to distract me so Lucky can fleece my mother. Sooner or later I'll make her see that."

"You already tried, didn't you? What did she say? Shape up or ship out? You're really in a difficult spot, aren't you, angel face?"

"The game isn't played out yet," Michelle said grimly.

"I'll be sorry to see it end—especially since you have to be nice to me now," he teased.

"Not for long. Mother only planned to stay till the end of the week, and the week is almost over."

He looked amused. "A lot can happen between now and then."

"Don't count on it," she said curtly.

"I hate to waste our remaining time together arguing, so I'll make a deal with you. I'll promise to make Lucky keep his hands off your mother's fortune, if you promise to be nice to me." When her eyes started to smolder, Jonathan laughed. "I mean nice in the purest sense of the word."

"Yeah, sure," she muttered.

His laughter died and he cupped her chin in his palm, looking deeply into her eyes. "I would never try to force you into my bed. It wouldn't be any good that way. Some-

day you'll come to me because you want me as much as I
want you, and I'll do everything in my power to make it
as wonderful for you as it will be for me.''

His deep velvety voice evoked pictures of a darkened
bedroom with filmy curtains floating in the breeze from an
open window. Moonlight glittered in Jonathan's eyes and
gilded his splendid nude body as he knelt over her, murmuring arousing words of love.

Michelle drew in her breath sharply, trying to banish the
erotic vision. It was difficult when he was only inches
away—here and now—promising more pleasure than she'd
ever known. When his lips touched hers, she didn't draw
away.

Jonathan kissed her gently, then raised his head to gaze
at her luminous face. Unaccountably, he was the one who
moved away and turned on the engine.

''Now that we understand each other, would you like to
stop somewhere for a drink?'' he asked, as though they'd
been having a normal conversation.

Michelle was totally confused. A man as experienced as
Jonathan had to realize the effect he'd had on her. He must
have known her resistance was weakened. Wasn't that his
purpose? He'd been relentlessly pursuing her all week, so
why had he drawn back when success was entirely possible?

Was he really an honorable man, as he claimed? Could
she have misjudged him that badly? It was possible. She
wasn't exactly a good judge of men, Michelle reminded
herself.

Excitement rose inside her like bubbles of champagne as
she considered the possibility of a relationship between
them. But the bubbles burst as suddenly as they'd surfaced.
She'd be more than willing to give Jonathan the benefit of
a doubt, if she was the only one who could get hurt. But
taking a chance with her mother's entire future was unac-
ceptable.

Michelle sighed deeply, wondering how she was going to make it until Sunday. That was when Evelyn's week was up. Michelle realized her own life would seem drab and uneventful after Jonathan, but at least she wouldn't be in this constant state of turmoil.

He glanced over at her and squeezed her hand. "Your problem is, you worry too much. Everything is going to turn out fine, angel face. Trust me."

Michelle decided to take the first part of Jonathan's advice and simply enjoy her last two days at Shorehaven. She hadn't changed her mother's opinion of Lucky, but it didn't really matter. She was fairly certain that Evelyn had been astute enough to have second thoughts about investing with him. Maybe their argument had done some good after all. Her mother would remember Lucky fondly after she went home, and then he'd be just a few snapshots in an album.

Michelle was completely relaxed that last Saturday night at Shorehaven. It had been a fun two days and she was inclined to be gracious in victory.

Glancing around the dinner table she said to the men, "You've both made this a very enjoyable week for Mother and me. I hate to go home."

"Then don't go," Lucky said. "I heard they're having another snowstorm in New York."

Michelle groaned. "That means the airports will be jammed and we'll have trouble getting a taxi."

"It sounds most unappealing. I'm glad Evie decided to stay longer," Lucky added casually.

"What?" Michelle looked at her mother in dismay. "That's not true, is it? You didn't say anything to me."

"I've been thinking about staying on, but I hadn't really made up my mind," Evelyn said evasively. "I was going to tell you tonight."

"Then it's definite? How long are you planning to stay here?" Michelle's heart sank at the prospect of remaining longer. Besides all the other trauma involved, she couldn't really afford it. But how could she leave her mother here alone?

"Well, actually I'm not staying on at Shorehaven," Evelyn said. "Lucky kindly invited me to visit him in Miami and I accepted."

"How could you do a thing like that?" Michelle exclaimed. "You hardly know the man! You have no idea what you'd be letting yourself in for."

"You're being impolite." Evelyn's voice had a steely quality. "Lucky is a fine gentleman and he's my friend. Kindly treat him as such."

"She's just concerned about you, which is understandable," Lucky said placatingly.

"I'm a mature woman," Evelyn replied. "I'm perfectly capable of making my own decisions."

"I never doubted that! I just want you to come home with me," Michelle wheedled. "You've been gone for two weeks already. I miss you when you're so far away."

"May I suggest a solution?" Lucky intervened. "Why don't you come for a visit, too? I have plenty of room for both of you."

"I can't do that," Michelle protested. "I have a job to get back to."

"Have you used up all of your vacation time?"

"Well, no, but I was saving some of it for this summer."

"You're entitled to four weeks and you've only taken one of them so far," her mother stated. "There's no reason for you to go back unless you want to."

"It isn't that. I just…it's inventory time at the store and I should be there." Even to Michelle's own ears that sounded like a weak excuse, especially when she knew her assistant could easily fill in for her. But it was the best one she could come up with.

"That's unfortunate," Evelyn said. "It would have been

lovely to have you along, but we'll keep in touch by phone.''

Jonathan hadn't taken part in the dispute, but his expression was compassionate as he watched Michelle's growing distress. Finally he said, ''Why don't you come to Miami for a couple of days? Surely you can spare that small amount of time. You might go home reassured.''

''You knew about this, didn't you?'' she asked in outrage. Michelle suddenly remembered Jonathan's secret smile when she'd confidently mentioned taking her mother home. ''You knew Lucky was going to invite Mother to visit!''

''He mentioned it to me,'' Jonathan admitted.

Or was it *your* idea, Michelle wondered silently? How naive she'd been to think Jonathan had given up. He'd merely gone to Plan B. So much for trusting him, she thought bitterly.

''Are you sure you won't take me up on my offer?'' Lucky coaxed. ''Miami is an easy drive from here. We can leave in the afternoon tomorrow and be at my place in time for a late dinner. You're welcome to stay as long as you like, but if you only want to stay overnight, I'll drive you to the airport in the morning. It would be a lot more convenient for you. You can get a direct flight out of Miami.''

''That makes sense, doesn't it?'' Evelyn asked her placatingly.

Michelle forced herself not to say what she really thought. What good would it do? Her mother had already decided to go. Any further criticism of Lucky—either implied or overt—could tip the balance in his favor.

''Will we have the pleasure of your company?'' he asked gallantly.

Michelle managed a smile and gave in—because she didn't have any other choice. The situation here had been bad enough. It would be even more dangerous to leave her mother alone with Lucky on his own turf. And Michelle knew that her boss would be very understanding when she phoned to extend her leave.

"I'll be happy to accept your kind invitation," she said.

It was a good thing she avoided glancing over at Jonathan. The look of satisfaction on his face might have snapped the fragile hold she had on her temper.

The two couples left Shorehaven separately on Sunday afternoon, since Jonathan and Lucky had each driven their own cars to the resort. That was another source of irritation to Michelle. She'd be a captive audience if Jonathan decided to gloat.

He didn't seem inclined to. He made small talk as they drove along the coast, unruffled by the fact that she replied in monosyllables.

Gradually, however, Michelle became so interested in the scenery that she forgot her resentment. The lightly traveled road took them through a series of picturesque small towns. Majestic trees had gray beards of Spanish moss drooping from their branches, and quaint houses with wide, screened verandas and old-fashioned porch swings could be seen from the road.

"These small towns are charming," she remarked. "It's such a change from the hustle and bustle of the big cities."

"I thought you might enjoy it," Jonathan answered. "That's why I took the coastal route instead of the expressway. It's a little longer, but you get to see more."

She turned her head to stare at his chiseled profile. "That was very thoughtful of you."

"I keep telling you I'm not such a bad fellow. Maybe you're starting to believe me."

"I wouldn't go that far. You could have told me what Lucky was planning."

"It would only have spoiled your last couple of days there, and you wouldn't have changed Evelyn's mind, anyway. The result would have been a rift between you and your mother, which I'm sure you want to avoid.''

''Of course I do! Why can't she see that I only want what's best for her?'' Michelle exclaimed in frustration.

''That's a decision you make for a child, not an adult.'' He reached over and squeezed her hand. ''Why don't you just relax and enjoy the ride? You might find you've been worrying over nothing.''

She didn't share his optimism, but the scenery was certainly intriguing. ''I wonder what it would be like to live in a town this small,'' she mused as they drove through a sleepy little village with a main street that was only three blocks long.

''I imagine it's very peaceful,'' Jonathan said.

''I can't picture you in a small town.''

''You think I spend all my time in nightclubs and fancy restaurants?''

''Yes,'' she said frankly.

''I don't know where you got the impression that I'm a playboy,'' he complained. ''You'd be surprised at the amount of nights I spend working late at the office. I'll bet you go out more than I do.''

''You'd lose that bet,'' she answered curtly.

He slanted a quick glance at her. ''You can't let one lemon sour you on the entire male population. We aren't all bad.''

''How did you—'' She stopped abruptly. ''I don't care to discuss my personal life.''

''You just told me you didn't have one,'' he teased.

''Then there's nothing to talk about.'' She turned her head to look out the window. ''Aren't those hibiscus beautiful? I wish we could grow them up north.''

''Okay, honey, I won't try to break down that wall you've built around yourself,'' Jonathan said as they left the village behind and drove down the two-lane, winding country road. ''Not now, anyway,'' he added.

As he slowed for a hairpin curve, a car came from the opposite direction. Suddenly another car overtook it and tried to pass on the blind curve. The second car was filled with young people who were shouting to each other over a blaring radio. Some of them started to scream when they realized their car was headed straight for Jonathan's.

A horrendous collision seemed inevitable, but Jonathan reacted with lightning speed. He turned the wheel sharply and their car left the road and crashed through a palmetto grove. Michelle held her breath as the convertible at first seemed about to flip over, then came to a jarring halt against the trunk of a tall tree.

The silence seemed eerie after the horror of the past few minutes. The car that almost caused the accident had left the scene swiftly. Only the sound of startled birds filled the air.

Jonathan released his seat belt and turned anxiously to Michelle. "Are you all right?"

"Yes, just a little shaken up. How could anybody be stupid enough to try to pass on a blind curve?"

He shrugged. "They probably live around here and know this road isn't used much. Not that it's any excuse. I'm just glad you weren't hurt."

"Thanks to you," she said gratefully. "You're magnificent in a crisis, Jonathan."

A smile lightened the concern on his face. "I never expected to hear words of praise from you. It was almost worth it." He opened his door and came around to her side of the car. "Get out and move around. I want to be sure you're all right."

"I'm in better shape than your car is," she said. One fender was crumpled against the tree, and something was dripping audibly from the engine. "Do you think it can be repaired?"

"I suppose so, but it will undoubtedly take some time.

We'll have to leave it at a shop in that town we just passed and rent a car to take us the rest of the way."

"How much farther is it to Miami?"

"Unfortunately we're only halfway there because I took the scenic route instead of the throughway," he said ruefully.

"It wasn't your fault. You meant well. Besides, we're in no hurry. We'll just call Lucky and tell them to have dinner without us."

"I guess that would be best. Can you make it back to town, or do you want to wait here and I'll come back for you?"

"No, I'll come with you. I have on flat shoes." She'd worn white pants and a red-and-white striped T-shirt for the trip.

It was a pleasant walk back to the village. Their close brush with death, or at least serious injury, left them both glad to be alive. When Jonathan took her hand, Michelle smiled contentedly at him.

Their thankfulness was diluted somewhat after they reached the little town. The one gas station was closing, and the owner said he couldn't tow the car until morning.

"My wife gets real put out if I'm not home on time for supper," he explained.

After trying, and failing, to convince him that this was an emergency, Jonathan was forced to give up. "All right." He sighed. "We don't want to wait around till it's repaired, anyway. I'll just leave you the keys and you can call me in Miami and tell me what the damage is. We're going to rent a car to finish the trip."

"Where are you gonna do that?"

Jonathan frowned. "Do what?"

"Where you gonna rent a car? The nearest place would be in one of the big towns up the coast."

Jonathan gave Michelle a resigned look. "Do you mind taking a bus? I could call Lucky to come and get us, but it would take him the same amount of time to get here as it would take us to get there on the bus."

Before she could voice an opinion, the man said, "There's no bus to Miami from here. You have to go up the road quite a piece to Parkersville. And then the bus don't run but twice a week." Having delivered his bad news, the station owner went to lock his gas pumps for the night.

"Well, that settles it," Jonathan said. "I'll have to call Lucky."

"It's too bad, but I don't see any other solution," Michelle agreed.

Lucky's houseman, Manuel, answered the phone. Lucky wasn't home yet, but he'd left a message. He intended to stop along the road for an early dinner, so Jonathan and Michelle should make their own plans. Lucky didn't know when he and Evelyn would get home.

"But he told me you're bringing a lady to stay. Her room is ready for her," Manuel assured him.

"Great!" Jonathan muttered as he hung up. "Now what? I guess we'll just have to go to a hotel. Tomorrow I'll call around and find someplace that will deliver a rental car. I know better than to expect them to be open tonight," he added sardonically.

"Will they deliver this far?" Michelle asked.

"I'll make it worth their while." As the station owner rejoined them, Jonathan said, "Where is the nearest hotel?"

"We don't have one."

"There must be a hotel in town!" Jonathan insisted.

"Nope. We don't have any use for one."

"Where do visitors stay?" Michelle asked.

"We don't get any tourists here."

"How about a rooming house?" she persisted. "We're not fussy. Just direct us to someplace that will put us up for the night."

"I guess you might try the widow Dancy. She's pretty

hard up since her husband died and left her with the two kids.''

"That sounds fine," Jonathan said. "How do we get there?"

"I'll give you a lift," the man offered. "It's on my way home."

Michelle was expecting the worst after all their other mishaps, but Caroline Dancy's house was surprisingly nice. The small yellow bungalow was neat and clean, and Caroline was soothingly sympathetic toward their problems.

"I'll just bet it was that Billy Bob Jenkins that ran you off the road. They ought to take away his license. It's the Lord's grace that you're both still alive!"

"And we're properly grateful." Jonathan smiled. "Unfortunately my car was badly damaged and there doesn't seem to be a hotel in town. We would appreciate it greatly if you'd rent us a couple of rooms for the night. We'll be out of here first thing in the morning."

Caroline looked at him doubtfully. "I only have two bedrooms, but you're welcome to the girls' room. Sue Ellen can bunk in with me, and Maybelle can sleep on the couch."

Michelle gave Jonathan a dismayed look. "We wouldn't think of putting you out like that," she told the woman.

"What else can we do?" he asked her helplessly.

"The mister is right," Caroline said. "The girls won't mind a bit, and you and your husband won't be any trouble at all."

"But we're not—" Jonathan clamped his hand around Michelle's wrist before she could finish the sentence.

"Since you put it that way, we'll be happy to accept your kind offer," he said smoothly.

Her two young daughters had been watching them with lively curiosity, although Maybelle's interest was mostly focused on Jonathan. She was a pretty girl, just barely in her teens, but she was clearly dazzled by him.

"You girls go and change the beds in your room," Caroline directed.

"Beds?" Michelle looked at her hopefully. "There's more than one?"

"The bedroom is kinda small, so Joe built bunk beds, figuring they'd take up less room. Joe was my husband, may he rest in peace."

"They're real neat beds," Sue Ellen, the younger girl, told Jonathan.

"The girls love them. I just hope they won't be too narrow for the mister." Caroline looked admiringly at his broad-shouldered frame.

"Please call me Jonathan. And I'm sure the beds will be perfect."

"Well, if you'll excuse me, I have to pop into the kitchen for a minute and take a look at our supper."

When they were alone, Michelle said to Jonathan, "Why didn't you let me tell her we aren't married?"

"Because she might have rescinded her offer, and then where would we have been? This is the only place in town to stay. Even if you preferred to sleep in the bus station, that's probably only a lean-to on the sidewalk."

"It just seems sort of dishonest," Michelle answered grudgingly.

Jonathan grinned suddenly. "Not unless you plan on having illicit relations."

Caroline returned at that moment. "Supper won't be ready for a bit," she said. "I hope you don't mind waiting."

Michelle suspected that the woman might have had trouble supplementing the meal to accommodate two more. "You weren't expecting us," she said. "Isn't there a restaurant in town?"

"Jody's Burger Joint has great hamburgers and pizza,"

Sue Ellen said as she and her sister came back into the living room.

"That sounds like a winner." Jonathan smiled at the little girl who was about ten or eleven. "Why don't I take all of us to the Burger Joint?"

"I already started dinner," Caroline protested.

"Save it for tomorrow night," he told her. "I'd feel a lot better about inconveniencing you if you'd let me take you out to dinner."

"Please, Mama, can we go?" Sue Ellen begged.

"It would be so much fun." Maybelle added her plea. "We never get to go there anymore."

"Well, I guess I could put the food in the fridge," Caroline said uncertainly.

Jody's Burger Joint was a family restaurant, as well as a hangout for young people. There was an ancient jukebox in the corner, and a cleared space in front of it where the youngsters could dance. Caroline and her daughters knew everybody in the place, which wasn't surprising in a town that small.

Jonathan insisted on ordering more than they could possibly eat. When Caroline objected he said, "You can take it home for tomorrow's lunch."

Michelle was once again struck by his sensitivity. Jonathan was a man who spent lavishly, yet he was aware of what it would be like to have to watch pennies. But best of all, his generosity was always unobtrusive.

Maybelle was fascinated by Jonathan, but Michelle was also an object of interest. During dinner the young girl inspected Michelle's hair and makeup critically. "What kind of mascara do you use to make your eyelashes so long and thick?" she asked. "Or are they false?"

"Maybelle! Mind your manners," Caroline exclaimed.

"It's all right." Michelle smiled. "No, they're not false."

"Mama won't let me use mascara," Maybelle said in a discontented voice.

"You don't need it, you have a natural beauty. Men like that in a woman," Jonathan said with a solemn face.

She looked at him with shining eyes. "Do you really mean it? I mean, about my being pretty?"

"You must know that already. I'll bet you drive all the boys wild."

"Tommy Hoskins helps her with her homework," Sue Ellen volunteered. "Maybelle can't do math, but I get good grades in it."

"Yours is easy," Maybelle muttered, shooting her sister a poisonous glance.

"Math isn't difficult once you get the hang of it," Jonathan said. "What kind of problems are giving you trouble?"

When she reluctantly told him, he took a paper place mat and showed her certain rules to follow. Maybelle's face lit up as she began to understand what he was telling her.

"Your husband is very good with youngsters," Caroline remarked. "Is he a teacher?"

"No, he's an engineer," Michelle replied. For all she knew, he might be.

Somebody put a coin in the jukebox while they were lingering over coffee and dessert. One of Maybelle's friends came by to ask her to dance, and Sue Ellen went to say hello to some of her own friends.

While the girls were gone, Caroline talked about her husband and the problems of raising two children alone. Michelle glanced over at Jonathan. If he was bored, it didn't show. He was giving Caroline his complete attention.

When the girls returned, Caroline glanced at her watch and gasped. "Just look at the time! I don't know how it got so late. These youngsters should have been home in bed an hour ago."

"Do we have to go, Mama? Can't we stay a little longer?" Maybelle pleaded.

Caroline shook her head. "You girls have school tomorrow."

As they walked back to the house laden with take-out cartons, Michelle had a sudden, disturbing thought. She and Jonathan had left their luggage in the trunk of the car. What were they going to sleep in? It was bad enough that they had to share a bedroom. This made things even worse!

He frowned as he noticed the perturbed look on her face. "What's wrong?" he asked in a low voice, lagging behind the others.

She told him the problem. "Can we go back to the car and get our suitcases?"

"It's a long walk and there are no lights on that rural road. I'm not even sure I could find the car in the dark. We traveled quite a distance into that grove. Even if we found it, there are probably snakes in there, maybe even a stray alligator."

She shuddered. "Okay, you convinced me. We'll have to do without."

"Please don't tell me you're going to sleep in the nude," he groaned. "The picture will stay with me and I'll never get any sleep."

"I don't want to know what you're wearing, either," she said tartly.

"Will it disturb you, too?" he asked softly.

It already had! Knowing Jonathan was lying nude just above her was a mind-blowing thought. "This has been such a traumatic day that I expect to fall asleep the minute my head touches the pillow," she answered, as coolly as possible.

"Lucky you." He chuckled.

When they were in their bedroom with the door closed, Jonathan began to get undressed. "Caroline is a nice lady, isn't she?'' he remarked, as though they were a normal couple coming home after an evening out. "I wish there was something I could do to make her life easier.''

Michelle avoided looking at him. "I feel sorry for her, too, but she's doing a good job raising those girls.''

"Yes, they're nice kids.''

"You made another conquest,'' Michelle said lightly, trying to match his casual attitude. "Maybelle thinks you're really cool.''

Jonathan laughed. "She's young enough to be pleased by any male attention. In a year or two she'll think I'm an old man.''

Michelle stole a quick look at him. Jonathan was years away from being old. He'd stripped off his T-shirt, revealing his broad, muscular shoulders and chest. His tapered, lean torso was as perfect as a bronze statue.

He glanced over at her and held out his shirt. "Do you want to sleep in my T-shirt?''

"No, thanks, I have my own.''

"Mine might be more comfortable. It's bigger.'' He stepped out of his jeans, then noticed that she was sitting on her bunk bed, still fully dressed. "Aren't you going to bed? I know it's early, but there's nothing else to do. We don't even have a newspaper.''

"It doesn't matter. We want to get up early, anyway.'' She took off her shoes, but nothing else.

Suddenly Jonathan realized what was bothering her. He came over and hunkered down in front of her, forcing her to look at him. "Aren't you being a little foolish, honey? You've seen me in bathing trunks, which were as brief as these jockey shorts, and I've seen you in a bikini bottom and nothing else.''

"Don't remind me.'' She smiled faintly.

"I'm trying not to think of it myself, or I might forget I promised not to seduce you. I want you so badly it hurts, but you have to want me the same way.''

Michelle's long lashes veiled her eyes. She wanted him every bit as much, but it was more than desire for her. She was in love with Jonathan; there was no use denying it. One night wouldn't be enough, but it was better than nothing. It was time to stop being cautious and follow her heart.

Michelle had delayed her decision too long. Jonathan straightened up and looked down at her. "Okay, angel, I get the message."

"I wasn't going to—" She stood so suddenly that she bumped her head on the upper bunk.

"Be careful!" He smoothed her hair gently. "Did you hurt yourself?" When she shook her head mutely he said, "Well, I'll climb up top so you can undress. Get some sleep, honey."

Michelle wanted to grab his legs as he went up the ladder, to prevent him from leaving, but she just watched wordlessly. Couldn't he see that she didn't want him to go? But how could he? She was always sending mixed messages. How was he to know tonight was different?

Jonathan squirmed around in the bunk bed, trying to adjust his long length to its narrow confines. When he saw her still watching him, he laughed. "It's a good thing you *didn't* want to make love. Only a couple of elves could make out in these beds."

Michelle forced a smile, realizing it was probably better this way. "See, I did you a favor." She turned out the light.

"Then why don't I feel grateful?" he teased.

She got undressed in the dark, trying not to think about how different it would be if Jonathan had undressed her. He wouldn't have left her panties and T-shirt on as she had. She'd be lying nude in his arms right now, while his hands moved in an intimate exploration of her body, and his mouth fanned the flames of desire.

Michelle turned over abruptly and banged her knee against the wall.

"Are you okay?" he called in a low voice.

"Yes, but you're right about these beds. They're built for munchkins."

"Just look at it as an adventure that's almost over. Tomorrow we'll be on our way again."

Almost over. The words were so final, as though they were written in stone.

Eventually Michelle fell into a troubled sleep. It was toward morning that her bed shook and something nudged her in the side, waking her abruptly. When her eyes flew open, she saw Jonathan. He was hanging onto the upper bunk, swearing under his breath while he struggled to get a footing on her mattress.

She stuck her head out and stared up at him. "What on earth is going on?"

"I turned over and fell out of the blasted bed!" he growled, letting go of the framework and sinking down beside her. He gingerly touched his scraped shin and swore some more. "If I hadn't grabbed the edge as I went over, I could have broken something vital."

Seeing Jonathan in a child's bed had been funny enough. Picturing him rolling out of it in the middle of the night struck Michelle as hilarious. She put her hands over her mouth to stifle her laughter.

"I'm glad you think it's so damn funny!" He scowled.

"I'll bet that's the first time you ever fell *out* of bed," she gasped.

"Fortunately, you're right." His smile broadened and he started to laugh as hard as she was.

"Shh." She put her hand over his mouth. "You'll wake the entire household."

They held onto each other, trying to stifle their merriment. Gradually it subsided and Michelle wiped her eyes. "I'm sorry. You could have gotten hurt."

"Not really. I was just looking for sympathy."

"And I laughed at you. That wasn't very nice."

"No, but this is." His lips brushed across her cheek.

The mood changed like lightning. Michelle was suddenly aware of being in Jonathan's arms, not as shared partners in a joke, but as a man and a woman with urgent needs.

When he lowered her head to the pillow she put her arms around his neck. They were wedged in the narrow bed facing each other, their bodies so closely joined that she could feel his passion. It echoed her own as he twined his legs around hers so they were like one person.

"Sweet beautiful Michelle," he murmured, sliding his hand under her T-shirt. "You're going to be mine, aren't you?"

"Yes," she breathed, arching her body as he caressed her breast.

"I've never wanted anyone this much." The pale moonlight was reflected in his golden eyes as he stripped off her T-shirt and gazed at her avidly. "You're so perfect." He touched his tongue delicately to one nipple, sending a ripple of pleasure through her. "I want to know every inch of you."

Michelle felt the same way. Her hands moved restlessly over his lithe torso, tracing the straining muscles in his back, the width of his shoulders.

"You're wonderful," he groaned before claiming her mouth for a deep kiss that engaged all her senses.

She was like a violin responding to his expert touch. Her body vibrated with pleasure as he explored it intimately. When he parted her legs and stroked her arousingly, Michelle's excitement escalated to a fever pitch.

She and Jonathan were in a secret world of mounting ecstasy where no one else existed. Then suddenly the real world intruded. A child's voice came from the other side of the wall.

"Mama! Where are you?" It was Sue Ellen.

Caroline's muffled voice answered her. "It's all right, baby. You're here in my bed, remember?"

"I woke up and I was scared. Everything looked different."

"Shh," Caroline said, as Michelle had earlier. "You'll wake everybody up."

Jonathan had stiffened momentarily. Then he relaxed and whispered in her ear. "They'll go back to sleep."

"No, we can't." Michelle drew back as far as possible in the narrow space, afraid to trust herself in his arms. She was going to suggest that they take the mattress to the far corner of the room, but Jonathan was staring in her incredulously.

"I don't believe this! How could you let things go this far and then suddenly change your mind? There's a word for women like you, and it isn't a pleasant one," he said bitingly.

"You don't understand! I didn't mean—"

He cut her off savagely. "You're right. I *didn't* understand, but I do now. I'm supposed to be the con man and you're the one who's been playing games. Did it amuse you to let me think you wanted me?"

"You know I wasn't pretending," she said in a low voice.

"No, for a few minutes you almost lost control, didn't you? I nearly got to you. Wouldn't that have been a laugh? The lady spider, caught in her own web." He picked up his jeans and shirt and went toward the door.

"Where are you going?" she whispered.

"What difference does it make?" he asked curtly.

Michelle hugged her knees to her chest and silently watched him leave the room. How could things have gone so wrong? Jonathan didn't give her a chance to explain that she didn't want their first time to be a hurried coupling with no opportunity to express tenderness and joy.

She forced herself to face the fact that there wouldn't be any first time—not now or ever. It would be useless to try to explain, even after he cooled down. Jonathan had made up his mind about her, and from the look of disgust on his face, he wasn't going to change it.

Michelle rested her forehead on her knees as waves of misery washed over her.

Chapter Six

Michelle stared into the darkness for a long time, but toward morning she fell into a deep sleep. She was awakened by sounds coming from the kitchen.

She dressed hurriedly, wondering if Jonathan had returned from wherever he'd gone during the night. What would she do if he just left her stranded here? It might be preferable to having to make conversation with him, she told herself wryly.

When Michelle reached the kitchen, Caroline was stirring something at the stove while talking to Jonathan, who was sitting at a square wooden table. His long body was relaxed and he had a smile on his face.

That wouldn't last long, Michelle thought as she hovered in the doorway.

Caroline turned and saw her. "Good morning, you're just in time for breakfast. Sit down and I'll serve it up in a jiffy."

"Thanks, but I'll just have coffee, if it's already made," Michelle said.

"The grits smell awfully good," Jonathan remarked. "You should try them. I'm going to have some."

Nobody could tell by his pleasant tone that anything was wrong between them. Michelle was grateful that he was being adult about it, but she missed the warmth and camaraderie they'd shared before. Be grateful for small favors, she told herself grimly.

"Coffee isn't enough to start the day right," Caroline scolded. "You'll get hungry halfway to Miami."

"I located a rental agency that agreed to deliver a car," Jonathan said. "It should be here within an hour."

"I'll bet you'll be glad to see the last of this place," Caroline said ruefully. "Jonathan told me what happened last night." As Michelle gave her a startled look she continued, "I'm just thankful he didn't get hurt falling out of that little bitty bed."

"I've survived worse things than that," he commented in a dry voice.

The rental car was delivered as they were finishing breakfast and they left soon after that. Caroline didn't want to accept payment for her hospitality, but Jonathan insisted.

"It's way too much," she protested. "I really shouldn't take it." She looked at the wad of bills, clearly torn.

"I'd be very upset if you don't," he insisted. "Say goodbye to the girls for us."

"I will. You drive safely now, you hear?" She stood on the porch waving until they were out of sight.

Michelle was dreading the trip to Miami. She and Jonathan had managed to talk civilly to each other while Caroline was there, but during the long ride they wouldn't have a buffer.

Her fears were ungrounded. He made idle small talk while they drove to the gas station where his car had been towed. After retrieving their luggage from the trunk and

making arrangements with the station owner, they were finally on their way.

Jonathan waited until they reached the highway before
broaching the subject that was on both their minds. "I want
to apologize for my behavior last night," he said quietly.

"I'd like to explain mine." Maybe he *would* listen to
reason, she thought hopefully. He seemed so much more
approachable this morning.

But Jonathan didn't give her a chance. "You have nothing to explain. For whatever reason, you changed your
mind. I'll admit it was a little difficult to accept at the
time," he said ironically. "But no means no. A real man
doesn't overreact."

"If you had only let me explain," she began desperately.

"I just told you, that shouldn't be necessary. It's a closed
incident, so let's drop it and talk about something else."

After a despairing look at his set face, Michelle knew
she had no choice.

Their conversation was a little stilted at first, but gradually they started to talk more naturally. Jonathan told her
about some festival that was going to be held in Miami the
following week.

"I think you'll enjoy it," he said. "It's very colorful."

"I don't expect to be there that long," she answered.
Surely her mother didn't plan to stay indefinitely.

Jonathan turned his head to gaze at her. "I'll miss you."

"Like a pain you've grown accustomed to?" she asked
wryly.

"Something like that." He smiled. "Maybe more like a
persistent itch I can't scratch."

"Either way, you should be glad to get rid of me," she
said lightly.

"I keep telling myself that." His tone matched hers.

About an hour later they reached Miami. Across from it
was Miami Beach with its line of tall luxury hotels facing

the ocean. Causeways connected the city with the beach.

He and Lucky actually lived on one of the islands between the two, Jonathan explained as he turned off the main causeway and drove along a quiet road lined with estates.

Michelle's eyes widened at the sight of stately mansions glimpsed through lush foliage. Lucky must live in one of the gatehouses, she decided. Some of the big estates on Long Island had them. They were small houses formerly used by gatekeepers and their families in the days when people had large staffs of servants.

She was admiring a sprawling pink mansion set amidst rolling green lawns, when Jonathan turned into the driveway leading to it.

"Well, we finally made it," he announced.

She gave him a puzzled look. "Where are we? I thought we were going to Lucky's house."

"This is it."

"You're joking!"

"I tried to tell you, but you wouldn't believe me."

Michelle was having difficulty adjusting her thinking. Only the very wealthy could afford even the upkeep on estates like these. If Jonathan had been telling her the truth all along, she'd done him a terrible injustice!

"It all sounded so improbable," she said helplessly. "I mean, inventors aren't usually wildly rich. And then when Lucky suggested that Mother invest in one of his new inventions, naturally I thought he was conning her."

"He didn't suggest it, *she* did. After you told me about it I asked Lucky if you'd misunderstood somehow. He said he'd mentioned his new invention to Evelyn, but he was sorry afterward. He didn't want her to risk even a small amount of money."

That was essentially what her mother had said. Evelyn was the better judge of character, but Michelle couldn't really fault herself. Maybe she'd been overly protective, but she'd acted out of love.

The front door opened and Lucky and Evelyn came out to greet them. "I'm glad you made it safely!" she exclaimed. "I was so worried when we got your message about the accident."

"I told Manuel to tell you it was a minor one," Jonathan said. "I wouldn't even have told you that much if we'd been able to rent a car last night. I knew you'd worry."

"That's what mothers do." Evelyn smiled. "Did you at least find a comfortable place to spend the night? It must have been a very small town if they didn't even have a car rental agency."

"It wasn't what either of us were expecting, but you learn to roll with the punches." Jonathan opened the car door. "I'll get the luggage out of the trunk."

Lucky's house was as magnificent indoors as out. The large entry hall had a pink marble floor, and the walls were covered in silk. Spacious rooms opened off a central hall that led from the entry.

While Jonathan and Lucky went into the den to talk business, Evelyn led Michelle up the curving staircase to the second floor.

"Isn't this house unbelievable?" Evelyn asked.

"It's magnificent, but isn't it awfully big for one person?"

"I suppose so, but Lucky has a wonderful staff to take care of the place. The cook and her husband have been with him for years, and so has Manuel. I don't exactly know how you'd describe his position." Evelyn laughed. "Manuel is unique."

As they walked down the upstairs hall, she said, "Wait until you see your room."

The bedroom assigned to Michelle looked like a picture out of a magazine. The bed had a crisp white eyelet bed skirt covered by a sapphire blue coverlet that coordinated with the drapes hanging at the tall French windows looking out on a terrace. The room also held a pale blue chaise and a delicate French writing desk.

"It was Lucky's idea to give you this room. There were others to choose from, but he said the blue matched your eyes," Evelyn said.

"He's a very thoughtful man," Michelle answered in a muted voice. "I guess I owe him an apology."

"Fortunately I never told him what you suspected him of."

She didn't have to; Jonathan must have. It was remarkably forgiving of Lucky to invite her to stay. She wouldn't be here long, however. Michelle just realized she had no reason to hang around.

She told her mother that when Evelyn started to talk about all the plans they'd made.

"You just got here!" Evelyn exclaimed. "Why do you want to leave so soon?"

"I do have a job to return to, and I feel funny about accepting Lucky's hospitality, under the circumstances."

"That's nonsense! He'd be amused if he knew. In fact, I'm not so sure he doesn't."

Lucky joined Evelyn in urging Michelle to stay, when she and her mother went downstairs a little later. Jonathan just listened without taking sides. That was enough to convince Michelle that he was a lost cause.

After a few minutes he stood, saying he wanted to go home and unpack. Almost as an afterthought, he asked Michelle if she'd like to come with him.

She declined, realizing his lack of enthusiasm meant he felt obliged to ask.

"You should go," Evelyn said. "Lucky and I have a date to meet some friends of his at the yacht club. You could come with us, but you'll have more fun with Jonathan."

"That's debatable," he said with a sardonic smile at Michelle. "But I thought she might like to see my house."

It seemed easier to agree than to argue about it, and she was curious to see if he lived on as grand a scale as his uncle. Nothing would have surprised Michelle at this point.

Jonathan's home was a great deal smaller than Lucky's, but equally elegant in a different way. It was a one-story house with wide glass windows facing the water where a sleek cabin cruiser was tied to his private dock.

The interior was modern, but not starkly so. Colorful paintings hung on the walls, and occasional tables held interesting art objects. Some of the crystal pieces were modern, but a small dagger with a jewel encrusted jade handle was an antique.

"I just love your house, Jonathan!" Michelle whirled around, trying to take in everything at once. "It's elegant, yet comfortable at the same time. You have beautiful things, but it doesn't feel like a museum."

"I'm glad you approve."

"Who wouldn't? It's exactly the kind of place I've dreamed about having someday."

"You've very kind," he answered graciously, but his face was expressionless.

"I know you want to unpack. Don't worry about me."

"It wouldn't be very hospitable to leave you alone. Perhaps you'd like to come in the bedroom with me."

Michelle trailed after him, accepting the fact that he didn't have any ulterior motive.

Jonathan's bedroom was spacious and also faced the water. While he unpacked, she wandered around the room, glancing at the books in his bookcase and a small sculpture on his bedside table. That was when she noticed the red number glowing in a small square on his telephone answering machine.

"You have a jillion phone messages waiting," she observed.

He glanced over indifferently. "They can wait."

"You never know. Some of them might be important. Go ahead and play them, I'll wait in the other room."

"That isn't necessary." He hesitated. "One of them might be a business call, though. If you don't mind, I think I will listen to them." He pushed the Play button.

The first voice was a woman's. "Hi, darling, it's Ashleigh. I'm simply furious at you for breaking our date! How could you just disappear without telling me where you were going? Call me the minute you get back from wherever. Love you. Bye."

Jonathan's face was inscrutable as he continued to unpack during the message. Michelle had pretended to be interested in the view outside, but when the machine beeped and another woman's voice sounded, she slid open the sliding glass door and went out on the deck.

Well, what did she expect, Michelle asked herself? A man like Jonathan would naturally be involved with a lot of women. She tried not to listen, but Ashleigh's affected drawl was unmistakable. She had left several messages. Finally Michelle walked down to the waterfront.

Jonathan joined her there a few minutes later. "Sorry it took so long. I was right, they weren't important," he remarked casually.

Who was he trying to kid? Michelle gazed at a small boat skimming down the canal. "If you have somewhere to go, you can take me back to Lucky's. I don't mind being alone."

"I really should stop by the office for a few minutes. Why don't you come along? I'd like to show you some of the things we're working on."

"Well...if you're sure I won't be in the way."

He gave her his first natural smile that day. "You're always a distraction, but you're never in the way."

* * *

His offices were in a tall building in the industrial section of Miami, an area tourists never saw. Richfield Enterprises occupied several floors of the modern glass building.

Jonathan and Lucky each had large corner offices, even though Lucky seldom used his. Jonathan's desk was piled high, but he took time to introduce Michelle to everyone. He also led her around an anteroom that was lined with glass cases.

With an arm draped around her shoulder, he showed her prototypes of Lucky's many inventions. "This is the one that started him on the road to success. It doesn't look like much, does it?"

Michelle stared at the unprepossessing little gadget. "It obviously serves a very important function."

He laughed and ruffled her hair playfully. "Would you have said the same thing if I'd shown it to you at Shorehaven?"

Michelle was pleased that he seemed to have forgotten their recent differences. He was like the old Jonathan. She smiled up at him happily. "Anybody can make a mistake."

"Don't think I intend to let you forget it," he teased.

His secretary came out of her office when she heard their voices. She was an attractive, efficient woman named Sharon, whom Michelle liked immediately. Unlike Pamela, the receptionist who sat at a desk in the anteroom. Her manner had been distant and unfriendly. Especially when Jonathan put his arm around Michelle's shoulders. It was only a friendly gesture. Was Pamela in love with the boss and automatically disliked any woman he paid attention to?

Sharon told Jonathan he needed to return some phone calls immediately.

"I'll do it later," he said. "I haven't finished showing Michelle around."

"I'm sure she'll wait for you," Sharon said.

"You don't know her as well as I do."

"Go ahead," Michelle told him. "I can amuse myself."

"Come into my office and I'll give you some magazines," Sharon offered.

The two women chatted instead. But when Sharon got involved in a business call that became lengthy, Michelle decided to take her magazine out to the anteroom.

Pamela was also on the phone, but her call sounded like a personal one. "I suppose you could call her attractive, but definitely not in your class," she was saying in a fawning tone. "I thought you should know, though, because he was acting very—" She paused abruptly when she saw Michelle. "Did you want something?" The woman stared at her with barely concealed hostility.

Michelle was annoyed enough to stay put. "I just came in here to read a magazine. Do you have a problem with that?" she asked sweetly, gazing directly at her.

Pamela's eyes shifted as she said, "No, certainly not." She swiveled in her chair and spoke softly into the phone. "I'll have to call you back."

Jonathan's phone calls dragged on. He'd been away so long that there were a lot of them. When he was finally through, Michelle sat in his office talking to him while he signed letters.

"We'll leave as soon as I finish these," he promised.

"I don't mind waiting. I don't get to sit in a V.I.P.'s office very often."

"Aren't any of your boyfriends executives?" he asked casually.

"None as successful as you." She glanced around happily. "This office is furnished better than my apartment."

Before he could answer, the door was flung open and a tall, beautiful blonde appeared. Her long hair was arranged perfectly, and her makeup was flawless.

"Surprise, darling!" she called, striking a dramatic pose in the doorway.

Jonathan stood abruptly. "What are you doing here, Ashleigh?"

Michelle didn't have to hear the name. She recognized the affected voice. His girlfriend Ashleigh was as glamorous as Michelle had known she'd be.

"I was driving by and I saw your car in the parking lot, so I decided to stop in," the blonde said gaily.

"You were driving in this neighborhood?" he asked sardonically.

"Yes, I, uh, I heard there's a fabulous bakery down here, of all places. I decided to try it."

Michelle was as skeptical as Jonathan was. She suddenly remembered Pamela's furtive conversation and fawning tone. Ashleigh evidently had a spy in the office looking out for her interests.

She crossed the room and put her arms around Jonathan's neck without glancing in Michelle's direction.

When she tried to kiss him, he moved away saying, "I'd like you to meet Michelle Lacey—Ashleigh Grant," he said completing the introduction.

The woman's eyes widened in pretended surprise as she turned to Michelle. "I didn't notice you had someone with you. I didn't mean to interrupt a business meeting."

"You haven't. Michelle and her mother are visiting Lucky," Jonathan said.

"How nice," Ashleigh replied tepidly before turning back to him. "I'm so glad you're back, darling. I missed you terribly."

"I wasn't gone that long."

"It seemed like an eternity. But I'll forgive you for simply disappearing like that if you take me out to dinner tonight."

"Well, I..." Jonathan slanted a glance at Michelle, who was pretending great interest in a cloud formation outside the window.

Ashleigh didn't wait for him to finish the sentence. "You owe me one for breaking our date."

"We didn't exactly have a date. As I remember, a group of us just planned to get together at the club."

"And you always take me," she insisted. "Everybody asked me where you were."

"Let's don't argue about it," he said a trifle irritably.

"You're right, I'm too happy to have you back. What time will you pick me up tonight?"

"I'm afraid this isn't a good night. I'm sure Lucky expects me to be available."

Like it was an obligation, Michelle thought indignantly! "I doubt if he expects you to disrupt your life because of his house guests. Go out on your date," she said coolly. "Lucky undoubtedly has something planned for Mother and me."

"She's right," Ashleigh said quickly. "When I have houseguests, I schedule every minute before they even arrive."

Jonathan's jaw set grimly as he was caught in the crossfire between the two women. "Most people aren't that organized," he told the blonde. "I'll still have to check with Lucky."

"I understand. I'll call you a little later." Turning to Michelle, she said, "How long do you expect to be here?"

"I haven't decided yet. Lucky invited me to stay indefinitely, and I just might do that," Michelle said blandly. "Everybody has been so nice to me." She gave Jonathan a melting smile.

Ashleigh's eyes narrowed, but her voice was honeyed as she remarked, "Southerners are noted for their hospitality. Sometimes outsiders take that to mean more than it really does."

"A perceptive woman can always tell the difference," Michelle answered confidently.

Jonathan looked at his watch. "Lucky and Evelyn should be back by now. I'd better take you home," he told Michelle.

Ashleigh glanced at her own watch. "Goodness, I had no idea it was so late! I have an appointment at the hairdresser. I'll talk to you shortly, darling."

After she left, Michelle dropped her act. "I meant it about keeping your date," she told him. "It isn't your job to entertain me."

"I don't consider it a job."

"It certainly sounded that way when you were explaining my presence to Ashleigh."

"But you made certain she got a different impression."

"I'm sure you can soothe her ruffled feelings. It shouldn't even stretch your inventiveness. She isn't very bright," Michelle said waspishly.

"I've never known you to be so uncharitable before." His hazel eyes brimmed with amusement. "It almost sounds as if you're jealous of Ashleigh, although I can't imagine why."

"I can't, either. She's affected and rude and obvious— and she's welcome to you!"

"You're very generous, but do you mind if I make my own choice?"

"That's your privilege." Michelle shrugged. "Can we go now?"

As they started to leave, Sharon stopped them with more papers for Jonathan to sign. She also wanted him to look over some estimates that had been faxed to the office.

"They can wait until tomorrow," he said. When his secretary tried to coax him into doing it right away, Jonathan declined firmly. "I'll come in early in the morning. Michelle has been patient long enough. We're leaving."

As they took the elevator down to the parking lot, Michelle regretted losing her temper. Jonathan didn't have to make time for her today. If it weren't for her, he would have spent the day at the office, taking care of all the work that had piled up during his absence.

As they drove out of the lot, she said in a muted voice, "I'm sorry for the things I said about Ashleigh."

"You don't think she's affected and rude?" He grinned.

"She's very beautiful," Michelle answered evasively. "I can see why you're attracted to her."

Jonathan's reply was equally evasive. "We've known each other for a long time. We share a lot of the same friends."

"That's nice. You have a lovely life here." Michelle was determined to sound positive.

"Don't you have the same thing in New York?"

"I don't have as many toys." She smiled.

He turned his head to look at her. "Are they important to you?"

"I can live without them, obviously, but I wouldn't mind being rich."

"Well, keep a good thought. If your mother marries Lucky, I'm sure you'll share in her good fortune."

"You still believe Mother went to Shorehaven to snare a rich husband!" Michelle exclaimed indignantly. "How can you continue to think such a thing after getting to know her? She doesn't have a devious bone in her body!"

"Oh, I don't know. I seem to remember they gave us the slip at Shorehaven on more than one occasion," he teased.

"They had to. We stuck to them like a bad cold," Michelle said wryly. "We weren't even good company. I can't blame them for wanting to be alone. But it wasn't because of any tricky plot of Mother's."

"I realize that now. Actually I think Evelyn would be very good for Lucky, and vice versa. They both need somebody in their lives."

"What brought about this change of heart?" Michelle asked skeptically. "You were so sure she didn't really care for Lucky."

"It was as valid an assumption as yours that we were

con artists. I've known for a long time that I was wrong about her.''

"How could you be sure?''

"I had someone run a check.''

"You had her investigated?'' Michelle asked incredulously.

"It was the only sensible thing to do. It's what you should have done the minute you became suspicious.''

"Ordinary people don't hire private detectives. That only happens in books or on TV.''

"Where do you think they get their ideas for plots?''

"Okay, *nice* people don't hire detectives,'' she said primly. "It's wrong to pry into other people's lives.''

"You have nothing to hide.''

"You had me investigated, too?'' she asked indignantly.

"I know you better than your mother does.'' He grinned.

"What do you know?'' she asked warily.

"Don't worry. Nothing I could blackmail you with. You've led an exemplary life.''

"You mean, dull.'' She sighed.

"There are ways to liven it up.''

"Thanks, but no thanks.''

"You can't say I didn't offer.'' He chuckled.

"I get offers like that all the time.''

"I don't doubt that a bit.'' Jonathan turned his head to glance at her.

Michelle's dark hair was blowing in the breeze, framing her delicate face and accentuating her petal soft skin. She looked like a gypsy princess, an exquisite one with sapphire eyes and a mouth that could drive a man wild. His hands tightened on the wheel and he looked away.

"Well, here we are,'' he said, turning into Lucky's driveway. He got out and opened her car door, but he didn't walk her to the entry. "Tell Lucky I'll check with him later.''

Michelle forced a smile. "Thanks for showing me around. I really enjoyed seeing your house."

"That's always nice to hear," he answered politely as he got back into the car.

She went inside, telling herself it was what she expected. The atmosphere was different between them today—even before Ashleigh showed up. Michelle realized she had to accept the fact that Jonathan was no longer interested in her. He was telling her that as kindly as possible. She lifted her chin and took a deep breath before going into the house.

Jonathan's face was somber as he drove away. A few days ago he would have been thrilled if Michelle had been as receptive as she was today. He'd spent most of the week romancing her, with very little success.

Not for lack of interest on her part. She could deny it to herself, but there was a vibrant attraction between them, an electricity that crackled when they were merely in the same room. He could awaken her lovely body with a touch, but she wouldn't allow herself to weaken for more than a few inflaming moments.

Jonathan could understand that. He could even find it admirable—if frustrating. What disturbed him was Michelle's complete turnaround once she found out he was wealthy. It might have merely amused him if sex was all he wanted. But it wasn't. He'd finally found the woman he wanted to marry.

Maybe he was overreacting, he told himself. Michelle's changed attitude could be due to the discovery that he wasn't the con man she suspected. But then he remembered her delight over his house, and her remark that it was just what she'd always wanted and hoped to have someday. His office had also impressed her. She'd even admitted that none of her boyfriends were as successful as he. There were so many things.

Too many to ignore. Jonathan's square jaw set grimly as

he pulled into his driveway. He wanted Michelle so badly that it was almost painful. But he wanted her to love him for who he was, not for his money.

The telephone was ringing when Jonathan walked into his house. He was tempted not to answer, in case it was Lucky calling to make plans for the evening. But his uncle would only keep trying.

When he picked up the phone, Ashleigh's voice greeted him instead. "Are you alone?" she asked cautiously.

"Yes, I just walked in the door."

"I was hoping you'd gotten rid of that woman. Entertaining out-of-towners is such a drag, isn't it? And she isn't even your obligation."

"Well, her mother is Lucky's houseguest."

"Michelle is rather obvious, isn't she?"

"In what way?" Jonathan asked sharply.

"She was certainly trying hard to give me the impression that you were interested in her. If you really were, she wouldn't have had to put on that act."

"You think she was only trying to irritate you?"

"Don't get miffed, darling. I'm sure Michelle would love to get her hooks into you. Why not? You're gorgeous and sexy—not to mention fabulously wealthy." She laughed merrily.

"Yes, I suppose that could be a consideration," he replied evenly.

"Not to me. I've always adored you for your own sweet self." Ashleigh dismissed Michelle as not worth their time. "I know you couldn't talk freely in your office. Did you miss me as much as I missed you?"

"It was a long week," he answered noncommittally.

"For me, too. Am I going to see you tonight, darling?"

Jonathan hesitated for only an instant before answering firmly, "I'm looking forward to it."

Michelle had found Evelyn and Lucky in the den, watching the early news. "We didn't know when to expect you.

Where did you go today?" Evelyn asked.

"Jonathan took me to see his house and then we went to his office," Michelle replied.

"That doesn't sound like much fun," Lucky commented. "Was that the best he could do?"

"It was very interesting," Michelle said brightly. "He showed me the prototype of your first invention. You really must see it, Mother."

"Yes, I want to. Lucky promised to show it to me." Evelyn looked over Michelle's shoulder. "Where is Jonathan?"

"He just dropped me off and went on. He said to tell you he'd talk to you later," Michelle told Lucky.

"I wonder why he didn't come in for a drink," Lucky said. "Oh, well, we'll see him this evening."

"I don't think so. I believe he has other plans." Michelle tried to deliver the information casually.

Lucky frowned. "He just got home. He didn't have time to make any plans. Where is he going?"

"I imagine he's taking Ashleigh out to dinner."

As Lucky's puzzled look changed to comprehension, he tried to make light of the matter. "I suppose he had a long-standing date with her and didn't feel he could break it."

There was nothing to be gained by correcting his mis-apprehension, so Michelle said, "That doesn't have to upset *your* plans. You and Mother do whatever you were planning to do. I'll just go to bed early and finish this great book I'm reading."

"Nonsense!" he said. "You'll come along with us. I thought we'd go to the country club for dinner."

Michelle tried to beg off. She really wasn't in a party mood—although that wasn't the reason she gave. But they both insisted she join them for the evening.

When they went upstairs a little later to change for dinner, Evelyn came into Michelle's room to chat for a few minutes.

"It's unfortunate that Jonathan was tied up tonight," she remarked. "It would have been nicer for you if he could have come with us, but we'll all do something tomorrow night."

"I wouldn't count on Jonathan to be around much from now on," Michelle said evenly. "He has a busy social life of his own."

"Naturally he dates a good deal. He's a handsome, eligible bachelor. But I'm sure he plans to spend time with you, too."

"If you saw his girlfriend, you'd change your mind."

"You met her? Where?"

"She just happened to stop by his office while I was there. It was quite uncomfortable. She made sure I knew Jonathan was already taken."

"That's too bad. I had hoped—" Evelyn paused. "Well, never mind. The three of us will have just as good a time without him."

"Come on! You can't wait to get rid of me," Michelle teased. "You know you want to be alone with Lucky."

"He's a very special man," Evelyn said softly. "You have changed your mind about him, haven't you?"

"I was never happier to be wrong about anybody," Michelle assured her. She hesitated, not quite knowing how to ask if her mother was really serious about Lucky. Instead she said, "This house is tremendous. Can you imagine living in a place this big?"

"I think I could get used to it." Evelyn smiled. "But I could be just as happy in a smaller house. Where you live isn't the important thing, it's whom you share it with."

Michelle couldn't agree more. She would be happy living in a tree house with Jonathan.

She turned away abruptly. "I guess we should change clothes."

"What are you going to wear?"

"Maybe a skirt and blouse," Michelle said indifferently.

"That's not dressy enough for a country club. Why don't you wear those white silk shantung pants you bought, and the short yellow jacket with the crystal beading."

"I never should have let you talk me into that outfit. It's much too glitzy. I probably won't ever have a place to wear it."

"This is your chance. Let's both get all gussied up. You'll feel better."

"I feel fine," Michelle answered coolly. "What made you think I didn't?"

"I simply meant, it's fun to get dressed up now and then. I'd better go and change," Evelyn said hastily, hurrying out the door.

Were her feelings for Jonathan that apparent to everyone, or only to her mother, Michelle asked herself? It would be a disaster if Jonathan guessed how she felt about him! She had to correct any possibility of that impression immediately.

Michelle went into the bathroom and washed her face before reapplying makeup carefully. She used all the tricks for looking radiant that the models at the store had taught her—concealer to hide the shadows under her eyes, blush on her high cheekbones for a rosy look. If Jonathan did happen to show up at the club tonight, he'd see she wasn't languishing over him. And even if he didn't drop by, Lucky might mention what a festive mood she'd been in.

Michelle also wore the outfit her mother had suggested. It was just right for the image she wanted to project—a glamorous sophisticate, someone without a care in the world.

She pinned a smile on her face and went downstairs to join the others.

Chapter Seven

Lucky was very flattering when Michelle joined him and her mother in the den. "You look spectacular, my dear! I'll be the envy of everybody at the club when I show up with two such gorgeous women."

They got the attention he predicted. Heads turned when they walked into the country club dining room. Lucky was well-known and popular. A lot of people came over to their table to say hello. They all looked speculatively at Evelyn and appreciatively at Michelle, who smiled brightly at everyone, pretending she was having a wonderful time.

Not all of the people who stopped by were Lucky's friends. Several young men were Jonathan's age. They pretended to be paying their respects to the older man, while they not-so-secretly seemed to be admiring Michelle's lovely face and alluringly curved figure. The one who dropped all pretense was a handsome young man named Carter Babcock.

"I went to Harvard with Lucky's nephew, Jonathan," he told her, after Lucky had introduced them.

"Are you an engineer, too?" she asked politely.

Lucky laughed. "That would take too much effort. Carter is a professional playboy."

"It's nice work if you can get it," she commented.

"Lucky makes me sound like a slacker," Carter protested. "Actually I'm performing a public service. It wouldn't be fair for me to take a job away from someone who needs it."

"You really don't work at all?" Michelle asked curiously.

"I wouldn't say that."

"Polo is very strenuous," Lucky drawled.

"So is waterskiing and tennis." Carter grinned. "I'm a man of many interests."

"If it works for you, that's fine. It would be nice to have some free time," she said. "But I'm not sure I'd know what to do with myself if I woke up every morning with nothing *but* free time."

He gave her a melting smile. "I'd be happy to help you fill it."

"Stop hustling my houseguest, Carter," Lucky ordered. "Don't you have somebody to get back to?"

"Actually I don't. I just stopped in for a drink because I didn't have anywhere else to go."

"Are those violins I hear?" Lucky asked dryly.

"That's the trouble with putting on a happy face." Carter sighed. "People don't realize I get lonely just like anybody else."

A waiter appeared with a first course for the other three. "Can I get you anything, Mr. Babcock?" he asked. "Another Scotch perhaps?"

"No, I was just leaving. Although…" Carter turned to Lucky as if a thought had just occurred to him. "Would you mind awfully if I joined you for dinner?"

Lucky frowned slightly, but before he could think of an excuse, Evelyn said, "That would be very nice. We can't leave the poor man to dine alone, can we?" She gave Lucky an appealing look.

There was nothing he could do about it, although Lucky was clearly not delighted by the idea. "We'd be pleased to have you join us." His tone wasn't as warm as the invitation.

If Carter noticed, he didn't mind. "Splendid! You've saved me from a long, solitary evening."

Michelle guessed that her mother thought Carter would take her mind off Jonathan. She only wished something could. Where were he and Ashleigh right now? Having dinner in some romantic restaurant? Or were they at his house, in an even more romantic setting? Michelle turned quickly to Carter, giving him a brilliant smile.

A small combo started to play while they were having dinner, and Carter asked Michelle to dance.

Lucky watched with dissatisfaction as Carter led her away with his arm around her shoulders. "I wish you hadn't asked him to have dinner with us," he told Evelyn.

"Why not? He seems like a nice young man," she said.

"I suppose so," Lucky agreed grudgingly. "I guess I disapprove of people who waste their potential. As far as I can tell, Carter's only aim in life is the pursuit of pleasure."

"So few people can attain that goal. How does he support himself?"

"He doesn't have to, that's the problem. Carter has trust funds that pour out a steady stream of cash. Both his parents came from extremely wealthy families."

"That could very well take away a young person's incentive," Evelyn commented.

"Not necessarily. Look at Jonathan, he's independently wealthy. He doesn't have to put in the long hours he does. But Jonathan is cut from a different piece of cloth," Lucky said proudly. "He works harder than any of our employees."

"He isn't a workaholic, though. It's nice that he still makes time for a social life," Evelyn remarked artlessly.

Lucky shot a glance at her. "You mean, like tonight? I'm sure that was something he couldn't get out of. I know he'd rather have been with Michelle."

"I wouldn't be too sure. She said this Ashleigh woman was quite possessive."

"That doesn't mean the feeling is mutual. Jonathan is very attracted to Michelle. I can tell. That was the reason I wasn't crazy about having Carter join us."

"I thought it would be nice for her. There's no reason for Michelle to be alone while Jonathan is out on a date," Evelyn said crisply.

"That's perfectly true. It would serve him right if Michelle did become interested in Carter." Lucky sighed. "I gather she and Jonathan had another argument. I don't know what's the matter with those two. Anybody can see they care about each other, but they're not happy unless they're miserable."

Evelyn smiled. "It certainly sounds like love."

"Maybe their version of it. I prefer the old-fashioned variety where two people in love enjoy each other's company and want to be together."

"I do, too, but that concept isn't popular today. If young people don't experience angst in a relationship they seem to feel something is lacking. Too bad they don't realize how wonderfully fulfilling love and marriage can be."

Lucky nodded. "We were both blessed with happy marriages. It's very lonely when your partner is gone."

"I know," Evelyn answered sadly.

"When Agatha died I didn't think I could ever fall in love again, but I was wrong." He covered her hand with his. "You're very special to me. I realize we haven't known each other long and I don't want to rush you, but can I hope you care about me a little?''

"More than a little," she said softly. "I felt the way you did, that I'd never be able to care deeply for another man. I suppose I thought it was disloyal even to consider it. But I know Richard would understand how lost I've been without him. I don't think he'd want me to spend the rest of my life alone."

"Dear Evie." Lucky's voice was husky. "We could have such a good life together. Will you—" He stopped short as Michelle and Carter returned to the table. Lucky hid his irritation with an effort, and the conversation became general.

Carter's obvious interest in Michelle was flattering. He couldn't take Jonathan's place, but Carter was delighted to be with her, whereas Jonathan wasn't. She accepted the fact and tried to enjoy the evening.

Carter could be very amusing. Even Lucky chuckled at some of his stories.

"You really didn't know you were proposing marriage to that girl in Tahiti?" Evelyn asked him.

"No, honestly! We were both victims of the language barrier," Carter said.

"She didn't know the difference between a proposition and a proposal," Lucky said.

"Not so! I have the utmost respect for women."

"You just don't want to be tied to one for life," Michelle joked.

"I'll admit I've never found that special someone I wanted to marry, but that could all change." He gave her a meaningful look.

Michelle knew better than to take him seriously, but Lucky wasn't pleased.

"Where is our waiter?" he asked abruptly. "He hasn't brought our coffee yet."

They lingered over dinner, but not too long afterward, Lucky suggested leaving.

"The evening is young yet," Carter protested.

"But I'm not," Lucky replied. "Are you ladies ready to leave?" he asked Evelyn and Michelle.

When Evelyn indicated that she was, Carter urged Michelle to stay and have an after-dinner drink with him. Since it was better than going home and wondering what Jonathan was doing, she agreed.

After they were alone, Carter's manner became more intimate. "Do you believe in Fate?" he asked, gazing compellingly into Michelle's eyes.

"Not really," she answered. "I believe we're the ones responsible for our own actions, not some unseen force that pulls our strings like a puppeteer."

"I disagree. I think it was Fate that brought me to the club tonight."

"Since you're a member and you come here so often the waiters even know what you drink, I doubt that Fate planned your evening," Michelle said ironically.

"I could just as easily have gone to the yacht club instead. But then I wouldn't have met *you*," he said deeply. "Fate meant for us to be together."

She gave him a disgusted look. "I heard better lines than that in high school."

Carter laughed unexpectedly. "You never know. Sometimes it works."

"In Tahitian maybe."

"Okay, I'll cut out the phony baloney. I really *am* attracted to you, though. I'm looking forward to getting to know you really well."

"You'd better be a quick study. I have to go back to New York."

"Didn't Lucky say you just got here today?"

"Yes, but I've been at Shorehaven for a week with my mother."

"A week is hardly a vacation," he said dismissively.

"I wasn't on vacation." When he gave her a puzzled look, Michelle regretted her unthinking statement. "I mean, it was just a spur of the moment thing. I got tired of the cold weather so I escaped to Florida for a short time."

"I knew we were kindred spirits. If you don't like where you are, go someplace else, I always say."

"That's easy for you, but I have a job waiting for me."

"Someone else did it while you were gone," he said pointedly. "Stay here. We'll have a blast. And if you get bored with Miami, we'll fly to Paris or Rome."

"It's cold in Europe at this time of year, and I don't have any winter clothes with me," she answered, pretending he was serious.

"That's no excuse. You can buy a whole new wardrobe in Paris. I'll phone now and make a reservation at the Ritz. Is that all right, or would you prefer the Meurice? Personally I think the pink marble bathrooms are a little much, but maybe that appeals to a woman. Which one shall it be?"

"You really *are* serious," Michelle said slowly.

"Of course." He looked at her in surprise.

"I was only joking. You live in a world all your own, Carter, but it's time for a reality check. I'm a working woman. I couldn't afford to flit all over the world, even if I had the time. And I don't intend to go as your close companion," she added firmly.

"We could have separate rooms," he said tentatively.

"With a connecting door? No, let's just enjoy this evening. I'll remember it, you can be sure. You have more bells and whistles than Jonathan—and I thought *he* was overprivileged."

"Johnny is a working stiff. You can't have any fun with guys like that."

"His girlfriend, Ashleigh, would disagree with you," Michelle commented lightly.

"She's been trying to land him for years, so naturally she thinks he's perfect."

"Does Jonathan have the same bias against marriage that you do?" Michelle tried to sound only mildly interested. "I mean, if they've been going together for a long time, you'd think they'd at least get engaged. Or are they?"

"I wouldn't know." Carter lost interest in the other couple. "If you won't go to Paris with me, how about the Bahamas? That's only fifty miles away. I have my own plane, so we can leave whenever we like and come back when we feel like it."

"Why not?" She laughed helplessly. "Nothing is real down here, anyway. I might as well be as crazy as the rest of you."

"That's my girl." Carter took her hand and led her onto the dance floor. "I'll teach you not to take life too seriously."

Michelle was a willing pupil, but she didn't have too much hope of success in forgetting Jonathan.

Jonathan couldn't get Michelle out of his mind, either. He'd taken Ashleigh to a lovely restaurant on the waterfront. A breeze was whispering through the palm trees, and soft dinner music was playing in the background, but Jonathan couldn't concentrate on either his companion or the excellent food.

Should he have joined Lucky and his party for dinner tonight? It wasn't very polite to just dump Michelle the minute he got home. His uncle wasn't too pleased about it. But he didn't know the whole story. No, he'd done the right thing, Jonathan assured himself.

For a while Ashleigh wasn't aware of his withdrawn mood, but she gradually showed her annoyance. "What's the matter with you tonight, Jonathan? You're not listening to a word I say."

"Of course I am."

"Then what did I just tell you?"

"You said, uh, you were talking about Isobel's cocktail party."

"That was half an hour ago! Do you mean you haven't paid attention to anything I said since then?" she asked indignantly.

"I heard every word, although I can't repeat them verbatim, if that's what you want."

He'd tried to sound humorous rather than impatient, but she looked at him warily. "Is anything wrong, darling? You seem so tense."

"There are a few problems at the office," he said vaguely. "But I shouldn't bring them home with me. I apologize."

"You don't have to," she said with relief. "I want to share the bad as well as the good with you."

"That's sweet, but my problems aren't really serious." He forced a smile. "What would you like for dessert?"

Once she was reassured, Ashleigh returned to the subjects dearest to her heart: gossip and social events. "Marlene is hoping Craig will invite her to the dance at the yacht club next week, but I happen to know he's planning to ask Tiffany."

Jonathan shrugged. "Marlene won't have any trouble getting a date. She goes out with a lot of men."

"But she already told a couple of people she expected Craig to ask her. It will be too embarrassing for words when he shows up with Tiffany." Ashleigh's eyes gleamed with malice. "I wouldn't want to be in Marlene's shoes."

"I imagine she'll survive." He tried to change the subject. "I haven't seen a Miami newspaper all week. Are the fishing boats still operating, or did the fishermen go out on strike the way they threatened?"

"I have no idea. Why on earth would fishermen strike?"

"Because they're grossly underpaid. They leave the dock before dawn, often in heavy seas and with no guarantee that they'll catch enough to make it worthwhile. Even when they do have a good catch, the brokers underpay them for fish they sell at many times the price."

Ashleigh looked at him admiringly. "You're so clever, Jonathan. How do you know all these things?"

"I read the newspaper."

"I do, too, but the news is so depressing. It's mostly just crime and violence. I think the media dwells on those things too much."

"How can you overemphasize murder and mayhem?" Jonathan asked sardonically.

"Is it so terrible of me to want to look on the bright side of things?" she asked plaintively.

"No, you're not alone there." He was sorry for being impatient with her. Ashleigh's attitude was no different than a lot of people's.

Jonathan made a point of being especially attentive after that, to make up for his earlier sharpness. He knew it hadn't been due to Ashleigh's insensitivity. He was used to that. But they'd been friends for a long time and he usually made allowances for her.

Michelle was the real reason he was tied up in knots, Jonathan admitted to himself. Why couldn't he simply write her off as a relationship that didn't work out? Sure, she was beautiful and sexy and utterly adorable, but so were a lot of women. He would forget about her. In time, Michelle would only be a distant memory—not even necessarily a pleasant one. Jonathan's jaw set rigidly as he tried to convince himself.

By the end of dinner, Jonathan found his mind wandering again as Ashleigh talked about upcoming parties, friends who were getting married, others who were getting divorced.

Finally he said, "If you've finished your coffee, why don't we go somewhere for an after-dinner drink?"

"That sounds lovely. Let's go to my place."

"Wouldn't you rather go someplace where we can dance? We could stop in at the Pelican Lounge, or perhaps drive out to the country club," Jonathan suggested casually.

"The club sounds good," she agreed. "Maybe some of our crowd will be there."

Unlike Jonathan, Michelle was relaxed and having a good time. It was impossible to be depressed around Carter. She didn't take his lavish compliments seriously, but his admiration was soothing and he was good company. He told her about all the famous places she hoped to visit someday. If they were glamorous, Carter had been there.

"I don't know why you want to just *hear* about Istanbul," he said while they were dancing. "We could be there in a matter of hours."

"Maybe next month," she said. "My belly dancer costume is at the cleaners."

Drawing her closer, he said in a seductive voice, "You'd make a gorgeous belly dancer. Will you give me a private performance?"

"It will cost you. I need lots of champagne first to get rid of my inhibitions."

"I'll buy you cases of it," he promised. "And anything else your little heart desires."

"You'd better be careful. I might have very expensive tastes."

"A woman as beautiful as you is entitled to the best." He folded both arms around her slender body. "I've never seen eyes that shade of cornflower blue, or skin with the glow of a pink pearl."

"That sounds like ad copy for nail polish or face powder." She laughed, while trying to put a little distance between them. "Maybe I—" Michelle's laughter died as she caught sight of Jonathan and Ashleigh in the doorway.

Carter could feel her body tense. "What's wrong, doll face?"

"Nothing, I just..." She tilted her head and gave him a brilliant smile. "Not a thing."

"That's good." He pulled her closer, and this time Michelle didn't resist. "I want you to be happy. Worry only produces wrinkles."

"Aren't those supposed to give your face character?" she asked brightly.

"That's a rumor started by people who can't afford plastic surgery." Carter glanced over at the couple who were cutting across a corner of the dance floor on their way to a table. "Hi, Johnny. This is a coincidence. I had dinner with your uncle earlier this evening."

"Really? Where is he?" Jonathan's face was set as he glanced around the room.

"He left quite a while ago."

When Carter started to introduce the two women, they told him they'd already met—both showing the same lack of enthusiasm. After the men exchanged a few words, Ashleigh linked her arm with Jonathan's and urged him toward the tables.

The dinner crowd had thinned out and there were leather booths along the wall, but Jonathan chose a table facing the dance floor.

Michelle was conscious of his eyes following her, and the disapproving look on his face. What did *he* have to be annoyed about, she wondered? Did he expect her to go home early with the older folks while he was out partying with his girlfriend?

Michelle was glad when the combo swung into a loud rock number and she could work off some of her frustration. Carter was an excellent dancer, and so was she. Gradually the other couples on the floor formed a ring around them to watch. When the number ended they all applauded.

"That was more strenuous than polo." Carter laughed. Putting his arm around Michelle's shoulders, he led her off the floor. "I think we deserve a drink."

As they passed his table, Jonathan said, "Why don't you join us?"

"We have a booth," Carter said. "It's more comfortable. Come and join *us*."

It was the last thing either woman wanted, but Ashleigh made an excuse before Michelle could think of one. "We already have our drinks here."

"I wouldn't expect you to carry anything that heavy," Carter said derisively. He raised a hand for the waiter. "Take these drinks over to our table, Jerry," he told the man who had answered his summons promptly.

It was bad enough that they had to share a table, but Michelle and Ashleigh were forced to sit next to each other in the close confines of the booth. The men each sat on an end, next to their own dates.

"Did you enjoy dinner?" Jonathan asked Michelle courteously.

"Yes, the food was divine," she answered, just as politely.

"The chef is good here, but the food can't compare to the Palm Court. That's where we had dinner," Ashleigh said. "The atmosphere is so romantic." She covered Jonathan's hand with hers.

"The atmosphere wasn't too bad right here." Carter commented, smiling at Michelle.

"I didn't know you were in town," Jonathan said to him. "I thought you'd be sailing in the yacht race to Hawaii."

"Been there, done that," Carter answered dismissively.

"Is there anything you *haven't* done?" Michelle asked.

"Held a job." Jonathan answered first.

"I don't know why my life-style irritates so many people," Carter complained. "I contribute money to the government instead of collecting it. I do my bit toward a healthy economy by keeping cash in circulation. Aren't those services to the community? The income of head waiters all over the world would suffer if I took a nine-to-five job.''

"So you're really a humanitarian." Michelle laughed.

"Or just plain lazy," Ashleigh sniffed.

"Do you work?" Michelle asked her innocently.

"Not at a regular job, but I do volunteer work."

"That's important, too," Michelle admitted. "There are so many people who need help, and so little money available. What kind of volunteer work do you do?"

"Well, I...I'm on the board of the garden club, and I'm chairman of the entertainment committee here at the country club. That reminds me, Jonathan." Ashleigh turned to him hurriedly. "We had to move the Spring dance back a week, so be sure and change your calendar."

Carter gave Michelle an amused look. "You won that match," he murmured in her ear.

She didn't feel triumphant. Ashleigh might be shallow and lacking in compassion, but she had Jonathan. It must be love if he couldn't see her flaws.

Michelle was glad when the combo started to play again. "Oh, good, the musicians are back," she said brightly. "Let's dance."

Carter stood to let her out of the booth. "You're tireless," he complained jokingly. "My heart rate was just settling down after the last set."

Jonathan got up quickly. "We wouldn't want you to have a coronary. I'll dance with Michelle."

"I don't really—" she began, but his hand fastened around her wrist and he pulled her away from the table.

When Jonathan took her in his arms on the dance floor, Michelle's protests were forgotten. She closed her eyes and let her body melt into his. For this short, enchanted time, he was hers alone.

Jonathan felt the same unrestrained bliss. They circled the floor silently, lost in the pleasure of being together again. Neither were aware of the couple back at the table watching them.

"It looks as if your boyfriend snapped the leash," Carter observed.

"That's ridiculous!" Ashleigh stated angrily. "Michelle is Lucky's guest. Jonathan just danced with her to be polite."

"If he was any more polite they'd have to throw a bucket of water over him," Carter drawled.

"Don't be crude," she said coldly. "You judge everybody by yourself, but Jonathan isn't like you. It takes more than a pretty face to attract him."

"Like that fantastic bod?" When he saw she was genuinely upset, Carter's tone softened. "Cheer up, Ash. You win some, you lose some. There are plenty of other guys around."

"Jonathan is *mine!*" she said in a hard voice. "I've invested a lot of time in him and I don't intend to let some little nobody walk off with my property."

"Ah, love, sweet love," Carter said mockingly. "Jonathan would be thrilled to know he's lumped in along with your convertible and your diamond watch."

Actually, Jonathan couldn't have cared less. He was as close to heaven as he hoped to get for a long time. How did he imagine he could ever forget Michelle? He'd yearned to hold her in his arms like this. And she felt the same about him, he thought joyfully. He could tell by her body language.

"I missed being with you tonight," he said softly.

Michelle had trouble returning to reality. She looked up at him, still lost in a dream. Then his words registered and the dream started to dissipate. Jonathan could have been with her if he'd wanted to.

"It's all right. I realize you had a commitment. Fortunately, Carter didn't," she said coolly.

"That's unusual for him. Carter is known for being quite a playboy."

"I think people misjudge him. I don't approve of putting a label on anyone."

Jonathan was unpleasantly reminded of how Michelle had been hanging on Carter's words just a short time ago, not objecting when he held her close. Unwelcome suspicions returned to devil him. Had she decided Carter was a better catch?

Jonathan's embrace loosened. "It seems my uncle picked the right date for you tonight," he remarked in a neutral tone.

"Carter isn't really a date," Michelle admitted reluctantly, because Jonathan would find out, anyway. "He was here alone and he asked Lucky if he could join us for dinner."

"That clears up something that was puzzling me. I was rather surprised that Lucky would try to fix you up with Carter."

"He didn't, but why wouldn't he?"

"Lucky doesn't have much respect for underachievers."

"Carter doesn't fit that category. He seems to be very good at what he does." She chuckled.

"You've very charitable."

"Why not? He's a charming man."

Jonathan's expression became more austere. "Would he be as charming without all those millions?"

His frosty tone lifted Michelle's drooping spirits. Jonathan was jealous! "I don't discriminate against the rich," she said demurely.

"That appears to make all the difference to you."

"You're the one who's hung up on money. Carter has been very pleasant to me tonight. I was enjoying myself. Is there anything wrong in that?"

"Not a thing." He released her. "Shall we go back to the table? I've kept you away from him too long."

Michelle didn't know what had happened. One minute everything was perfect between them, and the next minute Jonathan was cool and distant again. It was foolish to think he cared about her. This was the way things always ended between them, Michelle thought hopelessly as she accompanied him back to the table. It was time to give up the dream.

"I thought you'd forgotten who you came with." Ashleigh greeted Jonathan with a thin smile.

"I'm sorry. Michelle and I had some things to talk about," he explained.

"It must have been a fascinating conversation," Carter remarked.

"Depending on how you look at it," Jonathan drawled. "We were talking about you."

"You're more generous than I'd be." Carter gave him an amused look. "When I hold a beautiful woman in my arms, I guarantee you we don't talk about other men."

"I'm sure of that." Jonathan turned to Ashleigh. "Would you like another drink?"

"Not now," she said sulkily.

"We're ready for another." Carter signaled to the waiter.

"None for me, thanks," Michelle said. "I have to go home." She'd had enough of both Ashleigh and Jonathan.

"The evening is just starting," Carter protested. "I thought we'd go to a jazz joint I know of downtown. The place doesn't begin to rock until after midnight."

"It sounds lovely, but I'll have to take a rain check. I just arrived this morning and I've been on the go ever since. It's been a very long day."

"You do look as if you didn't get much sleep last night," Jonathan commented with an enigmatic expression.

"You're right, I had a miserable night," she answered.

"Then I'll take you home." Carter stood and helped her out of the booth. "Never let it be said that Carter Babcock isn't a compassionate man."

"I would never say that," Michelle told him. "You've been the brightest spot in this entire day." After saying a brief good-night to the other couple, she walked to the door with her head held high.

"They're perfect for each other," Ashleigh said waspishly. "I never did like Carter. I don't know what women see in him. Your friend was certainly dazzled by him, though."

"A lot of women find him charming," Jonathan answered neutrally.

"It's all that money, not his scintillating personality. He wouldn't be so smug if he realized that's all they're after—Michelle included. He couldn't get to first base with her if she thought he was poor."

"You're probably right." Jonathan looked at his watch. "Well, it's getting late. Shall we leave?"

"Where would you like to go?"

"I thought I'd take you home."

"It's barely midnight!" Ashleigh exclaimed. "And this is the first time I've seen you in a week."

"There will be other nights. I have a lot of things to do tomorrow."

"Is that the reason? Or is it just that you're bored, now that Michelle left?"

Jonathan sighed. "Don't be difficult, Ashleigh. I'm too tired to argue with you."

"But you weren't too tired to dance with *her!*" she said shrilly.

"Pick up your purse," he said in a steely voice. "We're leaving."

Her manner changed as she gazed at his rigid face. "I'm sorry I was such a shrew, darling. Will you forgive me? I can't bear it when you're angry at me."

"I'm not angry." He sighed. "Let's just go."

"I didn't mean to overreact, but you can't really blame

me,'' Ashleigh pleaded as they walked to the door. ''You
did dance with her for an awfully long time.''

''I explained about that. We were simply talking. You
could see us on the dance floor. What else did you imagine
we were doing?''

She didn't think this was the time to mention how close
he was holding Michelle. Instead, Ashleigh took a different
approach. ''It was all Carter's fault. I never would even
have noticed if he hadn't made such a big thing out of it.
When he told me you were romancing Michelle right there
on the dance floor, naturally I got upset. Wouldn't you if
you thought I was making a play for another man?''

They had reached the carport in front of the country club.
Before Jonathan was forced to answer, a parking attendant
came over to them.

''I'll have your car brought around right away, Mr. Richfield. Did you notice there's a scratch on the right rear
fender?''

''Yes, somebody dinged me in a parking lot,'' Jonathan
said. ''It wasn't your fault, Tommy. Don't worry about it.''
When the man had gone to get the car, Jonathan remarked,
''Some drivers are a menace to society.''

Ashleigh was aware of his evasion, but she decided not
to press him for an answer.

When Carter had driven away from the club a short time
earlier, he asked Michelle frankly, ''Are you really tired,
or did you make a late date with Johnny?''

''Certainly not! How could you think such a thing?''

''Very easily.'' He chuckled. ''Your performance on the
dance floor was quite revealing. Ashleigh was doing a slow
burn.''

''She's a very tiresome woman. I can't imagine what
Jonathan sees in her. Not that it matters to me,'' Michelle
added hastily.

''Which one of us are you trying to convince?''

"Believe me, there's nothing going on between us." Unfortunately that was true, she thought somberly. "Jonathan and I don't even get along very well, and tonight was no exception. We started out trying to be friendly toward each other—that's when you and Ashleigh got the wrong impression. If she hadn't jumped to conclusions she'd have seen that the only heavy breathing we were doing was out of annoyance with each other."

"What do you argue about?" Carter asked curiously.

She shrugged. "We had a misunderstanding when we first met, and everything went downhill from then on."

"How did you two meet?"

"My mother and Jonathan's uncle are interested in each other." Michelle gave him the abbreviated version. "That's why we try to get along, but I'm afraid it's a lost cause."

"I must admit I'm not sorry." Carter turned his head to smile warmly at her. "I hope this means we still have a date tomorrow. I said I'd show you the Bahamas."

Why not, Michelle asked herself? It would be a nice way to spend her last day in Miami. Tomorrow she intended to tell her mother that she was going home.

"I'd love to spend the day with you," she told Carter.

"Great! We'll fly to Nassau for lunch, then lie on the beach or drive around the island, whatever you like."

"It sounds delightful. I'd like to see a little of the Bahamas before I leave."

"Okay, we'll do it up right—sight-seeing, dinner and dancing, the works. Although I refuse to accept the fact that you're leaving so soon. Be prepared for a lot of gentle persuasion."

"As long as you're gentle." She smiled.

"Sweet little Michelle. I'll be anything you want me to be." He brought her hand to his mouth and kissed the palm.

"I don't want you to be any different than you were tonight," she answered firmly. "You've made this a very enjoyable evening."

"I'd like to do a lot more," he murmured.

"I suspected that," she said dryly. "But I'll be up-front with you, so there are no misunderstandings. I don't intend to sleep with you. It's no reflection on you, but we just met. If this means our date for tomorrow is off, I'll understand."

"I must say your candor is refreshing," he said with amusement.

Michelle shrugged as they turned into Lucky's driveway. "It saves a lot of unpleasantness." When he stopped the car in front of the house she unsnapped her seat belt and said, "It was really nice meeting you, Carter."

"You, too." He got out of the driver's side and came around to walk her to the door. "What time shall I pick you up tomorrow?"

She looked at him in surprise. "You still want to go?"

"More than ever. I enjoy people who are unpredictable. The women I know aren't noted for their originality. You're different. You don't play those stylized man-woman games. I like that."

Michelle looked at him skeptically. "I meant what I said. I get the feeling you're going to try to change my mind."

"Of course I am," he said cheerfully. "But you can always say no. One way or another, we'll have a fun time together." He put his arms around her and lowered his head.

Michelle didn't draw away. She wanted him to kiss her. Carter was a handsome, exciting man. He was exactly what she needed to forget Jonathan, who had become an obsession.

Carter's lips moved lightly over hers. When she put her arms tentatively around his neck, his embrace tightened and he made a male sound like a low growl.

His expertise was awesome, she thought clinically. Women must be incredibly aroused by his suggestive technique. Unfortunately it didn't work on her. She tried to feel something, but it just wasn't there. When his hand grazed her breast, she drew away.

He released her immediately, but his fingers caressed her cheek. "Okay, doll face," he said in a husky voice. "I won't rush you. But I'm not giving up, either."

Michelle went inside with a feeling of despair. If she couldn't respond to Carter, who was everything a normal woman could want, there was no hope for her. Maybe in time she would forget Jonathan—or at least it wouldn't hurt as much—but right now she doubted it.

Chapter Eight

Jonathan was as miserable as Michelle about the rift between them. After taking Ashleigh home, he drove around for hours, unable to get Michelle out of his mind. He thought his decision to forget about her and get on with his life ended the matter, but one glimpse of her tonight told him he couldn't.

Maybe it would be easier when she left town and wasn't a constant distraction, he told himself. But Jonathan knew that was only wishful thinking. The mere thought of her leaving made him desolate. How could he get through even one day without seeing her?

After hours of searching for a solution, he realized that since he couldn't live without her, he had to give Michelle the benefit of a doubt. She was welcome to his money; he simply wanted her to love him, as well. Maybe she would if he stopped acting like such a jerk.

Jonathan turned the car around and headed home, feeling a lot more cheerful.

Michelle slept late the next morning and then had to rush to get dressed, since Carter was picking her up at eleven. She had intended to tell her mother she was leaving the next day, or as soon as she could get a plane reservation. Now it would have to wait until she got back from the Bahamas, which meant she wouldn't be able to leave until Wednesday at the earliest. Thursday was probably more realistic.

Michelle hadn't asked Carter what to wear. She had read that dress was casual in the Bahamas, but he might want to have lunch in a fancy restaurant. There were also casinos and posh resorts in Nassau—Carter's kind of places. She finally settled on white linen pants with a ruffled, gauzy, turquoise-colored blouse and white sandals. A broad brimmed straw hat with flowers circling the crown completed her outfit.

When Michelle got downstairs, voices were coming from the sunroom. She left her hat and purse on a chair in the entry and went to tell her mother she was going out.

The sunroom was a cheerful solarium, furnished informally with comfortable furniture covered in a floral print. Wide glass windows looked out on the garden and the boat dock at the foot of the lawn.

It was a lovely view, but all Michelle saw was Jonathan. He was sprawled in a chair with his long legs stretched out and crossed at the ankles, looking completely relaxed. Obviously he hadn't spent the troubled night she had!

As Michelle froze in the doorway, her heart racing, Evelyn called to her. "Good morning, dear. I was starting to get worried. You don't usually sleep this late."

"Perhaps she was out late last night," Jonathan remarked pleasantly.

Michelle didn't notice the bleakness in his eyes. She was too upset over the fact that he didn't seem to care that she'd been with Carter. What time had Jonathan gotten in—if he went home, that is?

"Michelle is on vacation," Lucky said indulgently. "She doesn't need to keep set hours."

He had given her a perfect opening to mention that she was going home, but before she had a chance, Evelyn looked at her approvingly and said, "You look very nice. I don't think I've seen that blouse before."

"I brought it with me, but I never had a chance to wear it."

"It's very attractive," Jonathan said politely.

"Thank you," she answered formally.

Lucky tried to stifle his impatience with them. "Since Michelle is all dressed up, why don't you take her to lunch, Jonathan?" He kept his voice casual.

"I'm sure Jonathan has work piled up at the office," Michelle remarked hurriedly. "I'm surprised you're not there already," she said to him.

"I went in early this morning and took care of everything that was urgent, and then I took off for the day," he said. "Would you care to go to lunch?"

Michelle knew Jonathan was only asking her because Lucky all but told him to. She wanted to tell Jonathan he needn't bother.

Instead she said coolly, "Thanks, but I already have a luncheon date."

Evelyn gave her a surprised look. "With whom?"

"Carter asked me last night." Michelle looked at her watch. "He should be here any minute."

Lucky slanted a glance at his nephew. "Well, if you're both free tonight, maybe we'll all have dinner together."

"Perhaps you'd better not count on me," Michelle said. "I don't know what time I'll be back."

Lucky raised an eyebrow, but his only comment was "I see."

They were all staring at her speculatively. Michelle didn't want anyone to jump to the wrong conclusion, so she explained reluctantly. "We're going to Nassau. Carter said there's lots to see, which is why I don't know how long we'll be there.''

"Perhaps he'll suggest staying for a day or two," Jonathan remarked without expression. "There are some nice resorts on the island."

He was pushing her into Carter's bed! Michelle lifted her chin to hide the pain that caused. "What a good idea. Maybe we'll do that."

"You haven't even seen Miami yet," Evelyn said sharply. "Besides, you're a guest here. I don't think it would be polite to go running off somewhere."

"I'm sure Lucky wouldn't mind," Michelle said. She forced a smile. "I'm just in the way around here, anyhow."

"Not at all, my dear," Lucky said. "You're free to do anything you like, naturally, but it would be nice if you could join the rest of us for dinner tonight."

Jonathan stood abruptly. "You'd better make your plans without me, too. I might be busy, also."

When the doorbell rang, Michelle said a hasty goodbye. But Jonathan seemed determined to make her life miserable.

"I'll walk out with you and say hello to Carter," he said.

"Phone me if you change your mind about tonight," Lucky said to his nephew.

"I will, but I doubt it very seriously," Jonathan replied.

As they went down the hall together, Michelle said waspishly, "You just saw Carter last night and you didn't seem overly fond of him then. Why this sudden urge to say hello?"

"Is there any reason you don't want me to?"

"Why would there be?" she countered.

"You'd know that better than I. But you have nothing to worry about. Carter is a lot of things, but I've never known him to be indiscreet."

Michelle's eyes flashed blue fire. "Exactly what are you implying? That I slept with him last night?"

A muscle twitched in Jonathan's square jaw. "Did you?"

"It's none of your damn business!" She flung open the door and gave Carter a dazzling smile.

After kissing her cheek, he looked at the two of them quizzically. "I didn't get my dates mixed, did I?"

"Not at all," Michelle assured him. "Jonathan just happened to be leaving at the same time I was."

"That's good. I would have been very disappointed. I have our day all planned."

"I'm sure you could have found someone else to share it with you," Jonathan said, in what was supposed to be a joking tone. "This guy has a Rolodex full of names a sheik would pay a fortune for," he told Michelle.

"Don't be bitter, Johnny," Carter drawled. "You had your chance and you blew it."

Jonathan's eyes were somber as he watched them drive away. How could he have behaved like such a jerk? Was he *trying* to drive Michelle into Carter's arms? If she was wavering before, he'd given her a reason not to.

Michelle was seething after Jonathan's accusation. He, of all people, should know she didn't just fall into bed with anyone. She would have attributed it to jealousy if she didn't know better. For some reason, Jonathan's feelings toward her had changed. Maybe he thought she was freeloading off Lucky. If that was the case, he needn't worry. She couldn't get out of Miami fast enough!

Michelle regretted accepting this date with Carter, but as they flew to Nassau on his private plane, she changed her mind. Sitting in the cockpit next to him was exciting. The Atlantic Ocean was spread out below, dotted with groups of little islands, like small bits of confetti flung by a careless giant into the brilliant blue water.

"Bimini is that tiny cay over to the left, all by itself." Carter indicated an island much smaller than the rest. "Ernest Hemingway considered Bimini one of his homes away from home.''

Michelle stared out at the small dot surrounded by sparkling water. ''You'd think he would have preferred Nassau. It's supposed to have gambling and nightlife.''

''It does. People like Howard Hughes and the former Shah of Iran spent a lot of time on New Providence Island. That's where we're going.''

''I thought we were going to Nassau,'' Michelle said. ''Isn't it an island?''

''No, it's a city, the capital of the Bahamas, located on New Providence. And across a bridge is Paradise Island where a lot of famous people used to hang out, and some still do. We'll drive to Paradise for lunch.''

''It sounds so glamorous,'' she commented.

''That's what the developers thought when they changed the name from Hog Island.'' Carter laughed.

A car was waiting for them when they landed at the airstrip. Michelle couldn't help enjoying all the V.I.P. treatment. Carter was even more privileged than Jonathan. She quickly suppressed the thought of him before it could ruin her day.

There was so much to see and do that Jonathan was only a vague ache in the back of her mind. He was never completely absent from her thoughts, but Carter was a diverting companion.

He told her about the notorious pirates that once made the islands a lawless place of plundering and drunken revelry. ''The notorious Blackbeard, Henry Morgan, Captain Kidd and Anne Bonney all worked these waters.''

''There was a woman pirate?'' Michelle asked.

''One of the fiercest,'' Carter assured her. ''Anne was a hot-blooded beauty, conceived in Ireland on the wrong side of the quilt, as it was delicately called. She was born in South Carolina where her parents went to get married and start a new life on his plantation.''

"She should have turned out to be a southern belle rather than a pirate," Michelle observed.

"Southern gentlemen were too tame for Anne. She was one of the first liberated women. She decided she could do anything a man could do, and she did it even better."

Carter continued to tell her interesting stories about the Bahamas as they drove along the scenic road.

Nassau was a gracious city with Victorian mansions and a fort complete with a moat and dungeons. Michelle was charmed by the pastel buildings in the square, and especially by the Queen's Staircase. She wanted to climb the sixty-six steps to the top where the view had to be fantastic. But Carter said they had a lot more to see.

"You can't cover New Providence in a few hours. Perhaps we should stay over for a day or two," he suggested casually as they drove across the bridge to Paradise Island.

"Do you think you could get two hotel rooms on such short notice?" she asked innocently.

He laughed. "I've never been turned down so creatively."

"I didn't want the day to be spoiled by hurt feelings."

"You needn't worry. I don't sulk if I strike out."

"Because it doesn't mean that much to you," Michelle said matter-of-factly.

"You don't have a very high opinion of me, do you?"

"On the contrary. I've never met anyone like you," she answered evasively.

"Is that good or bad?"

"Do you have to ask? I'm here with you, having a wonderful time."

He turned his head to glance at her. "You wouldn't rather be with Johnny?"

"What a silly question." She changed the subject adroitly. "Are we going to have lunch soon? I'm famished."

"That's good, because the food at the Tropical Palms is terrific. It's one of the nicer resorts on the island."

"Nice" wasn't a strong enough description. The grounds could have been pictured in a travel brochure. Brilliant flowers made extravagant splashes of color, contrasting with the clipped green lawn. The glassed-in dining room looked out over azure blue water decorated with sailboats, and the hotel was surrounded by little thatched huts.

"Those are private bungalows," Carter explained. "Some of them have two bedrooms. Care to change your mind?"

"Do you promise not to walk in your sleep?"

"That's a promise I'd find hard to keep." He took her hand and squeezed it.

Michelle knew Carter wasn't serious about her. He just happened to like women—all kinds of women. But his admiration was just what she needed after Jonathan's rejection. Her eyes were somber with remembrance as she stared down at her plate.

"Don't you like your salad?" Carter asked.

"Oh, yes, it's delicious," she said, picking up her fork. "I've never had conch before."

"The natives pronounce it conk. I thought you'd prefer it to land crab. That's very tasty, too, but a lot of people feel squeamish when they find out they've eaten the same kind of crab they see skittering across the road at night."

She wrinkled her nose. "I might have been more than just squeamish. I've always thought the first person to eat a crab must have been very brave."

"Or very hungry. Although I suppose it isn't any different than eating a lobster. Those wouldn't win any beauty contests, either."

He told her about other Bahamian cuisine, and after lunch they drove around the island. Carter pointed out the limestone caves that might still contain a fortune in pirate gold.

"Isn't that just a myth?" Michelle asked.

"No, it's true. Henry Morgan was the most famous pirate whose treasure has never been found, but there were others. The Bahamas are spread out over 100,000 square miles of the Atlantic Ocean, and there are thousands of islands, some just little dots of land. So it's entirely possible that a fortune lies buried on more than one of them."

The day sped by enjoyably, but by late afternoon Michelle was ready to go home. She'd seen all she could absorb at one time. Each beautiful vista began to look like all the others.

When she mentioned it to Carter, he grinned. "I was waiting for you to feel that way. Okay, we've done the obligatory tourist bit. Now it's time for something more sophisticated."

The casino he took her to was brightly lit and pulsed with excitement. Well-dressed people crowded around green felt tables, shooting dice, playing blackjack or watching a little white ball rattle around a big roulette wheel.

Carter bought her a large stack of chips and suggested that she try her luck.

Michelle was a little surprised when he started to leave her. "What are you going to play?" she asked.

"I thought I'd try a few hands of chemin de fer."

"I've only seen it played in the movies," she said. "I think I'll watch for a while."

Only a handful of people were seated at the chemin de fer table, which was separated from the other gaming tables by a velvet rope. It was a complicated game where each person only received three cards. The players watched with expressionless faces as the croupier dealt the cards and moved stacks of chips around. Michelle had a feeling the stakes were very high.

Carter's former attentiveness to her was switched to the card table. Michelle watched for a while, but it seemed to be a very complicated game. When she wandered away, he didn't even notice.

He did notice the pretty cocktail waitress who brought him a drink, Michelle observed cynically. The seductive look he gave her was the same one he'd worn off and on all day with *her.*

Michelle didn't mind. She'd been under no illusions about Carter, nor were her emotions involved. He'd simply come along at a time when she needed him.

Eventually Carter came looking for her and Michelle thought he was ready to go home. But he wouldn't hear of it.

Ignoring her protests he said, "You can't leave without having dinner at the Coral Room. It's world famous."

"Then why haven't I heard of it?"

"Because you've led a sheltered life. Their rock lobster is a gastronomical adventure."

The Coral Room also had a floor show. When it was over and Carter suggested going to a club on the other side of the island, Michelle stated flatly that she wanted to go home. He was a little sulky at first, but it wasn't his nature to linger over minor disappointments.

It was almost midnight by the time they got back to Lucky's house. Michelle wanted to avoid a heated good-night, so she took the initiative. When Carter walked her to the door she kissed him lightly, then before he could reach for her, she took out her key.

"I had a really smashing time," she said brightly. "Thanks for everything."

He accepted her unspoken rejection. "I enjoyed it, too, although I could have made it even more fun for both of us." He grinned.

After they'd said good-night and she went inside, Michelle's polite smile faded. No wonder she couldn't forget

Jonathan. He'd told her he wanted to make love to her. Carter merely talked about having "fun."

The memories she'd suppressed all day came rushing back. She thought of Jonathan's compelling magnetism and his tenderness toward her. What had happened to change all that? She sighed heavily.

The house was quiet, so Michelle tiptoed across the marble floor. Before she reached the staircase, a door off the hall opened, flooding the entry with light. She was rooted to the spot as Jonathan appeared. Was he just a vision conjured up by her deep longing?

"Did you have a good time?" he asked, dispelling the notion.

"What are you doing here?" she whispered.

"I came to discuss some business matters with Lucky. He and Evelyn went out and I've been working in the den." When she continued to stare at him, he said, "I'm through now. Would you care to have a drink?"

"No, thanks." She finally pulled herself together. "I've had every kind of drink imaginable."

"Yes, I suppose Carter wined and dined you royally. Some coffee, then?"

"No, nothing." She turned away, afraid her emotions might show. Jonathan was very perceptive. "It's late. I'm going to bed."

"I don't blame you for being angry at me," he said quietly. "My behavior this morning was inexcusable. I'd like to apologize."

"Apology accepted," she said wearily, because it was easiest.

He looked dissatisfied. "You don't really mean that."

"It's late, Jonathan, and I'm tired. Can't we just leave it at that?"

"*I* can't. I've been miserable all day. I didn't come here to talk business with Lucky. That was the excuse I used, but he and your mother have been gone all evening. I've been waiting here for you to come home.''

"Were you sure I would?" Michelle asked sarcastically.

"I hoped you would." He hesitated for a moment. "Did you enjoy Nassau?"

"More than Carter did." She couldn't help smiling. "Sight-seeing isn't really his thing, but it was nice of him to put up with it for me."

"I didn't realize there was so much to see at night," Jonathan remarked casually.

"It would be difficult to see much in the dark. If you want to know what we were doing until this time of night, just come out and ask me," she said sharply.

"I don't have that right. You told me so this morning."

"I was angry. You were really out of line."

"You're absolutely correct. If I promise it will never happen again, can we at least be friends?"

"We've tried, but it never seems to work out." She sighed. "Sometimes the things we argue about aren't even important. There seems to be this constant tension between us."

"Why do you think that is?" he asked softly.

She knew perfectly well what he meant, but passion wasn't enough for her. Especially passion he shared with Ashleigh! Pretending not to understand, she gave him a crooked smile. "Maybe we just don't like each other."

"I'm sure that isn't the answer. We've had some great times together."

"Yes, those are the ones I'd like to remember," she said wistfully.

"We can add to them," he coaxed.

She shook her head, knowing whatever was wrong between them hadn't been resolved. "There isn't time," she told him.

"You're leaving? Evelyn didn't mention it."

"I haven't had a chance to tell her yet. Every time I start

to, something happens. I'm going to talk to her first thing in the morning.''

Jonathan stared at her moodily. ''I suppose there's nothing I can say to change your mind.'' A hint of a smile lightened his gloom for a moment. ''I haven't had much luck in the past.''

Before she could answer, the door opened and Lucky and Evelyn came in. ''I thought you'd have left long ago, Jonathan,'' he exclaimed. ''Is anything wrong?''

''No, after you went out I continued to work on those contracts. I didn't realize how late it had gotten,'' Jonathan said. ''I was just leaving when Michelle came home.''

''This late? You must have had a good time,'' Evelyn commented. ''How did you like the Bahamas?''

''Why are we all standing around in the hall?'' Lucky asked. ''Let's go into the den and have a nightcap.''

This was her chance to tell both of them she was leaving, Michelle thought. Why was she so reluctant to make it definite? Maybe she could have found an opportunity before this if she'd really wanted to. Her chin firmed as she was tempted to postpone her announcement until the next day. No, it wouldn't get any easier.

She didn't have an immediate chance. When the four of them were settled in the den, Lucky took a bottle of wine out of the refrigerator in the bar.

''Let's all have a glass of champagne,'' he said. ''I'm in a festive mood.''

''I'm glad somebody is,'' Jonathan muttered under his breath. ''Thanks, but I'll pass,'' he told his uncle.

''You have to take at least a sip. I'm going to propose a toast.'' Lucky smiled broadly at Evelyn. ''Do you want to tell them, or shall I?''

She returned his smile indulgently, saying, ''You can do the honors, darling.''

''Evie and I are getting married,'' he said. ''I hope you'll both be as happy about it as we are.''

"That's wonderful!" Michelle exclaimed.

"Are you really pleased?" Evelyn looked at her searchingly.

"Why wouldn't I be? I'll have a fabulous place to visit," Michelle joked, to hide her emotion.

"How about you?" Lucky asked his nephew. "Jonathan?" He frowned when the younger man didn't answer immediately.

"What?" Jonathan was staring at Michelle. "Oh...of course I'm pleased. I'm delighted for both of you."

"We hoped you would be." Lucky's frown disappeared.

"When is the happy event?" Jonathan asked.

"As soon as possible. At my age you don't make long-range plans." Lucky chuckled.

"Don't talk like that," Evelyn said reprovingly. "You're still a young man."

"If I am, it's due to you." He gazed at her tenderly.

"When *are* you getting married?" Michelle asked. "And where?" She was glad she had left her plans for returning to work so open-ended when she last spoke with her boss.

"The wedding will take place in New York in about a month," Evelyn said.

"So soon!" Michelle gasped.

"Lucky doesn't believe in long engagements." Her mother laughed.

"I'd settle for a quiet ceremony in a judge's chambers," he said. "The quicker the better, but I don't want to cheat Evie out of her day in the spotlight."

"It isn't that," she protested. "I just want you to meet all of my friends and family."

"I know, darlin', and it's fine with me," he said fondly.

Michelle seized the opportunity that had been presented to her. "There will be a lot to do in a very short space of time. Fortunately I can make some preliminary arrangements for you when I go home tomorrow."

"You can't leave now!" Evelyn exclaimed.

"I can't think of a better time. You two certainly don't need me around."

"*I* do. I was counting on you to go shopping with me for my wedding dress. You're the one who knows about clothes."

"You've always had good fashion sense, Mother."

"A wedding dress is different. What do I know about those?"

"As much as I do," Michelle answered dryly.

"It's not just shopping. I need you to help me make up a guest list. What if I forget one of the relatives? People are always so touchy about invitations. Your aunt Blanche didn't talk to her cousin for a year because she wasn't invited to her wedding."

"Anne was married in Japan where Uncle Donald was stationed at an air force base!" Michelle exclaimed. "Blanche wouldn't have gone anyway."

"It didn't stop her from holding a grudge."

"Your mother really wants you to be here," Lucky said. "And I do, too. Since we both want her to be happy, don't you think you could manage a few more days here?"

"I suppose so," Michelle answered reluctantly. How could she refuse when he was so good to her mother?

"Splendid! Then it's all settled."

A short time later Michelle said, "It's been a long, eventful day. If you'll all excuse me, I'm going to bed."

"I'll go with you," Evelyn said. "I've had a pretty exciting day myself."

But when they got upstairs she came into Michelle's room and closed the door. "Do you honestly feel comfortable with this?" She watched her daughter's face intently.

"I'm really thrilled for you, Mother," Michelle answered truthfully. "I know how sad you've been since Dad died. I think it's wonderful that you were able to find someone again."

"It doesn't mean that I love your father any less. He was my first love, and there will never be anyone like him. My feelings for Lucky are different. It isn't young love, but it's awfully nice. He's warm and funny. We enjoy each other's company. Can you understand that?"

"It sounds so nice and peaceful." Michelle sighed unconsciously.

"I wouldn't exactly describe it that way." Evelyn laughed. "Besides, you're too young to want peace. At your age you should be looking for a man who makes your heart race and your knees feel like spaghetti."

"What happens when you find him and he feels like that about somebody else?"

"Surely you're not still moping around after Stuart? I can't believe you were truly in love with him. I think just your pride was hurt."

"You're probably right," Michelle answered indifferently. "But men are all alike."

"Nonsense! You can't let one bad experience make you cynical. What you need is a real man. Somebody who doesn't need to romance every woman in sight to prove his masculinity. Someone like Jonathan," Evelyn added casually.

"Boy, are you ever a lousy judge of character! He collects women like other men collect stamps."

"I don't believe that," Evelyn protested.

"You should have heard the messages on his answering machine when he got home from Shorehaven. No wonder he's so spoiled."

"I never thought of Jonathan as spoiled. I think he's perfectly charming."

"You and the rest of the female population," Michelle replied curtly. She knew she was being unfair to Jonathan, but she didn't want to discuss him. "If you don't mind, Mother, I'd like to go to bed. I'm awfully tired."

"Yes, I imagine you must be after such a big day."

Evelyn hesitated at the door. "If you really dislike Jonathan, I'll ask Lucky not to include him in any of our plans while you're here."

"I might disapprove of some things about him, but I don't actually dislike him," Michelle said quickly. "You needn't say anything to Lucky. I wouldn't want to offend him after he's been so nice to me."

"But if you're going to be uncomfortable." Evelyn paused delicately.

"No, it's okay. I don't mind."

"In that case, I won't bother mentioning it to Lucky. Good night, dear. Get a good night's sleep."

Evelyn went down the hall to her own room, smiling wryly. "Young love," she murmured. "It's wonderful, but I wouldn't want to go through it again."

Nobody was around but Manuel when Michelle went downstairs the next morning. He was taking away the wilted flowers and replacing them with the fresh bouquets the house was always filled with.

"Good morning, Manuel," she called to him. "Where is everybody?"

He didn't give her his usual sunny smile. "Mr. Richfield and your mother went out," he answered, almost curtly.

Michelle was puzzled, but she figured he was concentrating on his task. "Do you know when they'll be back?"

"They didn't say, and it wasn't my place to ask."

"Is anything wrong, Manuel?" she asked tentatively.

"Not yet," he muttered. Before she could question him, he asked, "Where would you like to have breakfast, Miss Lacey, in the dining room or the sunroom?"

"The sunroom will be fine, but I only want juice and coffee."

"I will serve it to you there," he said formally.

What could be wrong with him, she wondered? He never called them by their last names. It was always, Mr. Lucky, or Miss Michelle. Maybe he had an argument with one of the staff, she decided, dismissing the matter.

Jonathan came in while she was having coffee and reading the morning newspaper. He looked very authoritative in a summer suit and a shirt and tie. But his manner this morning wasn't the distant one she'd come to dread.

After giving her a smile and a friendly greeting, he said, "Is there any more coffee in that pot? I could use a cup."

"I'm afraid it's lukewarm by now," she said. "But you're welcome to it."

"Thanks, but I'll have Manuel bring a fresh pot." Jonathan tugged on the bellpull to summon the man. "Is Lucky around?" he asked.

"No, he and Mother went out. I don't know where, or when they'll be back."

"I hope they're not gone for the day. I really do have business to discuss with Lucky today," he said wryly.

When Manuel answered the bell, Jonathan repeated his question about Lucky's whereabouts.

Manuel wasn't any warmer toward Jonathan. After he'd gone to get a fresh pot of coffee, Jonathan asked, "What's the matter with Manuel? He usually loves to hang around and talk to everyone like one of the guests. The problem most of the time is getting rid of him."

"He's been with your uncle a long time, hasn't he?"

"For years. Manuel is more than a servant. He started out as Lucky's valet, but he really runs the place now. I don't know what my uncle would do without him—or vice versa."

A short time later, Evelyn and Lucky returned.

"Did you forget that I was coming over with the Broderick contract for you to sign?" Jonathan asked his uncle. "It's a good thing one of us in this family pays attention to business," he joked.

"Sorry, Jonathan, I did forget about it," Lucky said. "But I had something more important to do."

"Where did you go?" Michelle asked her mother. "You didn't leave me a note, and Manuel only knew that you went out."

"Show them," Lucky told Evelyn, smiling broadly.

She held out her left hand. On the third finger was a huge emerald solitaire with a V of sparkling diamonds on each side. "Lucky took me to his jeweler."

"I was going to pick out a ring and surprise her with it," he said. "But I was afraid I might get something she didn't like."

"I don't know why you took me along. You didn't approve of any of my selections," she teased.

"You picked out little bitty keepsake rings," he said scornfully. "I wanted you to have something nice."

"I'd say you got your wish." Michelle whistled. "It looks like a traffic light. Next time you'll have to buy her a ruby so she'll have a matching set, stop and go."

"That's a great idea. Now I won't have to wonder what to get for our first anniversary," Lucky said.

"I hope you're not serious!" Evelyn said. "This is more than enough."

"You've heard that old saying, you can't be too rich or too thin. My version is, a woman can never have too much jewelry," Michelle quipped. She didn't notice that Jonathan wasn't laughing along with the rest of them.

While they were chatting, Manuel came in to clear away the coffee service.

"Show Manuel your little bauble," Lucky told Evelyn.

She held out her hand. "Isn't it beautiful?"

After a quick glance, Manuel's austerity deepened. "Very nice, Mrs. Lacey."

"Is that all you can say?" Lucky complained. "I'm officially engaged now. Where are the congratulations and good wishes?"

"I'm sure you'll be very happy together," Manuel said stiffly.

"What the devil is wrong with you?" Lucky gave him a perplexed look. "Are you worried that there will be a lot of extra work? Hire more help if you need it."

"That won't be my responsibility anymore," Manuel answered without expression.

Evelyn began to get a glimmering of what was wrong. "This house couldn't run without you, Manuel. *I* certainly wouldn't know what to do. I hope you're not thinking of leaving us."

Strong emotion finally broke through the man's rigid control. "Things won't be the same around here. You'll want to bring in your own people. I understand that, but there won't be enough for me to do." He drew himself up proudly. "I don't stay where I'm not needed. I don't take charity."

"That's absolutely—" Lucky began, but Evelyn held out a hand to silence him.

"You're the one who would be doing *me* a favor," she told Manuel earnestly. "I can't run this household. I wouldn't know who to call if the garbage disposal stopped working, or how to hire a new housemaid if one of them quit. I don't know how you handle so many different jobs. It's a real talent."

"Well...you sort of learn as you go along. I wasn't hired to do all the things I do around here. I was only supposed to be Mr. Lucky's gentleman's gentleman. But when I saw the way people were taking advantage of him, I couldn't let them get away with it."

"You see? That's what I mean. Tradespeople walk all over me. When they present an outrageous bill, I don't know what to do but pay it."

Manuel came over to lean against a table next to her. "That's a big mistake. They pad their bills because they think nobody will notice. You gotta call them on it."

"That's easy for *you* to say. I hope if you ever do leave,

you'll give us at least four or five years notice." Evelyn laughed merrily.

"Okay, you got yourself a deal, boss," he answered happily.

"We'll be having an early lunch out by the pool today, Manuel," Lucky said. "Maybe you'd better tell Bessie to get started."

When the man had gone, Lucky said to Evelyn, "I never realized Manuel was feeling insecure. You handled him beautifully."

"Everybody needs their ego stroked now and then." She smiled. "But Manuel really is indispensable. I couldn't run a house this size. The very idea is daunting."

"That's the difference between us." Michelle grinned. "It wouldn't take me long to get used to a big house and an eye-popping ring."

Evelyn held out her hand to admire the emerald. "It really is gorgeous. I can't wait to show it to Marian. She's my best friend in New York," she explained to the two men.

"And you can show it to *my* friends, too," Lucky said. "We'll give a big engagement party. I want you to meet everybody."

"I hope they'll like me."

"If they don't, we'll make new friends." His laughter turned to tenderness as he lifted her hand and kissed it. "How could anybody help loving you?"

Michelle's eyes were misty at their obvious devotion. She glanced at Jonathan, but he was lost in thought.

"I want you to invite all your friends, too, Jonathan," Lucky said.

"It's your party, not mine," his nephew objected.

"This has been a second home to your friends since they were in knee pants. I've watched them all grow up. Besides, it's a chance for Michelle to get to meet everybody, too. She'll be here a lot, I hope."

"As often as I'm asked," she said, without meaning it. Michelle was delighted for her mother, but she had no intention of intruding on her life.

"You're uncharacteristically quiet, Jonathan," Lucky remarked. "Is there something on your mind?"

"Yes, the Broderick contract. You still haven't signed it." Jonathan mustered a smile. "You're a great inventor, but a lousy businessman."

"Okay, okay, come into my study and I'll sign the blasted thing," Lucky grumbled. "You're a slave driver. At your age you ought to be less interested in business, and more interested in girls."

Lucky didn't realize he had nothing to worry about, Michelle thought sardonically.

Chapter Nine

After lunch on the patio beside the pool, Lucky returned to the subject of the party. "I think black tie would make it more festive, don't you, Evie?"

"Whatever you like, darling," she answered. "Although, Michelle and I don't have any evening clothes with us."

"That's one of the nice things about Miami. We have lots of stores," he said.

"When were you planning to have this party?" Michelle asked. "I said I'd help with arrangements for the wedding, but I can't stay indefinitely."

"Then we'll have it next week. Is that soon enough for you?" Lucky asked.

"You can't have a big party on such short notice," Evelyn protested.

"Sure, I can. I'll just have my secretary phone everyone instead of having invitations printed and mailed. That's more sensible, anyway. Then we'll know immediately how many people are coming.''

"It isn't just the invitations. You'll have to hire caterers and discuss a menu with them, and you'll probably want to have music. That means hiring musicians. You don't know how many things there are to do for as fancy a party as you have in mind."

"I have a good catering firm that takes care of everything. I've used them for years. They bring the food, help, flowers, the works. I just tell them how many people to prepare for."

"You let them choose the menu?" Evelyn asked.

"I always have, but you can do it if you like." Lucky looked at her in sudden concern. "I don't want you to feel I'm taking over your domain. I just want you to relax and have a good time at your party."

She smiled tenderly at him. "You dear man. How could I object to being so pampered?"

"All right then, I'll begin making up the list. You start to work on yours, too," he told his nephew.

"Later," Jonathan answered, without opening his eyes or moving off a chaise. He looked the picture of relaxation. He'd removed his tie and jacket and rolled up his shirt-sleeves.

"No, now!" Lucky insisted. "You're always after *me* to get things done."

"How often do I succeed?" Jonathan grumbled, but he sat up and took the paper and pen his uncle handed him.

After watching them both fill pages of paper with names, Evelyn said, "If even half of those people accept, it's going to be a large party."

"Most of my friends will be here," Lucky said. "I don't know about Jonathan's."

His nephew looked up and smiled. "They never miss a party—especially one of yours."

"I won't know anybody, except for Ashleigh and Carter," Michelle remarked casually.

Jonathan looked at her without expression. "You want me to invite Carter?"

"I don't care one way or the other. I just assumed you would. Isn't he a friend of yours?"

"I suppose you could call him that, although we don't see much of each other."

"Then I guess the only person I'll know will be Ashleigh," Michelle said. "You are inviting *her,* aren't you?"

He hesitated. "It would be awkward not to. I mean, most of our mutual friends will be coming. She'd be bound to find out. I don't like to hurt someone's feelings for no reason."

"But Carter wouldn't mind not being included. Is that it?" Michelle asked evenly.

Jonathan's jaw set. "All right, I'll invite him if it means that much to you!"

"I couldn't care less," she answered coldly. "I was just interested in your reasoning."

Evelyn and Lucky exchanged a glance. "We'll have to go shopping for gowns for the party," she said hastily. "And we'd better do it soon, in case we find something that needs alterations."

"Why don't we go now?" Michelle asked, rising.

Evelyn expected Michelle to look for something inexpensive, saying she didn't need another evening gown. She was surprised when her frugal daughter didn't look at the price tags in the elegant stores Lucky had suggested.

Evelyn got a glimmering of the reason after Michelle had turned up her nose at one dress after another.

"Don't you have something outstanding?" she asked the saleswoman. "I've seen the clothes these women wear. I don't intend to let them patronize me."

Since Ashleigh was the only woman friend of Jonathan's

that Michelle had met, Evelyn got the idea. It was a good sign, she thought happily. Maybe she and Jonathan would finally realize they were perfect for each other.

Michelle tried on and rejected one dress after another. The saleswoman was beginning to lose hope of a sale, but she refused to give up. About the time Michelle was starting to think they should look somewhere else, the woman returned with a length of flame-colored chiffon over her arm.

"This just came in," she said. "It hasn't even been tagged yet, but it's your size and I thought it might be what you're looking for."

As soon as Michelle tried it on, she knew this was the dress she had in mind. The strapless gown hugged her body closely before flaring out below the hips in layers of scarlet chiffon that fluttered when she moved. There was a matching scarf that the saleswoman draped around her throat, leaving the long ends to trail down her back.

"It's perfect!" Michelle exclaimed, twirling to look at herself from all angles in the three-way mirror. "Do you like it, Mother?"

"Yes, it's stunning," Evelyn agreed. "You'll be the belle of the ball."

"Hardly. You're the star of the show. But at least I'll get noticed."

"I knew this was right for you the minute I saw it," the saleswoman said happily. "And it doesn't even need alterations."

Michelle gulped a bit at the price. But this was a special occasion, she rationalized, not admitting her real purpose—to be more glamorous than Ashleigh.

Evelyn wasn't as fussy as her daughter. It didn't take her long to pick out a lovely beaded gown in a flattering shade of deep rose. Afterward they shopped for shoes and browsed through the cosmetic section of a department store, sampling different perfume sprays.

"This is such fun," Michelle said. "We always have a good time together. I'm going to miss our shopping excursions when you move to Florida."

"I'll miss you, too, dear," Evelyn said soberly. "I wish we didn't have to live so far apart."

"You and Lucky will be coming to New York to visit, and we can talk on the phone a lot."

"It won't be the same as having you right here. But life is full of surprises. Look at me. I certainly never expected to meet somebody and move to Florida. Maybe you will too," Evelyn said artlessly.

Yeah, sure, Michelle thought morosely. Jonathan will discover he's madly in love with me and we'll all live happily ever after. Unfortunately that was a romance novel; this was real life.

Jonathan was still at the house when they returned in the late afternoon, but he had evidently gone home at some point. He was now wearing white jeans and a navy T-shirt. He and Lucky were sipping tall, cool drinks under the umbrella table beside the pool.

They both sniffed appreciatively when Michelle and Evelyn came outside. "One of you smells like a flower garden," Jonathan observed.

"It must be Mother. I'm wearing Passionate Peony, but you're not likely to find it in a garden." Michelle laughed. "We sampled the department store's freebies."

"Let me see if that's what I smell." Jonathan rose and strolled over to her.

Cupping his hand around her nape, he sniffed behind her ear. Michelle caught her breath as his lips brushed her neck in a whisper-light caress. Their bodies weren't touching, but she was acutely aware of his hard, lean length, a few tantalizing inches away.

She moved back quickly. "Well, what's the verdict?" she asked brightly.

"You're the passionate one, all right." He looked at her flushed cheeks with a little smile.

"I didn't expect you to still be here," Michelle said abruptly. "Weren't you on your way to the office?"

"I went in and took care of the more pressing things so I could take the rest of the week off, more or less."

"It must be nice to be the boss. You were on vacation all last week, too."

"That wasn't a vacation." He grinned. "This week we can both relax and have fun."

Michelle didn't know what to make of Jonathan's rapid mood swings, or what she did to trigger them. She snapped back automatically when he was sarcastic, or even when he was simply cool, but it didn't change her feelings for him. Unfortunately Jonathan was the love of her life. It was sobering to realize nobody could ever take his place.

Michelle expected the coming week to be difficult, but for the next few days Jonathan couldn't have been more charming. She told herself not to count on it to last. It hurt too much when she allowed herself to hope.

It was heavenly to be with him when he was like this, however. Jonathan devoted all of his time to her—which meant he wasn't seeing Ashleigh, or any other woman. He acted as if he didn't want to. When they strolled along the beach, he held her hand, and when they walked off the tennis court at the country club, he put his arm around her shoulders.

That didn't mean anything of course. Those could have been merely friendly gestures. But there were other indications. When they danced together, a current of electricity flowed between them, creating sparks that threatened to ignite into a bonfire.

After several days, Michelle hoped it would happen. Why keep denying herself what she wanted so desperately? If this was all she'd ever have of Jonathan, well, it was better than nothing.

The problem was how to let him know she was receptive. Michelle had never had to do that with a man before, so she felt awkward about it. She could only hope that sooner or later Jonathan would pick up a clue.

On the days when Michelle was busy with her mother, Jonathan went to his office. But he always returned to have dinner and spend the evening with them. One night, none of them felt like getting dressed and going out, so they decided to have dinner at home on the patio.

The setting was informal, but the food wasn't. They started with vichyssoise served in thin china bowls. Then Maria, one of the maids, brought out a huge platter of cracked stone crabs and lobster tails with melted butter and aioli, the wonderful garlic-flavored mayonnaise.

"This seafood is divine," Michelle said. "Bessie outdid herself tonight."

"Anybody can prepare lobster," Jonathan remarked dismissively. "All you have to do is boil it."

"That's big talk from a man who probably can't even operate a can opener," she teased.

"It shows how little you know about me. I'm a great cook."

"Really? I'm impressed."

"Well, I doubt if any of the famous chefs are losing sleep because of me. But I do barbecue a mean steak."

"That's quite an accomplishment," Michelle said. "People always ask for their steak a certain way, like rare or medium rare. How do you know when it's done just right?"

"If I told you, you might not be impressed. What if I cook dinner for you one night instead?"

"It's a date," she said happily.

After dinner, Evelyn and Lucky went to a movie. The younger couple declined their invitation to go along.

"What do you want to do instead?" Jonathan asked Michelle when they were alone.

"Nothing very strenuous," she answered. "How would

you like to pop popcorn and watch television? Or is that too boring? If you'd rather go out I'll get dressed."

"No, a restful evening sounds good to me for a change. Let's see if Bessie has any popcorn. If not, I'll go out and get some."

"I can live without it," Michelle said. "I just thought it might be fun."

"Everything is fun with you." Jonathan put his arm around her waist. Before she could turn toward him, he led her into the kitchen.

When he started rummaging through the pantry, Michelle said, "I don't think you should be doing that. Mother just averted a crisis with Manuel. We don't want Bessie to get upset now."

"Not to worry. She likes me."

"Everybody does." Michelle had spoken without thinking, but she wasn't sorry. Maybe Jonathan would take the hint.

Something flared in his eyes as he looked at her lovely face. She was so beautiful and he wanted her so much. Not for one night, but forever. It was a commitment he had to be very sure of, however. If he made love to her he'd never be able to let her go. And he still had unresolved doubts.

Jonathan turned back to the pantry and reached for a cardboard box. "Here it is. It was right in front of my nose."

She had trouble hiding her disappointment. Wasn't he ever going to forgive her for rejecting him that night at Caroline's house? That had to be what it was.

Michelle had been staring blindly at the box. When her eyes focused she said, "This isn't popcorn, it's cake mix."

"So it is." Jonathan laughed awkwardly. "I don't suppose you'd like to make a cake instead."

Bessie came into the kitchen, looking surprised at seeing them there. She glanced disapprovingly at her disordered shelves. "Can I get you something, Mr. Jonathan?"

"We were looking for popcorn, Bessie," he said. "The kind you pop in the microwave. Do we have any?"

"I'll make it for you," she said, starting to rearrange her pantry.

"We don't want you to go to any trouble," Michelle said.

"It's no trouble," the woman said firmly. "You and Mr. Jonathan go do whatever you were doing. I'll bring it to you." Her implication was plain: Stay out of my kitchen.

"I guess I'm not as lovable as I thought." Jonathan chuckled as they walked back to the den.

"You'd be more lovable if you hadn't made a mess of her shelves," Michelle answered.

The charged moment in the kitchen was forgotten—or at least glossed over—as they watched television and shared a bowl of popcorn, sitting on the couch next to each other.

A popular sitcom helped them relax. Then they watched a movie. The television log said it was a mystery, which they both agreed they liked. What it didn't mention was the steamy love story that was part of the plot.

Jonathan avoided looking at her as the couple on the screen kissed and caressed each other erotically. After shifting restlessly on the couch he finally said, "I thought this was supposed to be a mystery story."

"I did, too, but it's boring." If the sensuous lovemaking he was watching didn't give him ideas, what more could she add? "Switch the channel," Michelle said, suppressing a sigh.

"I have a better idea." He stood and turned off the set. "Let's walk down to the water. I feel like some fresh air."

"Me, too."

They strolled across the extensive lawn to the boat dock. A soft breeze had sprung up, ruffling Michelle's long hair and perfuming the air with the scent of orange blossoms and jasmine.

She sniffed appreciatively. "I don't know why we

wasted time indoors when it's so beautiful out. Look at the way the moon makes a path on the water.''

The canal was almost glassy. Only a few ripples marred the mirrorlike perfection as tethered boats rocked gently in the breeze. Suddenly a fish broke the surface of the water, leaping for a mosquito.

"He was a big one, wasn't he?" Michelle exclaimed. "Let's go out on the landing and see if he jumps again.''

"Do you like to fish?" Jonathan asked as they walked side by side.

"I don't know. I never tried it.''

"You might enjoy it. I'll take you out on my boat if you like.''

"Is that the nifty cabin cruiser I saw tied up to your dock?''

"That's the one," he answered. "I like it better than Lucky's. I can take mine out alone, but he needs a crew for his.''

"It sounds like his boat is a yacht. I never knew anyone who owned a yacht," Michelle commented.

"Lucky is already spoken for, so you'll have to settle for a cabin cruiser," Jonathan said lightly.

"I wouldn't—'' she began, when suddenly her heel caught in the decking and she pitched forward.

Jonathan caught her before she hurtled off the pier. "Are you all right? What did you trip over?" He glanced down at the wooden pier, but there were no coiled ropes or other hazards.

"I caught my heel between the boards. Look, I came right out of my shoe." She kept an arm around his neck while she tried to step back into her shoe.

"I'll get that for you. Can you stand alone for a minute?" His arm was around her waist and he put a hand on her shoulder to steady her.

His face was so close that she could feel his warm breath on her cheek. Without conscious thought, Michelle clasped her other arm around his neck and gazed up at him with parted lips.

Jonathan inhaled sharply and his embrace tightened. "Lovely Michelle," he said huskily. "Do you know how exquisite you are in the moonlight?"

"Tell me," she whispered.

"Words can't do you justice. You're like a dream that tantalizes me, a rainbow I can never reach."

"I'm a woman, Jonathan," she said softly. "And I'm very real."

His hand wandered feverishly down her back, cupping her bottom and urging her against his rigid loins. "I don't know what's sensible and what isn't anymore," he muttered. "I've wanted to hold you like this since the moment I first saw you."

"There's nothing stopping you any longer," she murmured, kissing the hollow in his throat.

"No. Nothing important."

His mouth covered hers hungrily, expressing all his pent-up longing. Michelle responded in the same way. The time for rationalizing was over for both of them.

While Jonathan's tongue probed deeply, his hands caressed her, fueling her already heated desire. When his hand slipped under her T-shirt and cupped her breast, Michelle arched her body into his.

"You do want me, darling, don't you?" he said. "That part is real."

She was too lost in the magic he was creating to question anything he said. It didn't even register. "I've never wanted any man like this," she whispered.

"We're going to be so good together, sweetheart."

As his mouth trailed a line of kisses down her neck, his fingers slipped inside her bra and circled her taut nipple. When Michelle cried out in pleasure he looked at her with eyes that were almost incandescent.

"I'll make you happy, darling, I promise."

Jonathan was lifting her shirt when a speedboat came around the bend. It slowed as the noisy teenagers aboard saw them silhouetted in the moonlight.

"Way to go, man!" one of them shouted raucously.

"Get a room," another yelled.

There were other ribald comments before the boat roared away down the canal.

Michelle and Jonathan looked at each other in bewilderment for a moment before drawing apart. The rude catcalls had cheapened what they felt for each other.

She straightened her shirt without looking at him. "I guess we should go back to the house. Mother and Lucky ought to be home soon."

"Michelle, wait!" He put his hand on her arm as she turned away.

"What?" she asked without facing him.

After a moment's hesitation, he said, "I'm sorry."

It wasn't what she wanted to hear. Did he mean he was sorry for almost making love to her? She was the one who instigated it, Michelle realized forlornly. "It's all right," she said, beginning to walk off the dock.

When they reached the house, Evelyn and Lucky hadn't returned yet, which would have made things easier. They made small talk for a while, feeling uncomfortable with each other.

Finally Jonathan said, "I think I'll make it an early night if you don't mind. I brought some work home from the office, and I haven't had a chance to look at it."

"I don't mind," she answered. "I'll go to bed and read for a while."

He kissed her on the cheek before he left, but it was just a formality.

Michelle's face was somber as she climbed the stairs to her room. She might as well stop hoping for a miracle, because it wasn't going to happen. Jonathan wanted her, but for some reason he wouldn't allow himself to make love to her.

Perhaps he realized—in spite of her attempt to hide it—that she was in love with him. Jonathan was an honorable man, no matter what faults he might have. Maybe he always checked himself in time because he wouldn't want her to think he was making a commitment.

Michelle sighed heavily as she began to get undressed. Tonight might have marked the end of even a casual relationship between them. He didn't enjoy going through this any more than she did. It was probably best if he didn't come around, although she found it difficult to convince herself of that.

Jonathan drove home in the same somber mood as Michelle's. She had guessed correctly about a couple of things. He couldn't go through many more traumatic incidents like tonight. And he shouldn't make love to her while he still felt some ambivalence.

Michelle might want to marry him for the wrong reason, but she didn't fall into bed with just anyone, rich or otherwise. Carter was proof of that. So if he couldn't accept her unconditionally, he would be just using her. And he loved her too much for that.

Some of Michelle's fears were unjustified. Jonathan came by as usual the next day, acting as though nothing had happened the night before. But Michelle wasn't fooled. His smile seemed forced and he kept his distance. No more tugging playfully on her hair, or putting his arm casually around her waist.

She must have succeeded in treating him just as casually, because neither her mother nor Lucky appeared to notice any difference. Thankfully the engagement party was drawing near, and after that this ordeal would be over.

Preparations were already started for the party. Trucks

came to the service entrance delivering folding chairs to be stored out of sight, and the housemaids were polishing quantities of silver.

None of these preparations involved the family, but they tried not to make extra work for the servants. "Let's take the boat out today," Lucky suggested. "We can either have lunch on board or at some marina that looks inviting. Then Bessie won't have to stop whatever she's doing to prepare lunch."

"That sounds lovely, but Mother and I really need to go shopping," Michelle said.

"Again?" Lucky chuckled. "I thought you went through the stores like a plague of locusts on your last shopping trip."

"I'm afraid we spent most of the day finding a dress for me. This time we have to concentrate on Mother's trousseau."

"She's right. I do want Michelle's help and she won't be here that much longer," Evelyn said artlessly.

"Stop pushing her out," Lucky complained. "I like having her around."

"So do I, but we can't be selfish. Michelle has a full life of her own in New York." Evelyn flicked a glance at Jonathan, then returned her gaze to Lucky.

He smiled broadly as he got her message. "I suppose we can't hope to keep her much longer. There must be a lot of young men waiting impatiently for her to come home. Isn't that so, Michelle?"

"Hordes of them," she answered brightly.

"When you finally pick the one and only, perhaps you'll let us have the wedding down here," Lucky said.

Jonathan stood. "I'd better check in at the office. Do you have any plans for tonight?" he asked his uncle.

"I thought I'd take the girls to dinner at the Tropicana. You're welcome to join us, of course."

Evelyn smiled. "I haven't been called a girl in years."

"You're *my* girl," he said fondly.

When Jonathan had left and Michelle had gone upstairs, Lucky said, "You can't say we didn't try."

Evelyn laughed. "Don't you think that part about having the wedding here was laying it on a little thick?"

"Subtlety hasn't worked noticeably well," he answered dryly. "I'm tempted to propose to her for him myself."

"Your nose isn't big enough to play Cyrano," she teased. "Perhaps we should stop meddling. They *are* adults."

"Until they start acting like it, we'll just have to help them along."

Michelle's spirits couldn't help lifting on the night of the party. The house had been bustling with activity all day. Beautiful floral arrangements were displayed everywhere throughout the spacious rooms, and she could hear musicians tuning their instruments.

A portable dance floor had been laid on the extensive lawn in back. It was circled by round tables and chairs. Off to one side was a red-and-white striped tent where the bar was being set up. In just a short time the house and grounds would be filled with glamorous, well-dressed guests.

Michelle was glad she'd decided to splurge on the red dress. Ashleigh had accepted—naturally. But so had Carter; that was a bonus. At least she wouldn't have to depend on Jonathan for a partner if Ashleigh decided to monopolize him—which was a foregone conclusion.

Michelle spent so much time perfecting her hair and makeup that the party was already in full swing by the time she got downstairs.

"What took you so long?" Evelyn demanded when Michelle joined her and Lucky on the patio.

"Whatever it was, it was worth it." Carter had appeared at her side. He held her arms out and looked her over avidly. "You're always gorgeous, but tonight you're positively ravishing," he declared.

"Are you looking for another acquisition?" Jonathan drawled. He'd come over to join their group. "I thought your dance card was already filled."

"Isn't that funny? I thought the same thing about yours." Carter smiled maliciously.

As the two men measured each other, Ashleigh provided an only partially welcome diversion. She came over and linked her arm through Jonathan's.

"What a fabulous affair!" she told their host. "I always love it when outsiders come to visit. It's such a good excuse for a party."

"I prefer to think of Evie and her daughter as guests rather than outsiders," Lucky said.

"Yes, of course. I do, too. I just meant that Northerners and Southerners don't really have anything in common. Oh, dear!" Ashleigh laughed gaily. "That doesn't sound much better. Come and dance with me, Jonathan, before I make an utter idiot of myself."

"God got there first," Carter murmured sardonically as she pulled Jonathan away. "Would you care to dance?" he asked Michelle.

She needn't have worried about being a wallflower. Men flocked around her, drawn like a magnet to the scarlet gown that beckoned to them from the sea of white and pastels the other women had on. Michelle was like an exotic bird, beautiful and prized. Men paid her extravagant compliments, from the trite to the poetic. They praised her deep blue eyes and grew lyrical about the creamy skin of her throat and bare shoulders.

She enjoyed it. What woman wouldn't? But her flirty eyelashes and alluring smile masked a persistent hurt. Why couldn't Jonathan feel this way?

She saw him on the dance floor, not always with Ashleigh. But most of the women looked at him in the same way. And Jonathan was charming to all of them. Michelle's heart twisted as she watched him smile, as if he was having a wonderful time—which he undoubtedly was.

She might not even be there for all he cared. Was it because of Carter's lavish compliments? Was Jonathan avoiding her because he thought she preferred Carter? Michelle wanted to believe that, but she wasn't into self-delusion.

"May I cut in?" a low male voice asked, as she tried to focus on her partner.

"Only because it's your uncle's party." Michelle's partner laughed, relinquishing her reluctantly to Jonathan.

Neither spoke for a few minutes as he folded her in a close embrace. They were content just to be together. Jonathan rested his lips on her temple and moved one hand sensuously over her back. They were oblivious to all the other couples on the floor, lost in their own private world of pleasure in each other.

"Are you having a good time?" he asked finally.

"I'm having a wonderful time," she answered, determined not to air her grievances. "Everyone has been so nice to me."

"Yes, I noticed." He smiled. "You're the most beautiful woman here. The men have been swarming around you like bees around a fragrant flower—which you resemble."

"Thanks, I didn't think you noticed."

"You can't believe that. No matter what else you can say about us, we've never been indifferent to each other," he said wryly.

Michelle forgot about appearing unconcerned. "Then why haven't you danced with me tonight?"

"You were having such a good time. I didn't want to monopolize you."

"One dance isn't a monopoly," she remarked tartly.

"Once wouldn't have been enough," he said in a husky voice.

She was crazy to believe him, but Michelle wanted to. "Does that mean you're going to dance with me again?" she asked, gazing provocatively through her long lashes.

"I'm through being noble." He kissed the tip of her nose playfully. "I've given those other guys all the chances they're going to get."

Michelle knew it was insane to let him play with her like a yo-yo, but the surge of pleasure that rushed through her was irresistible.

"Uh-oh," Jonathan said. "I see Mitchell Thomasen heading this way. Let's get out of here." He took her hand and led her off the floor.

There was no place where they could be alone, but Michelle was content just to be with him. Jonathan didn't let go of her hand as they strolled around the grounds, stopping to talk to different groups of people.

The pool looked spectacular with the underwater lights on and lotus blossoms floating on the surface. They were admiring them along with some other guests when there was a drumroll and the orchestra leader took the microphone and asked for everyone's attention.

"Will you all gather around," he requested. "Your host would like to say a few words."

"This is it." Jonathan smiled at Michelle.

Ashleigh appeared beside them. "What's going on?" she asked sharply.

"You'll find out in a few minutes," he replied, refusing to answer her insistent questions.

People drifted over to stand around the floor as Lucky walked up to the microphone. After thanking everyone for coming, he held out a hand to Evelyn.

When she was standing beside him, he said, "I asked all of you here this evening to meet Evie—the wonderful woman I'm going to marry." When excited exclamations broke out, he smiled and held up a hand. "I'm sure you're all wondering how I convinced this lovely lady to be my bride. I can hardly believe it myself. She's made me the happiest man in the world.'' He put an arm around her shoulders and hugged her close. ''I'm not going to make a speech. I just wanted to announce our engagement and tell you how fortunate I feel. Now let's get back to the party. We invite you all to drink a toast and celebrate along with us.''

Waiters were circulating through the crowd, carrying trays of glasses filled with champagne. An excited buzz filled the air, and people crowded around Lucky and Evelyn.

''You're getting a real prince,'' a man told her.

''I know that,'' Evelyn answered softly.

''Have you set a date for the wedding yet?'' A woman named Beth asked. ''If you need any help with the arrangements, please don't hesitate to call me. I'm one of Lucky's oldest friends.''

''I never thought I'd hear you admit it.'' Her husband chuckled.

''That's going to cost you,'' she told him with a mock frown. Turning back to Evelyn, she said, ''I've married off three daughters, so I know everything you need to know about weddings.''

''It's awfully kind of you to offer, but we plan to be married in New York,'' Evelyn said. ''That's where I'm from.''

When they all protested at being left out of the festivities, Lucky promised to have a big reception when they got back from their honeymoon.

Beth and some of the others told Evelyn they wanted to give her a bridal shower. She was touched that Lucky's friends had accepted her so warmly.

Not everyone was pleased with Lucky's announcement. Ashleigh was less than thrilled about Michelle's mother marrying Jonathan's uncle.

''Isn't it delicious?'' she remarked to a group of their

friends, turning to Jonathan. "Lucky's been like a father to Jonathan, so that will make him and Michelle brother and sister."

"Not exactly." He smiled at Michelle. "We'll be more like kissing cousins."

Ashleigh tried unsuccessfully to hide her fury. "Really, Jonathan! Wouldn't any relationship between you two be a little tacky?"

"Is that a question, or a statement?" Carter drawled.

"Don't you have somebody else to annoy?" she snapped. "Why is it always me?"

"It's like the reason people climb Mount Everest—because it's there. You're here." He grinned.

Michelle couldn't help feeling sorry for the woman. She wasn't a very nice person, but neither was Carter. And Ashleigh was no match for him.

Jonathan took pity on her. "Your humor is getting old, Carter. Take a hike."

"Is the decision unanimous?" Carter asked Michelle.

She couldn't be rude, even if he deserved it, so she answered indirectly. "Why don't you have something to eat before they clear away the buffet? The food is delicious."

"Okay, doll face, for you, anything."

Jonathan looked at her enigmatically as Carter ambled away, but he didn't comment.

The rest of the evening was a delight. Jonathan stayed by her side most of the time. When Lucky called her away to meet one or another of the guests, Michelle would look over to find Jonathan watching her, as though she was the only person there who mattered to him. It was intensely gratifying, yet puzzling.

Michelle knew she should just accept her blessings and leave it at that. But she couldn't. While they were dancing she approached the subject gingerly.

"It's funny the way you think you know someone and you don't really," she said with a little laugh.

"You mean, like when you see a person on the street and you think they're somebody else?" Jonathan asked.

"No, I meant someone you see all the time, someone whose moods change and you don't know why."

His expression was unreadable. "Were you referring to anyone in particular?"

"Well…you're an example. Some days I can't do anything to please you, and other times you couldn't be nicer to me. I'm not saying our arguments aren't partly my fault," she admitted. "But at least you always know why *I'm* angry."

"Our quarrels are all over," he murmured, drawing her closer.

"I doubt that. If there's something bothering you that I don't know about, we're going to keep having misunderstandings."

"Not anymore. They were mostly my fault to begin with."

"I don't want you to take the blame, Jonathan," she said earnestly. "I want to know why you blow hot and cold."

He hesitated for a moment, choosing his words carefully. "If I've seemed distant at times it was because I was wrestling with my own private devils. I guess I was looking for an ironclad guarantee, when I know they don't exist. I've had big contracts fall apart on me, but it hasn't stopped me from taking chances."

Michelle stared at him in bewilderment. "You mean, some problem at the office has been bothering you?"

It didn't seem possible that would affect their relationship, yet Jonathan must be under great pressure as C.E.O. of a multimillion dollar company. She was so relieved to find out it was nothing personal that she didn't question his explanation.

"It doesn't matter anymore." He cradled her head on his shoulder. "I've worked everything out."

After many sleepless nights, Jonathan had finally realized

how bereft he'd feel if he lost Michelle. Lucky's remark about giving her a gala wedding had been a dose of reality. The thought of her belonging to another man was unthinkable. But he had to make up his mind, because once she left here he might lose her forever. It no longer mattered if her feelings weren't as deep as his. He would make her so happy that in time she'd come to love him as totally as he loved her.

Lucky was beckoning to them from the grass. "Come over here for a minute, Michelle," he called. "There's someone here who says she hasn't met you yet."

"Lucky certainly has a lot of friends," Michelle remarked as they threaded their way through the other couples on the dance floor.

"And they all want to get better acquainted with Evelyn. Before they rope you into their plans, I'd like you to save tomorrow night for me," Jonathan said.

"They'd probably include you, too."

"I'm sure they would, but I'd prefer a quiet evening alone with you. I thought perhaps we could have dinner at my house."

"Are you going to barbecue your famous steak?"

"If you like."

"You're the host, so you get to choose. Surprise me." She smiled.

Michelle didn't care what they ate—or *if* they ate. An uninterrupted evening alone with Jonathan would be a small slice of heaven.

Chapter Ten

The party didn't break up until the early hours, so everybody slept late the next morning. Lucky and the two women gathered in the sunroom for a late brunch, and to talk over details of the party.

"Your friends are simply delightful," Evelyn said.

"They approve of you, too," Lucky answered fondly. "A lot of them wanted to come to New York for the wedding, but I told them it's going to be a small affair."

She looked at him doubtfully. "Maybe it's selfish of me to want to be married in New York. Michelle could fly back here for the wedding. She's the one who is really important to me. It doesn't matter if the others aren't here."

"How about your cranky relative, Blanche?" he teased. "You don't want her to stop talking to you."

"I could live with it," Evelyn said dryly.

"Maybe so, but your good friends would be disappointed, too, if they didn't get invited to your wedding," Michelle remarked. "You grew up with a lot of them."

"Of course you should have your family and friends around," Lucky said. "That part is decided. Now you have to choose where you want to go on our honeymoon."

It was fun to plan a trip where money was no object, but as her mother and Lucky discussed romantic locales like Venice and Rome, Michelle's attention wandered. Where was Jonathan? He usually checked in every morning to see what their plans were. If Michelle was busy he went to the office. Otherwise he was available. It was a little strange that he hadn't phoned.

The telephone had rung steadily that morning, but all the calls were from Lucky's friends, thanking him for the party. Michelle no longer had high expectations when Lucky answered yet another call.

"This one is for you," he said with a smile as he handed her the phone.

"I've been trying to get through to you all morning, but the line has been busy," Jonathan said.

"Everyone has been phoning to say what a good time they had last night," she said.

"That's what I figured. I wanted to tell you there's a minor problem at the office. I won't be able to see you today."

Michelle's heart plunged, but she tried to keep her voice unconcerned. "It's okay, I understand. I hope it's nothing serious."

"Nothing I can't handle. You win some, you lose some," he said dismissively. "It's no big deal, but it's going to take me time to straighten things out."

"So, you're telling me our date for tonight is off," she said evenly.

"When did I say that? Of course not! I'm looking forward to it."

"I am, too." Michelle's heart bounded back to its rightful place.

"Good. Is it all right if I pick you up at seven-thirty?

That will give me plenty of time to get straightened away here at the office.''

"Seven-thirty sounds fine," she answered in a vibrant voice. "But would you rather go out to dinner, since you'll be tied up all day? Then you won't have to bother barbecuing.''

"Don't give it another thought. I have the evening all planned.''

Jonathan's house looked inviting when they arrived. The lamps in the living room cast a welcoming glow through the wide windows, and soft music was playing on the stereo.

Michelle gazed around at the softly lit room and the bottle of champagne chilling in a silver ice bucket on the coffee table. "This looks like the seduction scene from a movie," she teased.

"What gave me away?" He grinned. "The wine? The music? Maybe Kenny G. was a tad too much.''

"No, I like it. And I love this house." She straightened an ornament on an end table a fraction. "You don't know how fortunate you are.''

"Why is that?" he asked as he uncorked the champagne.

"I live in a small apartment. Of course most people in New York do, but it must be wonderful to have all this room.''

"It isn't a large house, compared to someplace like Lucky's. Or even Carter's penthouse," Jonathan added casually. "He has a triplex.''

"Those are both too big for my taste. This is a perfect size." Michelle didn't intend to let Carter spoil another evening for her, so she changed the subject. "Where do you keep the barbecue? I didn't notice it on the patio when I was here that first time.''

"It's usually put away in the gardening shed. Are you getting hungry?''

"No, I just wondered because I didn't smell smoke. At home people light the charcoal hours before they intend to use it. So the coals will be just right, I'm told."

"But they never are until after you're all through barbecuing."

"Exactly!" she said, and they both laughed.

"Actually I took your advice. I'll have to give you a rain check on that steak I promised you."

"We're going out?" Michelle tried to hide her disappointment. In a restaurant or one of Jonathan's clubs, they were always running across his friends. For at least this one night, she wanted to be alone with him.

It was a relief when he said, "No, we're dining in, but I didn't have time to mess around in the kitchen. Carlos is preparing dinner. He's my version of Manuel, except that he isn't as chatty."

A slender man appeared, carrying a tray of hors d'oeuvres. He was wearing a white coat, something Manuel didn't always bother with, and his manner was friendly yet reserved. After serving them both, he set the tray on the coffee table and returned to the kitchen.

"He *is* different from Manuel." Michelle laughed. "By now, Manuel would have told us all about the confrontation he had at the supermarket, and how to pick a ripe avocado."

"Carlos isn't that gregarious, but he does a good job for me. He's also a pretty good cook."

The man was a lot better than that, Michelle discovered when they sat down to dinner a little later. Two places were set at a small table by a window looking out on the water. Soft candlelight illuminated the wineglasses and the single rose in a crystal vase.

"I thought this would be more comfortable than shouting at each other down the length of the dining-room table," Jonathan said.

"It's also romantic," she said lightly.

"I hoped you'd think so." The candle flame reflected in his eyes as he said, "But the setting isn't really important. It's the person you're with."

"That's true," she agreed, gazing back at him.

They were acutely aware of each other as they sipped their wine and ate the excellent dinner Carlos had prepared. The conversation flowed as easily as the wine, but underneath it was a current of excitement and anticipation.

This time nothing was going to go wrong, Michelle vowed! They'd had so many misunderstandings, but they had worked through their problems. Nothing more could happen to keep them apart.

Carlos cleared away the dinner as quietly and efficiently as he'd served it. While he was cleaning up the kitchen, Jonathan and Michelle took their coffee into the living room.

They talked easily, but after Carlos said good-night and left, the atmosphere changed—for Michelle, at least. Her coffee cup clattered in the saucer when she set it down on the table.

"Relax, sweetheart," Jonathan said. "I'm not going to turn into a sex-crazed maniac just because we're alone."

"I didn't expect you to," she answered.

"I wonder." He chuckled. "I suppose I can't really blame you. I haven't shown a lot of restraint in the past."

"I wouldn't say that," she protested. "You've always been a perfect gentleman."

"You don't know the self-control it took," he answered wryly.

"That earns you even more Brownie points," she teased.

"I don't want a medal." He threaded his fingers through her hair, pulling her face closer to his. "I want to make love to you."

"That sounds like a fine idea." She smiled alluringly.

"I was hoping it would."

His mouth brushed across hers. Then the tip of his tongue

traced the line of her closed lips, teasing them open. She linked her arms around his neck as his tongue erotically explored the moist recess of her mouth. When she made a low sound of pleasure, he drew back slightly to look at her with glowing eyes.

"Darling Michelle, I can't believe you're finally going to be mine."

"I can't, either. Everything seemed to be conspiring against us. But I couldn't bear it if something happened this time." She ran her hands feverishly over his shoulders, tracing their solid width.

"Nothing is ever going to keep us apart again."

"Oh, Jonathan—" Michelle was about to tell him how much she loved him, but his mouth covered hers and she was sure he knew.

While his mouth possessed hers, his hands slipped under her cropped top and caressed her body. She moved restlessly as his fingers left a burning trail across the soft skin of her midsection. When he finally cupped her breasts in his hands, her pulse was beating rapidly.

She waited for him to unclasp her bra, needing to feel his touch on her bare skin. But unaccountably, Jonathan drew back, then stood. Michelle watched in bewilderment as he crossed the room.

"This time I don't want any interruptions," he said deeply, closing the drapes. "I've waited too long for this."

"We both have."

She rose and pulled her top over her head. As Jonathan watched with glittering eyes, she reached in back and unhooked her bra. The look on his face urged her on. No man had ever made her feel or act like this before.

After kicking off her shoes, she unzipped her pants and let them slither over her hips to the floor. While their eyes held, Michelle stepped out of the pool of silk and walked slowly toward him.

When she began to unbutton his shirt, Jonathan reached

for her, but she evaded his grasp. "No, let me do this," she said.

"Whatever you like, my love," he said huskily. "I'm all yours."

After she'd removed his shirt, baring his splendid torso, she leaned toward him and brushed her nipples lightly across his chest.

He drew in his breath sharply and jerked her hips against his. "You're driving me wild," he said in a ragged voice.

"I hope so," she answered with a seductive smile as she unbuckled his belt. "I want to make you lose control so you're completely in my power."

"I always have been."

Jonathan's body was rigid as Michelle hooked two fingers inside the waistband of his briefs and eased them over his hips. He tried to remain still, but when his bursting manhood sprang free and she cradled it in her hands, he uttered a hoarse cry and pulled her into his arms.

"You don't know what you're doing to me. I'm not made of steel."

"I'm glad." She laughed softly. "I like you just like this." Pulling his head down, she plunged her tongue into his mouth.

Jonathan tore off her panties and molded her to his long length. The sensation of their naked bodies touching at every point was electric. They moved feverishly against each other, accelerating their desire.

"This isn't the way I wanted it to be," he groaned. "But you're irresistible. I need to be part of you."

He lowered her to the carpet and positioned himself between her legs. For one breathless instant they stared into each other's eyes in tantalizing anticipation. Then their lips met and Jonathan entered her, bringing such molten pleasure that she gasped with delight.

Their bodies rose and fell in a heated dance that grew faster and more out of control as their urgent need took them to ever greater heights. Their bodies writhed in boundless ecstasy that culminated in a bursting sensation that rocketed through both at the same time.

Michelle was limp in Jonathan's arms afterward, completely and utterly fulfilled. His body was relaxed against hers and they remained joined together, too contented to move.

He finally rolled over on his side, keeping her in a close embrace. "Darling Michelle." He kissed her closed eyelids. "I knew it would be like this. Did I make you happy?"

"Couldn't you tell?" She smiled without opening her eyes. "I practically attacked you."

"Feel free at anytime." He chuckled.

"It might be a problem at the country club," she said mischievously.

"Then I'll drop out of the club." He smoothed the damp hair off her forehead lovingly. "I always knew you were as passionate as you are beautiful."

"Only with you. I've never acted like this before. Maybe it was the champagne." But Michelle knew that wasn't the reason.

"In that case, I'm going to open another bottle." He grinned, rising and lifting her in his arms. As he carried her into the bedroom, Jonathan said, "This is where I intended to make love to you—and not so rapidly," he added with a laugh.

"I've waited a long time for this." She kissed the hollow in his throat. "I couldn't have waited much longer."

After placing her gently on the bed, he leaned over and stroked her cheek tenderly. "It should have happened a lot sooner, but that's all in the past."

When he kissed her briefly, then started toward the door, she asked, "Where are you going?"

"To get the champagne," he answered, giving her an

impish look. "The night is young yet, and I have plans for us."

Michelle could have told him she didn't need any incentive. The wine wasn't responsible for her uninhibited behavior. She'd followed her heart instead of her head for once, and it was the right thing to do. No matter what developed between them—or didn't—this night was worth it.

Jonathan returned carrying a silver tray with two glasses and a bottle of champagne. Michelle watched admiringly as he walked around the room, splendidly nude and completely at ease.

He looked up to see her gazing at him. "You're so quiet. What are you thinking?"

"How wonderfully unselfconscious you are." She had covered herself with the sheet in his absence.

"I want you to know everything about me." He walked over to the bed and brushed aside the sheet. "The way I want to know you." His hands caressed her body. "You're so exquisite. I love to touch you."

Her entire body heated as he gazed at every intimate part of it.

When a normal reflex made her twine her legs together, Jonathan separated them and stroked her thighs. "You can't be shy with me, darling, after giving yourself to me so totally."

She smiled wryly. "It doesn't go with my earlier behavior, does it? But I told you, I'm not usually like that."

"I'm glad you are with me." He leaned down to kiss her breasts.

When his warm tongue curled around one nipple, Michelle arched her body and tangled her fingers in his thick hair.

"You're so wonderfully responsive, sweetheart." His voice was husky with desire. "You're like a beautiful flower, unfolding just for me."

"Only you." She sighed, knowing no other man could ever awaken her like Jonathan.

"I want to know every inch of your exquisite body."

His fingertips traced the fullness of her breasts, then trailed an arousing path to her thighs, like a blind man discovering the contours of a lovely statue.

But Michelle was very much alive. She quivered as he parted the damp curls between her legs for an intimate exploration that made her cry out in delight.

"Yes, angel, tell me when I please you." His expression was molten as he stared at her parted lips and dreamy eyes.

"You already have," she answered in a breathy voice.

Her passion rose as he lifted one of her knees and strung a line of kisses across her inner thigh. The sensuous feeling was a sweet agony that she wanted to go on forever. But when his mouth moved to the core of her desire, she felt like a volcano threatening to erupt.

Tugging frantically at his shoulders she gasped, "Please, Jonathan, I need you now!"

He moved up and covered her taut body with his. "You'll never have to ask twice. I'll always be here for you, my love," he murmured, gathering her close.

Their lovemaking wasn't concluded as rapidly this time. Jonathan filled the throbbing void inside her with slow thrusts that built the excitement. Every movement brought tantalizing joy. Gradually the tempo increased as their passion escalated. Michelle dug her fingers into his buttocks and raised her hips to keep their bodies welded together as they reached completion. It came in an electrifying jolt that sent waves of sensation spiraling through them.

Michelle clung to Jonathan as the storm subsided. When her body was vibrating gently in the aftermath of passion she relaxed with a sigh of utter happiness. "This is what heaven must be like."

"As long as I'm with you, anyplace is heaven," he murmured, stroking her tenderly.

They felt too peaceful to move for a long time. Finally Jonathan stirred halfheartedly. "You never got to drink your champagne. Would you like some now?"

"Don't tell me you're feeling macho again," she said mischievously.

"Not right at the moment," he admitted, grinning. "But we have a whole night ahead of us."

And after tonight what, she wondered? Jonathan hadn't told her he loved her, even at the height of their lovemaking. Was this all he wanted? It was a hurtful thought, but Michelle couldn't regret what had just happened. She'd known this might be all there was.

"I'm glad we managed to have this night together," she said wistfully.

"Yes, we finally broke the jinx." He scissored one leg around both of hers so their bodies were more closely joined.

"It did seem as if somebody put a hex on us. Especially after we returned to Miami."

"I'd say our troubles began before that," he answered, after a moment's pause.

"Well, yes, but at Shorehaven they were due to a misunderstanding. It seems funny now, doesn't it?"

"Not especially."

"Don't sulk," she teased. "You thought Mother and I were fortune hunters, too."

"It was a natural assumption on my part. Women have tried to marry Lucky for his money before."

"Mother might not be that rich, but it could have happened to her, as well. Money is a powerful magnet."

"Evidently." Jonathan released her and turned on his back.

Michelle looked at him with a slight frown. "You don't still think that's the reason she's marrying him?"

"No, they appear to be very much in love. I'm happy for both of them. Your mother is a nice person."

"*Something* seems to be bothering you, though. What is it?"

"Nothing," he insisted. "It's been a wonderful evening. Let's don't spoil it."

"That's the last thing I want to do! I don't even know what we're arguing about."

"We're not arguing."

"We will be any minute. Why does this always happen to us?" she asked in frustration.

"I'm not going to let it," he said firmly. "I don't want to lose you."

There was one sure way to keep her, but it hadn't occurred to him, Michelle thought sadly. Pride made her hide the pain.

"We won't have much more time together, anyway," she said matter-of-factly. "I really do have to go back to New York shortly."

"You make it sound as if you're just going away for the weekend. Could you simply walk away from me? Don't I mean anything to you?"

Why was he doing this to her? It wasn't fair! Her nerves were starting to wind tightly. "What do you want me to say, Jonathan? That I'm madly in love with you?"

"I know how you feel about me," he said heavily. "You made that clear at Shorehaven."

"I can't believe that's still bothering you!" she exclaimed. "Didn't my attitude change when we got to Miami?"

"The attraction between us was always strong. You wanted me as much as I wanted you. I could tell. But you wouldn't give in to it until now."

"If you were as perceptive as you claim to be, you should know the reason. Your girlfriend, Ashleigh, made it clear that you were already taken—and you didn't make any great effort to deny it."

"I was talking about before this. There were so many

times when we almost made love, but you changed your mind at the last minute.''

"Something always happened," she murmured.

"What about when the car broke down and we had to share a room? That's a night that will live in my memory," he observed sardonically.

"I'd prefer to forget about it." She sighed.

It was useless to explain what really happened that night. Jonathan hadn't listened to her then, and he wouldn't believe her now. Men had fragile egos. But that was the only thing that had been involved for him.

"I suppose I shouldn't complain. You had a revelation and we're here now." His voice had a brittle quality that rasped on her nerves.

She gave him a bewildered look. "I don't understand. What was my revelation?"

He waved one arm, including the luxurious room and the expensive waterfront beyond the closed drapes. "You found out I have more toys than your other admirers. Wasn't that the way you put it?"

Michelle stared at him incredulously. "You think I slept with you because you're rich?" She purposely didn't call it making love, since that wasn't what it was for him.

Jonathan regretted his words instantly. "I'm sorry, darling, I didn't mean that the way it sounded."

He reached for her, but she drew back. "Yes, you did! That's been the problem between us ever since we got here, only I didn't realize it."

"Maybe it did bother me a little," he admitted. "But you, yourself said your attitude changed when you found out my life-style was...different than you'd expected," he concluded delicately, but it was too late.

She was taut with anger. "I wouldn't have cared if you'd been out of a job and lived in a one-room apartment," she raged. "Money didn't enter into it then, and it doesn't now.

No amount would make up for your insulting opinion of me!"

"Please, Michelle, I—"

She didn't let him finish. "If you really want to know the reason I didn't fall into bed with you before, it had more to do with scruples than economics. I didn't think it was sporting to go to bed with a man I might later have to report to the police," she said witheringly. Wrapping the sheet around herself, she got up and stalked into the living room.

He trailed after her, trying to reason with her. "I understand why you're upset, but can't you see how I could jump to a wrong conclusion?"

"It didn't stop you from having sex with me," she said bitterly as she gathered up her strewn clothing.

"It was more than sex for me. I'd hoped it would be for you, too, although it no longer made any difference. I was willing to settle for whatever feelings you had for me." He started toward her, but he stopped when she glared at him.

Michelle was struggling into her clothes, jerking angrily on her zipper. "Why are you bothering to pretend? We both got what we wanted. And it didn't cost you a penny," she added mockingly.

Jonathan flinched. "I'm sorry that I've hurt you so badly," he said quietly.

She lifted her chin, determined not to let him see *how* badly. "You're wrong about me as usual. My emotions would have to be involved for me to be hurt. Give me your car keys," she demanded abruptly. Michelle was afraid she couldn't keep up her caustic act of indifference much longer.

After realizing she was in no mood to talk things out calmly, he said, "I'll take you home. Just give me a minute to throw on some clothes."

"Are you afraid I'll steal your expensive car?" she taunted.

Jonathan's jaw set grimly as her barbs began to rankle. "Aren't you overreacting pretty drastically? If you don't care about me, what does my opinion of you matter? Maybe you're angry because I made you face the truth about yourself."

"I won't dignify that with an answer." She turned toward the door. "If you won't give me your keys, I'll walk."

"Wait." Jonathan picked up his discarded slacks and reached into the pocket. "Here," he said, tossing her the keys.

She caught them deftly. With her hand on the doorknob she said, "Goodbye, Jonathan. Enjoy your toys. Sorry I don't want to be one of them."

Jonathan stared at the door for a long time, trying to figure out how things had gone so wrong. He had decided to take Michelle on any terms. God knows he'd agonized over it long enough! So why hadn't he kept his mouth shut?

Naturally she'd be offended and upset. But people often told the truth when they were too angry to be cautious. Michelle sounded believable when she said her emotions weren't involved. How could he doubt her? She never once mentioned the word love.

Jonathan paced the floor, telling himself he was lucky to have uncovered her true feelings before the wedding rather than after. It would never have worked out. They wanted different things from a marriage. And then he remembered the passion they'd shared. Her responsiveness. The way she'd made him feel like king of the universe.

He wavered for a moment before his expression hardened. Sex was fine for a short-term affair, but it wasn't enough for a successful marriage. He'd been a fool to think Michelle would ever grow to love him.

She'd been painfully blunt about her feelings. The scornful words still rang in his ears: "We both got what we wanted tonight." That was clear enough. All tonight had meant to her was good hot sex.

Jonathan told himself he'd forget her. Or maybe the bitterness would fade and he'd only remember the part of their relationship that was what he'd hoped for. Like the beginning of this evening when Michelle had shed her inhibitions along with her clothes. His groin throbbed at the memory of her exquisite body and what he had mistaken for love in her eyes.

Turning abruptly, Jonathan stalked into the bathroom and turned on the shower.

Michelle had stormed out of Jonathan's house holding onto her anger so the desolation underneath wouldn't surface and overwhelm her. When that happened she wanted to be alone in her room, away from well-meaning questions and sympathetic looks.

It began to seem as if she would get her wish. Lucky's car wasn't in the driveway, which meant he and her mother hadn't gotten home yet. He never bothered to put his car in the garage.

Michelle parked her own car and dashed for the house, intent on getting upstairs before they returned. She was closing the door with a sigh of relief when Manuel came through the entry carrying a tray with a pitcher of juice.

"You're home early," he observed. "In my day, a date that ended before midnight was a bummer." He laughed merrily.

"Oh, well, it's almost twelve o'clock." Michelle started across the marble floor toward the staircase.

"The boss and your mom aren't back yet," Manuel remarked unnecessarily. "I was just taking a pitcher of orange juice to the den. Would you like some?"

"No, thanks. I'm going to bed."

"I always leave a pitcher of juice for Mr. Lucky. He likes a glass before he turns in. The oranges are fresh squeezed, right off our own trees. Are you sure you don't want some?"

"No, really."

"Well, okay. Can I get you anything else?"

Manuel was in one of his chattier moods, Michelle thought in despair. "Not a thing," she answered brightly. "I've had enough of everything tonight."

"I'll probably be up when your mom gets back. Do you want me to give her any message?"

"Just tell her I'll see her in the morning."

Manuel cocked his head. "You can tell her yourself. They just drove up."

Michelle was considering a dash for the stairs, when he opened the door wide. The staircase was in full view of the entry. She would never make it to the top before her mother and Lucky got inside. How could she explain not waiting to say hello? While she hesitated, the older couple appeared in the doorway.

"Hello, dear. Did you have a nice time tonight?" Evelyn asked.

Lucky glanced around. "Where's Jonathan?"

"He...he isn't here," Michelle said.

"That's his car in the driveway, isn't it?"

"Well, yes, I...he left it for me." Michelle reproached herself silently. Even in her highly charged state, she should have thought to put Jonathan's car in the garage. Naturally it would provoke questions.

Lucky was looking at her with a slight frown. "He drove you home, and then you drove *him* home? Isn't that a little strange? If you needed a car tomorrow you could have taken one of mine."

"He didn't actually drive me home," Michelle said slowly, searching wildly for a believable explanation without finding one. "Jonathan was, uh, he was having trouble with his back, so I told him I'd drive myself home. It was no big deal."

"Jonathan has never had trouble with his back," Lucky stated. "He's in perfect shape. Even the doctor was impressed when he gave him his last physical."

Evelyn was aware of her daughter's tension and the strain on her face that Michelle was unable to hide. Not from her mother, anyway.

"Backs are tricky things," Evelyn remarked casually. "I knew a man who threw his back out just bending down to pick up his briefcase. He was in good shape, too, so you never can tell."

"Maybe I should phone Jonathan," Lucky said hesitantly.

"I'd leave him alone," Evelyn said. "I'm sure it's nothing serious and he might be asleep by now."

"I'm going to bed, too." Michelle was grateful to her mother for averting Lucky's questions and not asking any of her own.

But Evelyn had only postponed them. "I'll go upstairs with you," she said. "I want to change into more comfortable shoes."

Michelle wasn't surprised when her mother came into her room instead. "Lucky is waiting for you downstairs, so we'd better not get started talking," she said with a forced smile. "You know how we can go on for hours."

"What happened tonight?" Evelyn asked quietly.

"I already told you."

"I'd like the truth. I can see that you're upset about something. Did you and Jonathan have an argument?"

"Another one, you mean?" Michelle asked bitterly.

Evelyn sighed. "I know the path of true love isn't supposed to run smoothly, but you two are the absolute limit! What do you quarrel about all the time?"

"In the first place, love has nothing to do with it."

"Oh, please, Michelle! It would be obvious to a blind man that you're in love with Jonathan and he feels the same about you."

"You need a refresher course in the birds and the bees, Mother," Michelle said mockingly.

"If sex was all you wanted from each other, neither of you would be this miserable," Evelyn answered calmly. "It's quick, it's satisfying and it's over."

"That isn't what you told me in our mother-daughter talk," Michelle said in a brittle voice. "In your version, sex and love were a package deal. I grew up believing in fairy tales, but my Prince Charming always turns into a frog. I seem to have a knack for choosing the wrong men."

"I can't believe Jonathan was a bad choice. I'm sorry to see you so unhappy, dear, but you'll work things out," Evelyn said soothingly. "You always do."

"Not this time. I'm going home tomorrow."

"That would be a mistake. You can't run away from a problem."

"I'm not running away. I'm finally facing reality. Maybe I did think Jonathan and I had a future together, but it was strictly in my own mind," Michelle said bitterly. "All I want to do now is go home and get back to a normal life."

Evelyn realized, as Jonathan had, that Michelle was beyond reach in her present mood. "All right, dear. It's your decision to make. But do think about it. You might change your mind in the next day or two."

"You weren't listening to me! I just told you, I'm leaving tomorrow."

"You might not be able to get on a plane that soon," Evelyn said, hoping that was true.

"I intend to call the airport right now. Surely they'll have one seat available. But if they don't, I'll ask to be put on standby. Either way, I'll be packed and out of here in the morning."

Evelyn looked at her daughter's set face and knew any further argument would be futile. What could have happened to hurt Michelle this badly? If only there were something she could do. But she couldn't think of anything.

"Well, I'll let you make your phone call." She paused at the door. "I *will* see you in the morning, won't I?"

"Of course! I wouldn't leave without saying goodbye." Michelle managed a smile. "Don't look so tragic, Mother. This isn't the end of the world. I'll survive."

"I know you will." Evelyn tried to hide her concern. "Get a good night's sleep. You have a busy day ahead of you tomorrow."

Evelyn and Lucky discussed the situation when she went downstairs a few minutes later.

"I knew that story about the car didn't make sense." He sighed. "What did they fight about tonight?"

"I don't know. I've never known what they find to quarrel about."

"Well, they'll make up, like they always do."

"Not this time, I'm afraid. Michelle is going back to New York tomorrow."

"That does sound serious. But don't worry. I'll tell her I'm having trouble getting a reservation. That will delay her, and maybe this will all blow over."

Evelyn shook her head. "When I left her room, Michelle said she was going to make her own reservation. She's so determined to leave that I think she'd take a plane to almost anywhere."

"That doesn't sound good," Lucky admitted.

"Whatever happened must have been really traumatic. I've never seen Michelle this upset."

He frowned. "Jonathan has always been a gentleman. It's hard to believe he got out of line. But if he did, he'll have to answer to me. I'm going to phone him right now!"

"You can't do that."

"Watch me!" Lucky barked.

"I have nothing against meddling when people don't know what's good for them." A hint of a smile lightened Evelyn's sober expression. "But you can't do it openly—

especially with young people. They think they know more than we do to begin with.''

"What do you propose, then? That we just sit back and let them make the mistake of their lives?''

"I'm not any happier about it than you are. But short of locking Michelle in her bedroom, I don't think we can stop her from leaving.''

"That might be the solution. Or better yet, why don't we lock them up together?''

"The way they've been acting, I'm afraid only one of them would come out alive,'' Evelyn said wryly. "No, we have to let her go. But perhaps after she's gone they'll discover their differences aren't really that important.''

"Or maybe one or both of them will get involved with someone else to prove they're not hurting. It would be just the kind of foolish thing they'd do.''

"That's a possibility,'' she admitted. "But at this moment, I don't have any answers. If you do, I'd be happy to listen.''

"Let me think. I can't believe there isn't a solution. The trick is to get them together,'' he mused.

"Unfortunately there isn't enough time. Michelle was very firm about leaving in the morning.''

"How is she getting to the airport?''

"I'll borrow one of your cars and drive her. I'd ask you to come along, but I think it would be better if you didn't. Michelle might feel defensive because you're Jonathan's uncle.''

"What if the Mercedes had a dead battery and I'd taken the Lincoln to go to the golf course?''

Evelyn gave him a puzzled look. "Then I suppose we'd have to call a taxi.''

"Or you could call Jonathan.'' Lucky smiled broadly.

"They're probably not speaking,'' she said doubtfully. "Do you think he'd take her?''

"I believe he'd jump at the chance. I'll bet he's already

trying to figure out some way to get Michelle back and still keep his pride intact. This will give them a perfect opportunity to see each other again without either having to make the first move.''

Evelyn's face lit with excitement that only lasted a moment. "It's a wonderful idea but it won't work. Jonathan's car is right outside. If both of *your* cars were unavailable, it would be logical for me to borrow his car to drive her to the airport.''

Lucky frowned as he realized she was right. Then his face cleared. ''No problem. I'll take Jonathan's car back to him tonight and slip a note under his front door telling him it's in his driveway. You can follow me in my car and drive me home.''

''You're a genius!'' Evelyn exclaimed. ''And a very nice man,'' she added fondly. ''Somebody else might have decided Jonathan was well rid of Michelle.''

''Your daughter is very much like you,'' Lucky said tenderly. ''I want the best for my nephew.''

Chapter Eleven

Michelle was up early after a sleepless night. When she opened the drapes, a heartbreakingly beautiful day greeted her. The sun shone brightly from a clear blue sky, edging the fronds of the palm trees with gold. Little sailboats bounced over the ocean and birds sang joyously, as though glad to be alive.

Michelle didn't share their sentiment. There were dark shadows under her eyes that she lightened with makeup so her mother and Lucky wouldn't guess how forlorn she felt.

The pain would ease, Michelle assured herself. She just had to keep reminding herself of what a smug, insensitive jerk Jonathan was! But she kept remembering the tender lover instead. He had seemed concerned only about her pleasure, making sure he satisfied her completely. Michelle's pulse quickened as she remembered the ecstasy his hands and mouth had brought her.

It was only an act, she reminded herself. Jonathan was an experienced man. By now, every heated caress was probably automatic, she thought bitterly. They had nothing to do with tenderness. Snapping her suitcase shut, she picked up her purse and went out the door.

Evelyn was alone in the sunroom. She glanced up with a bright smile when Michelle joined her. "Good morning, dear. I'll ring for Manuel to bring your breakfast."

"Don't bother, I won't have time. I got a confirmed seat on a plane this morning, but I have to pick up my ticket half an hour before the flight."

"Weren't you fortunate," Evelyn murmured.

"Yes, I was. The booking agent said she'd just had a cancellation." Michelle glanced around. "Where is Lucky? Isn't he down yet? I want to say goodbye and thank him for his hospitality."

"I'm afraid you'll have to write him a note. He had an early golf game."

"Did you tell him I was leaving? Not that I would expect him to give up his golf game for me. I just wondered," Michelle said casually. Had Evelyn told Lucky about last night's disaster—the little she knew? Was Lucky annoyed?

"I haven't had a chance to tell him," Evelyn said. "I didn't mention it last night, because I thought you might change your mind."

"I didn't," Michelle said grimly.

"So I see." Evelyn glanced at the suitcase. "Anyway, Lucky was gone this morning before I got up. He slipped a note under my door saying he'd be back for lunch."

"I'm sorry I missed him." Michelle glanced at her watch. "I sort of assumed one of you would take me to the airport. Is that all right? I'd be nervous waiting for a cab to arrive. You never know when they're going to show up."

"I'll be happy to drive you, dear. It will give us a last chance to visit on the way. We'll have to take the little Mercedes, because Lucky has the Lincoln."

"I don't mind roughing it." Michelle smiled. "It's going

to be hard to go back to my old life after living in luxury for so long.''

"You're welcome to stay. You know that."

Michelle's smile faded. "I've stayed too long already. Can we get started? I'm in rather a hurry."

"I'll have Manuel bring the car around."

Michelle fidgeted while she waited, walking to the window several times. When he returned, she gave a sigh of relief that soon turned to anguish. Manuel, who was in on the plot, reported with a broad smile that the Mercedes had a dead battery. Evelyn was sure he'd given them away, but Michelle was too upset to notice.

Gritting her teeth she said, "I hate to do it but we'll just have to borrow Jonathan's car. It's right outside."

"I'm so sorry, dear, but Lucky took his car back to him last night. He thought Jonathan might need it to go to the office this morning."

Michelle groaned. "Then I'll just have to take a taxi. Why didn't I leave myself more time?" she wailed. "I just hope the cab company will send one immediately."

"I hope so, too, for your sake," Evelyn said. "But you'd better be prepared to wait as much as half an hour."

"That's too long! I'd never get to the airport in time. What am I going to do?"

"I could call Jonathan. He's only five minutes away. I'm sure he'd be glad to give you a lift."

"I doubt that very seriously. But in any case, I don't intend to find out." Michelle's soft mouth thinned. "I'll just have to call a cab."

Her anxiety increased after she phoned several taxi companies and was told the wait might be as much as forty-five minutes.

"If you expect to make your plane you'd better let me call Jonathan. Or you can wait for another cancellation," Evelyn said artlessly. "I'd love to keep you here longer."

"No...go ahead and call him," Michelle said grudgingly. "Chances are, he isn't even home."

Jonathan was out on his deck, staring moodily at the water when the telephone rang. He didn't move from his deck chair. Let the answering machine pick up. The one person he wanted to talk to wasn't going to call. But after a moment, annoyance mixed with his gloom. Did he intend to allow Michelle to cripple him emotionally? No, damn it! He could function perfectly well without her.

Striding into the house, Jonathan grabbed the phone just before the message began to play.

"I'm so glad I caught you," Evelyn said. "I was beginning to think you weren't home."

"I was out on the deck drinking coffee," he replied warily. Evelyn had never phoned him before. How much had Michelle told her mother about last night?

"I hate to disturb you, but I have a big favor to ask." Evelyn explained Michelle's predicament.

"You want *me* to drive her to the airport?" he asked incredulously. "Does Michelle know you're calling me?"

"Yes, she's right here. I'd let you talk to her, but she's in a tearing hurry. If you can't take her, I'll have to call someone else immediately."

"No! I'll be there."

Jonathan hung up and raced for his car, filled with jubilation. Until the full import of Evelyn's phone call hit him. Michelle was leaving! His heart plunged, although he should have known that's what she'd do.

And yet...if she was really through with him, she wouldn't let him get within a mile of her. Maybe this was her way of saying she regretted all the bitterness and didn't want to see their relationship end on that note. If Michelle gave him an opening even an inch wide, he would apologize for everything he had said and done, or ever would do in the future!

* * *

"You see? I told you Jonathan would be delighted," Evelyn said after hanging up.

Michelle doubted it. He probably couldn't think of an excuse fast enough. But she didn't want to argue about it. "At least come with us, Mother."

"Isn't Jonathan's car a two-seater?"

Michelle had forgotten that. This just wasn't her day.

She was waiting on the doorstep with her suitcase when he drove up a few minutes later. Her tense body and remote expression wasn't what he'd been hoping for, but Jonathan told himself that was to be expected. It must have been hard for her to take the first step. He intended to make it easier for her, though.

His optimism soon evaporated. Staring out the front window as they drove away, Michelle said coolly, "Thank you for giving me a ride."

"You don't have to thank me. I was glad to do it."

She turned her head to give him a sardonic look. "You want to be sure I don't miss my plane?"

"That's not what I meant!"

"It doesn't matter. I'm still grateful," she said indifferently.

"I don't want gratitude," he rasped.

She shrugged. "Okay, I was desperate and you were the only ride available."

"I should have figured that out for myself."

"What does it matter? It's almost over."

He was goaded into saying, "Almost? You mean there's something else you forgot to tell me last night?"

"I'm surprised you'd want to talk about that," she flared.

"Why not? It was quite a night. I've rarely had a partner who displayed such enthusiasm," he drawled.

Michelle turned her head to stare out the windshield again. Jonathan made what happened between them last night seem cheap, a meaningless roll in the hay.

He slanted a glance at her rigid profile, cursing himself

for being an insensitive clod. Was this how he expected to make up? Even if that seemed a remote possibility now, the last thing he wanted to do was hurt her.

"I don't want to argue with you, Michelle," he began tentatively. "I was hoping we could at least be friends."

"We never were. Why start now? Because of a casual one-night stand?"

Jonathan's eyes were bleak. "It was more than that for me," he said in a low voice.

He must have realized he'd been less than gallant. But Michelle didn't want him to be kind. If she allowed herself to remember the man she fell in love with, she'd lose control of her tightly reined emotions.

"I don't want to talk about it," she said flatly. "We said more than enough last night."

"Including some things we didn't mean—at least I didn't." He paused, hoping for a crumb of hope. When none was forthcoming he changed the subject. "You're going to miss this warm weather. I heard on the news that New York is expecting more snow."

"It isn't too bad when you live in the city. They clear the streets right away."

During the rest of the drive they discussed the weather and the benefits of living in a big city as opposed to the inconveniences.

When they reached the airport it was too hectic for conversation. Cars were double-parked, trying to let off passengers, and people were weaving through the traffic, lugging suitcases and tote bags while policemen blew their whistles shrilly to try to keep the traffic moving.

The skycaps were all besieged by travelers clamoring for their attention, but Jonathan managed to get one to take Michelle's luggage. While the man was writing her flight number on a tag and attaching it to her suitcase, they said goodbye.

"I hope you have a nice flight," Jonathan said politely.

"Thanks, I'm sure I will," Michelle answered just as formally. She clutched her purse tightly, grateful that the ordeal was almost over.

"Maybe I'll give you a call once in a while," he said casually. "Just to keep in touch."

"You could do that, but it's rather hard to reach me."

"I know," he answered somberly.

"Goodbye, Jonathan," she said with finality, turning away.

"Michelle, wait!" He didn't get to say any more.

A policeman came over to them. "You'll have to move along. This area is for loading and unloading passengers only."

As he got into his car, Jonathan watched Michelle disappear inside the airport.

She forced herself not to look back. She didn't need a last glimpse of Jonathan. He would remain in her memory forever.

After watching from his upstairs window as Michelle and Jonathan drove away, Lucky went down to the sunroom to join Evelyn.

"I see everything went off perfectly," he said with a smile.

"Our part did, anyway," she replied. "I only hope it works."

"It will," he answered confidently. "They'll be back here in an hour. Ring for Manuel, will you? I feel like a big breakfast."

Manuel was just as cheerful when he arrived. "How about my performance? Wasn't I fantastic? I could have been an actor."

"You'd better not quit your day job," Evelyn said dryly. "Most people don't look that happy when they announce that a car has a dead battery."

"Jeez! Everybody's a critic," he grumbled.

"I'm sure you did fine," Lucky said. "Tell Bessie I'd like waffles and bacon this morning. And you can bring me some juice and coffee while I'm waiting."

He and Evelyn talked over their plans for the day while he waited for his breakfast. By the time he'd finished eating, almost an hour had passed.

Evelyn tried not to fidget. Finally she sneaked a surreptitious peek at her watch, but Lucky noticed. "Don't worry. Jonathan and Michelle will be back any minute now," he said reassuringly.

"I'm sure you're right, darling," she replied as the phone rang.

It was Jonathan's secretary. "Mr. Richfield told me to call and leave a message," she said. "He didn't think you'd be home. Would you like to speak to him?"

"He's there in the office?" Lucky asked. "Yes, put him on."

"I thought you'd be on the golf course," Jonathan remarked when he came on the line.

"I, uh, my game was called off. Ed Harrison got sick. Did you take Michelle to the airport?"

"Yes. Tell Evelyn I got her there in plenty of time."

"Dandy!" Lucky muttered.

They talked business for a few minutes. Then Lucky hung up and looked at Evelyn regretfully. "I guess I was overly optimistic. Michelle is gone."

"Only to New York. It's disappointing, but scarcely disastrous. Let's wait a few days and give them both a chance to cool down. I still think they'll be so miserable that they'll get in touch with each other."

Evelyn was right about one thing. Both Michelle and Jonathan were miserable.

Michelle had always considered winter's ice and snow part of the trade-off for living in an exciting city like New

York. But when she returned from Florida, the days seemed grayer and the nights colder than she remembered.

Everyone envied her tan and wanted to hear all about her trip. The women also asked if she'd met anyone interesting. It was difficult to lie when images of Jonathan tormented her night and day.

The nights were the worst. Jonathan came to her in dreams that seemed poignantly real. He held her in his arms and caressed her intimately, whispering such tender words that she clung to him tightly. And then she would wake up, clutching a pillow. The sense of loss made her reluctant to go to sleep again.

Jonathan was suffering equal tortures. Everything reminded him of Michelle: the way she smiled, the flower-fresh scent of her skin—her responsiveness when they made love. He masked his despair under an uncharacteristically curt manner that baffled people.

Lucky was concerned about the change in Jonathan's personality. His unhappiness proved how much he cared about Michelle. But Jonathan avoided all his attempts to talk about her.

"This can't go on," Lucky told Evelyn. "Your theory wasn't any better than mine. You were right about them discovering they miss each other, but Jonathan is too stubborn to do anything about it."

"Michelle is, too. I can tell how unhappy she is when I talk to her on the phone, but she pretends everything is just dandy at home."

Lucky looked thoughtful. "We can't give up just because a couple of things didn't work. How about the jealousy angle? We could tell each of them the other one is seeing somebody else. Then they'd realize they could lose each other forever."

"It's an idea," Evelyn said doubtfully. "But maybe it would be better to say they were asking about each other.

That wouldn't make either feel rejected, and it leaves the door open for a reconciliation."

"Except that neither is willing to make the first move. How about a compromise? I'll tell Jonathan that Michelle has been asking about him, and you tell her he's seeing somebody else, maybe Ashleigh."

"That just might do it. Michelle detests her."

"Good! Then let's try it. What do we have to lose?"

Michelle was just walking in the door that evening when her mother phoned. She was tired and out of sorts, and the last thing she wanted to do was appear upbeat. But she forced herself. She made suitable, approving comments as Evelyn told her about the parties and luncheons she'd been invited to. Until her mother mentioned seeing Jonathan at a country club dance.

"He's so handsome and charming. It's no wonder the women are crazy about him."

"I'm really not interested in hearing about Jonathan," Michelle said sharply.

"I'm sorry, dear. That was insensitive of me. How could I have forgotten how you feel about him? You always sound so cheerful when I talk to you. I suppose I thought you'd decided it was just a physical attraction between you."

"That about sums it up." On his part, anyway, Michelle thought grimly.

"You're certainly not alone there!" Evelyn laughed merrily. "Ashleigh did everything but take off her clothes to get his attention."

"I'm sure she's done that, too."

"We mustn't be judgmental. They have been seeing each other for quite a while. Lucky says Jonathan has been dating her for years. I'm always skeptical when things drag on too long, but you never can tell. If Ashleigh catches him in just the right mood, maybe something permanent *will* develop.''

"They should be very happy together. They deserve each other.''

"I don't agree. Jonathan deserves better, but we don't always know what's good for us,'' Evelyn observed innocently. "Anyway, I'll keep you informed. I'm glad everything is going so well for you, too, dear. I'll talk to you again in a couple of days.''

She hung up with a pensive look at Lucky. "I feel terrible about making my own child so unhappy. But if it brings them together it will be worth it.''

"It's time for me to do my part.'' He picked up the phone and called his nephew.

They talked for a few minutes, as Evelyn had done. Then Lucky said casually, "Oh, by the way, I have a message for you from Michelle. Evie was talking to her tonight and she asked how you were.''

"Michelle asked about *me?*'' Jonathan's voice was suddenly taut. "What did she say?''

"I think she asked Evie if she'd seen you lately, and how you looked, that sort of thing. Just a friendly inquiry.''

"She sounded friendly?'' Jonathan asked cautiously.

"Of course. Why shouldn't she?''

"We, uh, we didn't always get along. I'm rather surprised that she'd be interested enough to ask about me.''

"Maybe you took your little spats more seriously than she did.''

"I doubt that,'' Jonathan stated grimly.

"You're obviously wrong. Why else would she ask? It might be nice if you gave her a call sometime, just to stay in touch.''

"I would if I thought she wanted to hear from me,'' Jonathan answered slowly.

"You'll never know unless you call. Of course it's up to you. Don't feel you have to call her for Evie's sake. If you're not interested in keeping up the friendship it's all right with us."

"I'll think about it," Jonathan muttered.

"I believe the fish took the bait," Lucky told Evelyn jubilantly after he hung up. "And unlike you, I don't feel a bit guilty. If Jonathan's spirits were any lower he'd need a block and tackle to lift them. He'll phone Michelle, I guarantee it."

"Let's just hope she's smart enough to meet him half-way." Evelyn sighed.

Jonathan paced the floor, his body taut as he wrestled with a dilemma. Was Michelle merely being polite because her mother was marrying his uncle? It could have been an offhand question. Where did you have dinner last night and, oh, by the way, how is Jonathan? If that was the case, he'd look like a fool if he called her.

But suppose Michelle regretted their argument and wanted to make up? She couldn't miss him as much as he missed her, but she wasn't indifferent to him. Maybe this was her way of extending an olive branch. If he refused it, they really would be finished.

As he strode to the phone, Jonathan's face was alive with hope.

Michelle didn't share his emotion. She'd been feeling low when she came home, and her mother's call had put the cherry on the cupcake. It shouldn't surprise her that Jonathan was dating—or even that his main squeeze was Ashleigh. She'd had the inside track all along.

If Michelle needed any proof of how little he was affected by their breakup, his behavior since then provided it. While she was moping around as if the world had come to an end, Jonathan was doing what he did best: charming the ladies, Michelle thought bitterly.

When the phone rang a few minutes later, she picked up the receiver, spoiling for an argument.

Jonathan was so happy to hear her voice that he didn't notice the edge. "I'm glad I caught you in. I didn't know what time you got home from work."

Michelle's breath caught in her throat. The sound of his voice brought him vividly to life. She could almost see his lean, intelligent face and lithe body. The longing that filled her was almost unbearable. But then she remembered Ashleigh, and all the other women he'd been romancing. Did he have that husky little note in his voice when he talked to them? Of course he did!

"Michelle?" Jonathan asked uncertainly, when she didn't reply immediately. "Did I catch you at a bad time?"

"No, it's all right. I'm going out shortly, but I can talk for a couple of minutes. What's on your mind?" she asked coolly.

He felt as if he'd been doused with a pitcher of cold water, but he reminded himself that Michelle had made the first move, in a roundabout sort of way. Maybe she didn't know how receptive *he'd* be. He mustn't overreact or he'd spoil everything.

"I was just sitting here listening to some music and I started thinking about you," he said.

"I'm surprised to hear you have a free night. Mother said she saw you at the country club and the women were swarming around you like gnats."

Michelle sounded jealous, he thought joyfully! "That's an exaggeration," he told her. "I didn't even have a date that night. I was with a group of friends."

"You aren't dating Ashleigh anymore?"

"Well, I...as I told you, she's an old friend."

"We must have a different definition for the word friend," Michelle said mockingly.

"What can I say to convince you? You always believe what you want to believe, anyway."

"I'm sorry if I'm not as gullible as your girlfriends—at least, I'm not anymore."

Jonathan sighed. "We're doing it again. Why can't we talk for five minutes without getting into an argument? I'd hoped things would be different between us, but they obviously aren't."

"Why would you think anything had changed?"

"When Evelyn said you'd asked about me, I thought it meant you wanted to hear from me. Clearly you didn't."

"My mother told you that?" Michelle asked in outrage.

"Indirectly. Lucky thought I'd like to know."

"The kindest thing I can say is that your uncle misunderstood," she said in a biting voice. "I thought I made it clear to you on our last memorable night together that I don't want anything further to do with you. *Ever!* Is that clear?"

"Perfectly," he answered coldly. "I should have known it was all a mistake. You'd rather dwell on your imagined insults than admit I had some valid questions."

"Forgive me if I object to being quizzed after I make love—I mean, have sex." She corrected herself hastily.

Jonathan's anger died abruptly. "You had it right the first time," he said softly. "We made love."

"Maybe your version of it, not mine. Love implies trust, something neither of us has in the other." When tears threatened, Michelle said abruptly, "I have to get ready for my date. Goodbye, Jonathan." The finality in her tone was unmistakable.

He was torn between anger and despair as he hung up. The anger was directed at his uncle. How could Lucky have set him up like that? Jonathan's jaw was rigid as he reached for the phone.

His conversation with Lucky was short and bitter. "What made you think you had the right to meddle in my life?"

Lucky feigned innocence. "I don't know what you're talking about."

"Don't hand me that! If you and your partner want to play merry little matchmakers, find somebody else's lives to louse up. Michelle and I are through, it's over, we're not even speaking any longer. I don't know how to put it any plainer than that."

"You talked to her?" Lucky gave Evelyn an apprehensive glance. "What happened?"

"It doesn't matter. I could have told you it wouldn't work." Jonathan's desolation showed through before he hardened his voice. "Just don't ever do anything like that again." He hung up abruptly.

"Well, back to the old drawing board," Lucky said heavily. He told Evelyn what Jonathan had told him.

"If only we knew what the problem is between them. We know they love each other, so what is keeping them apart? The whole thing is ridiculous! I'd like to—" The phone rang before she could finish her intention.

It had been a crushing blow to Michelle to find out Jonathan hadn't called her on his own. She realized, as he had, who the culprits were and her anger matched his. She couldn't wait to call her mother, but Jonathan got to the phone first. After getting a busy signal, she paced the floor, pausing only to press Redial every couple of minutes.

When she finally reached her mother, Michelle's grief and frustration boiled over. "This is probably the worst thing you've ever done to me! Do you know how demeaning it was to find out you told Jonathan to call me?" She rushed on without waiting for an answer. "Thanks to you, he thinks I'm sitting by the telephone every night, pining to hear from him. How would you like somebody to pity *you?*"

"I'm sure that wasn't the reason he phoned you," Evelyn said placatingly. "I'll admit Lucky gave him a little nudge, but he wouldn't have called if he hadn't wanted to."

"Our affairs don't concern either of you. You have a full satisfying life. Why can't you leave mine alone?"

"Because I want the same thing for you," Evelyn answered quietly. "You and Jonathan love each other. That much I'm sure of. I don't know what happened between you, but it can't be important enough to cause all this unhappiness."

"That's a matter of opinion. You don't know what this is all about."

"Then *tell* me!"

"I'd rather not talk about it," Michelle said stiffly.

"Because you're at fault?" Evelyn asked guilelessly.

"I am not! *He's* the one who accused me of being a fortune hunter. Just because I wasn't friendly toward him until we got to Miami, he assumed it was because I found out he was rich. But that had nothing to do with it. Naturally I was wary of him at Shorehaven. I thought he was a shady character!"

"Is *that* what this is all about?" Evelyn asked incredulously. "I can't believe it!"

"Well, there was a little more to it," Michelle mumbled.

"I should hope so," her mother exclaimed. "Otherwise you two sound like backward children."

Michelle was in a quandary. How could she tell her mother that Jonathan had waited to make his accusations until after he'd gotten what he wanted from her? Or the hurtful way he'd degraded her passion by calling it "enthusiasm," compounding the insult by comparing her to his other partners. Although he did give her performance high marks, Michelle thought bitterly. But those weren't the kind of things you told your mother.

"All I can say is, you don't really know Jonathan," she said evenly. "He uses people for his own purposes. I'll admit I was taken in by his charm, but I'm not stupid enough to believe he was ever serious about me.''

"You're wrong about him," Evelyn protested. "He jumped at the excuse to call you.''

"That just proves even womanizers have a conscience," Michelle said curtly. "The only thing good about our relationship was the—'' She stopped abruptly. "Let's just say I wouldn't have anything to do with him now if he got down on his knees and begged. Tell him to read his bankbook every night. That will make up for any loss he might feel.''

Evelyn could tell that nothing she said would make a difference. At the conclusion of the call she said to Lucky, "At least now I know what the problem is."

"That's a relief!" he exclaimed.

"Not really. Somehow, Jonathan got the idea that Michelle was interested in him only for his money. Unfortunately he didn't mention it to her until after they'd made love.''

"That young jackass," Lucky said disgustedly.

"True, but it proves how much he cares. Jonathan wants Michelle to love him for himself. Which she does, but torture on the rack wouldn't make her admit it now.''

"What can we do about it?" Lucky asked helplessly.

"Nothing, that's the sad part. If we interfere again, we might lose them. Michelle has never been this angry with me.''

"Jonathan, either. He never talked to me like that before.''

"We're lucky they're still talking to us at all. It breaks my heart to see them ruining their lives this way, but we'll have to stay out of it or risk losing them forever.''

It was difficult to sit back and do nothing. As the days passed, Jonathan became more and more withdrawn. He was meticulously polite to both his uncle and Evelyn, but the joy had clearly gone out of his life. He functioned, nothing more.

Michelle wasn't faring any better. She was like a wary stranger when Evelyn talked to her on the phone. Their former warm relationship was gone.

"I wish it was because she hasn't forgiven me yet, but I know that's not the reason," Evelyn lamented to Lucky. "It will be a disaster when they have to see each other at the wedding. At one time I might have thought it would solve everything, but I realize that isn't going to happen. I just hope they'll be civil to each other."

"I won't have those two ruining one of the happiest days of our lives," Lucky stated. "If necessary, I'll tell Jonathan he isn't invited."

"You can't do that! He's as dear to you as a son."

"It would sadden me greatly," he admitted. "The only other solution would be if Jonathan went broke and begged Michelle to take pity on him. But I know neither of those things are likely."

"No, I suppose—" Evelyn stopped, staring at him intently. "But what if she *thought* he lost all his money? What if she thought he was suicidal over it?"

"That's ridiculous! Jonathan doesn't care that much about money. He'd just go out and make more."

"People in love don't think clearly." Evelyn smiled. "Michelle wouldn't let pride keep her from preventing a tragedy. She'd tell him how much he has to live for and they'd both see how foolish they'd been."

"It's risky," Lucky said dubiously. "If the plan backfired again they might never forgive us. Besides, Michelle wouldn't believe such a wild story."

"Maybe not if I told it to her, but she'd believe it if she read it in the newspaper." Evelyn laughed delightedly at his bewildered expression. "All we have to do is take the front page of the financial section to a printer and have him change one of the paper's articles to one of our own. The demise of Richfield Enterprises would certainly be news.''

"Do you have to wipe us out completely?" he joked.

"It's for a good cause." She picked up the morning paper and scanned the financial section. "This article on the rise in interest rates is about the right length. Take this down." She handed him a notepad and pen. "How does this sound for a headline? 'Local Millionaire Goes Bankrupt.' Then we can say something like: 'The financial world was rocked by the news that millionaire socialite Warren "Lucky" Richfield and his nephew and partner Jonathan Richfield have filed for Chapter Eleven.' The rest of the article can explain that the company suffered reverses due to overextension and bad investments. You can write that part."

"It's like asking me to write my own obituary," he remarked in humorous complaint.

"It's only money," she teased. "Do you think you can have this printed up soon? I want to fax it to Michelle as fast as possible."

"I'll see that it's done today," he promised.

Michelle was shocked when she got home from work that Friday and received Evelyn's fax. She telephoned her mother immediately.

"How could a thing like this happen? Richfield Enterprises must have been worth millions!"

"That's what I couldn't understand," Evelyn said. "Lucky explained that it was a high risk business. They were overextended in the expectation that a new invention of his would make a fortune. When it didn't, the bank called in a huge loan. There was no way they could meet it."

Michelle vaguely remembered Jonathan saying he was used to taking chances, but everything always worked out. Evidently not this time. "I'm so sorry," she said.

"Yes, things look pretty grim. Everything will have to go, the estate, the yacht. We plan to live in my house in New York."

"Things are that bad?" Michelle exclaimed.

"It could be worse. At least we still have each other. That's all that really matters. I'm proud of the way Lucky is taking adversity. It's Jonathan we're worried about."

"It isn't as bad for him. He's young. He can start over."

"That's what we keep telling him, but he blames himself for what happened, even though it wasn't his fault. We don't know what to do for him anymore. He's become more and more withdrawn and depressed. I've avoided mentioning it to Lucky, but I'm really afraid Jonathan might do something drastic."

Michelle felt as if a cold hand had clutched her heart. "He's not a quitter," she protested. "After he gets through moping around, he'll start over."

"I'd agree with you if this only concerned him. But you know how he idolizes Lucky. Jonathan can't live with the notion that he let his uncle down."

"Don't say that!" Michelle said sharply.

"I'm telling you his state of mind." Evelyn pretended to sniffle. "I have to appear calm for Lucky's sake, but I don't know how much longer I can take all this tension. I really need you, Michelle. I hate to ask, but could you possibly come back and help me deal with all the problems?"

"I'll get the first plane out of New York," Michelle promised.

Her tense body refused to relax during the interminable flight and the long taxi ride to Lucky's house. Surely her mother had exaggerated the extent of Jonathan's depression. But suppose she hadn't? A world without Jonathan was unthinkable! Never to see his laughing face again or hear his deep husky voice? But even if that wasn't to be, she couldn't bear it if anything happened to him.

Evelyn and Lucky were waiting for her in the front hall. When Michelle saw the doleful look on their faces her heart almost stopped beating.

"What's wrong?" she asked apprehensively. "Jonathan is all right, isn't he?"

"I hope so." Lucky sighed. "He's stopped answering the telephone."

"Didn't you go to his house to check on him?" Michelle demanded. "How do you know he's okay? He may be— you can't just sit here and do nothing!"

"I'm the last person he wants to see," Lucky said.

"We were hoping you might go over and talk to Jonathan," Evelyn said.

"He doesn't want to see me, either."

"Then I don't know what to do," Lucky said. "I guess we'll just have to wait till he calls *us*."

"Give me your car keys," Michelle ordered. "Somebody has to act responsibly around here."

She was too frantic with worry to realize that both her mother and Lucky were acting out of character. They were decisive people who should have been able to cope better.

Jonathan was out on his deck, morosely watching the sun go down. He was glad Carlos had finally left and he had the house to himself. He didn't want to talk to anyone.

When the doorbell rang, he swore pungently on his way to answer it. Why couldn't everyone just leave him alone? The breath was knocked out of him when he opened the door and saw Michelle.

They stared at each other speechlessly, both having difficulty controlling the wave of longing that swept over them.

Finally Michelle said quietly, "May I come in?"

"Of course." He opened the door wider and stood aside.

"Forgive my manners. I was just surprised. I didn't expect to see you here."

"I had to come when I heard. Are you all right?"

"I'm fine." He didn't know what she was talking about, but he wasn't about to question his good fortune. "I don't need to ask how you are. You look wonderful!"

"You don't have to put on an act for me, Jonathan," she said earnestly. "I know it's been rough for you, but things are going to get better."

"I used to hope they would," he said hesitantly, afraid of saying the wrong thing.

"They will, I promise you. You're not a quitter. You have everything to live for."

"Not everything," he answered softly.

"You mustn't think that way," she said urgently. "You're young and talented. You have a bright future ahead of you. You're not responsible for what happened."

"Yes, I am. I was a fool! I know that now." He gazed at her yearningly. "Is there any chance you'd consider taking me back?"

"I thought you'd never ask!" She threw her arms around his neck.

They kissed frantically, murmuring endearments and apologies as they caressed each other restlessly. Michelle touched his face, his hair. She kneaded the taut muscles in his back, arching her body into his when Jonathan moved sensuously against her.

"You will marry me, won't you, sweetheart?" he asked in a husky voice.

She laughed breathlessly. "You couldn't get away from me now if you tried!"

"That's something you'll never have to worry about."

When they eventually came down to earth, Jonathan continued to hold her close. "This is what I hoped would happen," he said blissfully. "I don't even want to know why you changed your mind. It's enough that you did."

"It wasn't pity, darling. You're not to think that," she said firmly.

"It wouldn't matter to me if it was. I don't want to talk about it." His mouth closed over hers again, silencing her in the best possible way.

When she could catch her breath, Michelle said, "We do have to talk, Jonathan. There's so much to discuss. Like where we're going to live. Lucky will be in New York with Mother, but I don't mind moving down here. This is where your contacts are. We'll find a little apartment somewhere and I know I won't have any trouble getting a job."

He lifted his head to stare at her. "I don't understand."

"Don't go all macho on me." She smiled. "We'll need my salary until you get established again."

"You want me to leave the company?" he asked slowly. "And what's all this about Lucky moving to New York?"

"If you answered your phone, you'd know," she teased. "They're moving into Mother's house after the estate is sold. She said Lucky is taking it very well. If he can, you can, too."

He gave her a baffled look. "What are you saying? Lucky wouldn't sell his home without telling me about it first."

"I guess he didn't want to upset you. But you must have known he couldn't keep it after the company went bankrupt."

"*Our* company? I just negotiated a multimillion-dollar deal. We were never in better financial shape."

"You don't have to keep up a front for me, darling," Michelle said gently. "Mother told me you had to declare bankruptcy. She even faxed me the article that appeared on the financial page of the newspaper. I know you and Lucky are wiped out, but it doesn't matter to either Mother or me."

Jonathan folded her in his arms and kissed her tenderly. "Darling Michelle, I'm covered with shame when I think of what I accused you of. Can you ever forgive me? Even if I am still rich,'' he added with a wry smile.

She couldn't have heard correctly. "What did you say?"

"All I lost was you, sweetheart. I still have the money that got me into all this grief." He stroked her cheek lovingly. "I hope you don't mind."

Michelle continued to look bewildered. "But that can't be. I saw it right there in the newspaper!"

He shook his head admiringly. "That was a masterful touch. They knew you might not take Evelyn's word for it, so they gave you proof you wouldn't think to question."

She stared at him in amazement. "You mean they did it to us again?"

"Yeah, isn't it wonderful?" He put his arms around her waist and swung her around. "But don't think this changes anything. You're still going to marry me."

"It's what I've always hoped for," she said softly.

When Jonathan lifted her in his arms and carried her into the bedroom, Michelle knew all of her dreams would come true.

* * * * *

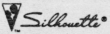

Take 4 bestselling love stories FREE
Plus get a FREE surprise gift!

Special Limited-time Offer

Mail to Silhouette Reader Service™

3010 Walden Avenue
P.O. Box 1867
Buffalo, N.Y. 14240-1867

YES! Please send me 4 free Silhouette Special Edition® novels and my free surprise gift. Then send me 6 brand-new novels every month, which I will receive months before they appear in bookstores. Bill me at the low price of $3.57 each plus 25¢ delivery and applicable sales tax, if any.* That's the complete price and a savings of over 10% off the cover prices—quite a bargain! I understand that accepting the books and gift places me under no obligation ever to buy any books. I can always return a shipment and cancel at any time. Even if I never buy another book from Silhouette, the 4 free books and the surprise gift are mine to keep forever.

235 SEN CF2T

Name	(PLEASE PRINT)	
Address	Apt. No.	
City	State	Zip

This offer is limited to one order per household and not valid to present Silhouette Special Edition® subscribers. *Terms and prices are subject to change without notice. Sales tax applicable in N.Y.

USPED-696

©1990 Harlequin Enterprises Limited

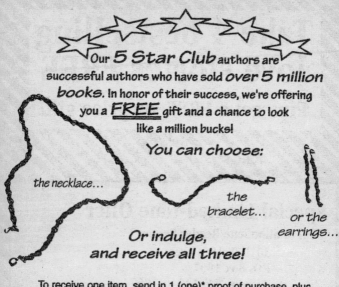

FIVE STARS
MEAN SUCCESS

If you see the "5 Star Club" flash on a book,
it means we're introducing you to one of our
most STELLAR authors!

Every one of our Harlequin and Silhouette
authors who has sold over 5 MILLION BOOKS
has been selected for our "5 Star Club."

We've created the club so you won't miss
any of our bestsellers. So, each month
we'll be highlighting every original book within
Harlequin and Silhouette written by our
bestselling authors.

NOW THERE'S NO WAY ON EARTH OUR STARS WON'T BE SEEN!

OVER
5 MILLION
BOOKS SOLD
SPECIAL OFFER INSIDE

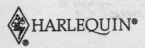 HARLEQUIN®

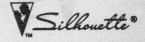 Silhouette®

BEVERLY BARTON

**Continues the
twelve-book series—
36 Hours—in April 1998
with Book Ten**

NINE MONTHS

Paige Summers couldn't have been more shocked when she learned that the man with whom she had spent one passionate, stormy night was none other than her arrogant new boss! And just because he was the father of her unborn baby didn't give him the right to claim her as his wife. Especially when he wasn't offering the one thing she wanted: his heart.

For Jared and Paige and *all* the residents of Grand Springs, Colorado, the storm-induced blackout was just the beginning of 36 Hours that changed *everything!* You won't want to miss a single book.

Available at your favorite retail outlet.

COMING NEXT MONTH

#1171 UNEXPECTED MOMMY—Sherryl Woods
That Special Woman!
And Baby Makes Three: The Next Generation
Single father Chance Adams was hell-bent on claiming his share of
the family ranch. Even if it meant trying to seduce his uncle's lovely
stepdaughter. But when Chance fell in love with the spirited beauty for real,
could he convince Jenny to be his wife—and his son's new mommy?

#1172 A FATHER'S VOW—Myrna Temte
Montana Mavericks: Return to Whitehorn
Traditional Native American Sam Brightwater was perfectly content
with his life. Until vivacious schoolteacher Julia Stedman stormed into
Whitehorn and wrapped herself around his hardened heart. With fatherhood
beckoning, Sam vowed to swallow his pride and fight for his woman and
child....

#1173 STALLION TAMER—Lindsay McKenna
Cowboys of the Southwest
Vulnerable Jessica Donovan sought solace on the home front, but what she
found was a soul mate in lone horse wrangler Dan Black. She identified
with the war veteran's pain, as well as with the secret yearning in his eyes.
Would the healing force of their love grant them a beautiful life together?

#1174 PRACTICALLY MARRIED—Christine Rimmer
Conveniently Yours
Rancher Zach Bravo vowed to never get burned by a woman again. But he
knew that soft-spoken single mom Tess DeMarley would be the perfect
wife. And he was positively *livid* at the notion that Tess's heart belonged to
someone else. Could he turn this practical union into a true love match?

#1175 THE PATERNITY QUESTION—Andrea Edwards
Double Wedding
Sophisticated city-dweller Neal Sheridan was elated when he secretly
swapped places with his country-based twin. Until he accidentally agreed to
father gorgeous Lisa Hughes's child! He had no intention of fulfilling that
promise, but could he really resist Lisa's baby-making seduction?

#1176 BABY IN HIS CRADLE—Diana Whitney
Stork Express
On the run from her manipulative ex, very pregnant Ellie Malone wound up
on the doorstep of Samuel Evans's mountain retreat. When the brooding
recluse delivered her baby and tenderly nursed her back to health, her heart
filled with hope. Would love bring joy and laughter back into their lives?